Lies

A Black Orchid Series Novel

BOOK I

APRIL RODGERS

PAGE PUBLISHING, INC.
New York, NY

First originally published by Page Publishing, Inc. 2017

ISBN 978-1-68348-744-9 (Paperback)
ISBN 978-1-68348-745-6 (Digital)

Printed in the United States of America

Dedicated to the most powerful woman I know... Mom.

JORJA

They say when you die, your life flashes before your eyes. Well, that was not the case the first time I died, so why does it seem to be happening now? My eyelids feel so heavy, every blink getting longer and longer. "Cavan." My throat feeling as dry as the Sahara Desert as I try to say his name again. The poison making its way through my stone body is making my mind see things I had long left behind. My husband, my beloved Leland, I miss you so much. My beautiful daughters, how innocent you both were.

"Cavan, please," I beg, "just let me die!"

With every moment passing, the flashes of my past getting clearer as the dimly lit stone room where I lay fades behind me.

"My love," Cavan whispers as he leans over my nearly lifeless body. "This is only temporary." I try to comprehend what he is telling me, but the poison in my veins has taken over. Cavan's words became a jumbled mess in my mind as I try to open my eyes again. If I am going to die here tonight, at least my final thoughts are of my family, and knowing that they are safe now, I can close my eyes and finally let go.

Jade's voice fills my mind, "Mom, where are you?" Her voice, so soft and sweet, is this what heaven sounds like?

"I'm right here, I'll always be right here," I whisper as my heavy eyelids close one last time. "I love you, girls."

CHAPTER 1

1854

"MOTHER!" Rayne's voice rang through Jorja's ears. "Mother, get up." Jorja let out a sigh, pulling the blankets over her head and rolling over to burry herself in Leland's chest. Rayne yelled again from her bedroom across the hall. "Mother! Get up; we have so much to do today." Jorja curled into the warm arms of her beloved husband as he laughed.

"My love, I believe we have created a monster."

"Leland!" She giggled. "I would hardly call your daughter a monster. You forget what it's like to turn eighteen."

"No." He smiled. "I remember quite clearly how happy my eighteenth year was." Leland wrapped his arms around his wife tightly. "That was the year you finally agreed to marry me."

Kissing him softly, Jorja smiled and added playfully. "Yes, I suppose it was a good year for me as well, my love."

"Mother! Will you please come in here? Jade is making fun of everything I am trying on."

Leland smiled at Jorja as she pulled herself out of bed and searched for her dress. "Still as beautiful as the day I married you, my love," he said, leaning back on his pillow watching Jorja slip into her day clothes. Kissing him quickly, she added, "Flattery will not get you out of setting up today."

With the decorations in place, Jorja left Leland to greet the guests who were beginning to arrive. She found her daughters, Rayne and Jade, in the upstairs bedroom getting ready. Clothes were all over the bed, hung over the chairs and some on the floor.

"Mother, I have nothing to wear." Rayne cried, fear filling her voice.

"My dear, I thought we chose a dress this morning?" Jorja placed her hand on her panicked daughter's cheek.

"I can't wear the same-old dresses if *he* will be here."

With tears filling her eyes, Rayne looked up at her mother, and Jorja smiled softly. Not long ago, she was the frightened girl trying to be perfect for the man she loved.

"Come with me, my dear." Jorja took Rayne by the hand and led her across the hall to the master bedroom. Jade followed with curiosity. Leland had asked her to wait to give her his gift until it was almost time for her party. Jorja guessed this would be the perfect time.

On the master bed, there lay a box with a thin white envelope sitting on top that read.

To my beautiful little girl on your birthday.

Rayne's eyes widened, as she opened the box, she saw what she described as the most beautiful dress in the world. It was an off the shoulders gown; Rayne always admired these dresses when she would watch the women coming off the ships at the docks where her father worked.

"Rayne," Jade said, stunned, her hands covering her mouth when her sister put the dress on. Rayne's long curly brown hair fell over her shoulders leaving just a hint of soft flesh.

"You don't like it." Rayne paused for a moment "*He* won't like it?" she panicked; her lips pressed closely together, and her eyes shut as she turned toward the long mirror.

"No, that's not it at all." Jade gasped. "You are stunning."

"Then what's wrong?" Rayne cried still afraid to open her eyes.

"I think tonight I am going to lose my sister; he will surely ask you to marry him," Jade answered with tears in her voice.

"Mother, do you think he will like it?" Rayne asked, holding her breath.

Jorja could not say a word; she just smiled trying to hold back her own tears. Surely, her child was now a woman, and she assumed without doubt, a soon-to-be-married woman.

Rayne opened her eyes and looked at herself. With so much emotion flowing across her face, they could tell she was pleased.

"I think I will have to restrain your father from beating this boy half to death for looking at you in such a way when he sees you like this tonight," Jorja said with a giggle.

"There will not be a man, a woman nor child tonight that will be able to take their eyes off you, my dear." She felt her eyes start to tear up but quickly pulled together.

"Jade," Jorja said quickly taking in a deep breath, "please help your sister with her hair; you know what she is like when she is nervous." Then she turned with a smile and headed back downstairs.

"You know I will, Mother," she said happily.

As Jorja walked down the stairs, she could hear her girls talking and laughing with each other. They are so close with each other, more so than most sisters are. She reached the kitchen in time to see her husband Leland standing in the window looking out with a bottle of irish whisky in one hand and his glass in the other. He was dressed in a handsome suit and hat. Jorja smiled and walked up behind him and reached her arms around his chest, taking a deep breath he sighed.

"What is the matter, darling?" she asked as if she did not know what he was thinking.

"That is my baby girl up there, you know I do not like the idea of her growing up!" he said in a stern yet sincere voice. "And this Charles—"

Jorja cut him off with a light kiss on his back, and her hand moved up to his mouth. He turned his body slowly to face her, still not looking her in the eyes. Much like with his daughters, he could not seem to say no to her nor could he stay mad or upset when they would lock eyes; he would always turn away quickly with a sharp *"you win."* These three women had his heart, body and soul. There was no denying that.

The guests slowly started to arrive, Leland turned to slip outside to greet the guests, Jorja reminded him to behave tonight and let Rayne have her moment. She knew he had a hard time understanding that his first-born child was a woman now, but he would have to accept it when Charles asked for her hand in marriage tonight.

Jorja watched out the glass door as Charles crossed the yard to speak with Leland then she turned away and went upstairs to change; the girls were still in their room putting on the final touches to their already perfect attire. Jorja changed quickly then went to assist them.

"Jade, darling, please give me a moment with your sister. I think your father might need a hand out back," Jorja said in a low voice.

"Yes, Mother." She gave her a kiss on the forehead then hurried down the stairs to find her father in the ever-growing crowd of people.

"Mother . . . I'm um . . . nervous," Rayne said, trembling with her words.

"My dear, you have no reason to be nervous," Jorja told her daughter softly trying to hold back her own tears. "You are beautiful, and Charles is already here and speaking with your father." A look of horror crossed Rayne's face.

"Don't worry, I have already told him to behave," Jorja added with a quiet laugh. "You know your father has no intent to make you unhappy, not tonight . . . not any night!"

"Thank you, I just hope everything goes well," Rayne answered worried. "I have waited so long for this. I will be absolutely horrified if he does not ask me to be his wife."

"My darling, you worry too much," Jorja said with a soft smile. "Take my hand, I will walk you down."

"Mother, one more thing." She paused.

"Yes, my dear?"

"No matter what happens tonight, I never want us to end up like you and Grandmother and Grandfather." Rayne locked eyes with Jorja. "Please promise me that we will always be close."

"Rayne Sullivan, wild horses could not pull us apart!" Jorja said firmly, keeping eyes with hers.

Music was playing, and people were dancing when Jorja walked through the french doors of their home leading out onto a patio overlooking the large green lawn now covered with people. Rayne stopped at the bottom of the stairs in the house; she asked her mother to give her a moment. Jorja walked outside and looked for her husband; she knew he would want to see his daughter's entrance. Leland and Jade came out of the crowd and met her at the gate to the patio. Jorja could see the fear in his face.

Jade touched her father's hand. "Father, it will be okay, trust me," she said with her devious smile.

Just then, every head in a hundred-foot radius turned and faced them; Jorja knew exactly what they were looking at. Jorja turned her body and faced the french doors; she saw a grown woman where her child once stood.

Leland walked over and wrapped his arms around his daughter and kissed her on the forehead. "Happy birthday, darling, you look amazing," he whispered. "Charles has already spoken with me, my dear, and he is now waiting for you by the water."

Rayne slowly walked through the crowd receiving her birthday wishes from everyone; she made her way to the edge of the yard and onto a wooden platform where Charles was standing. If he was nervous, he did not show it.

Charles was a tall boy with a muscular toned build. His strong arms and upper body took her breath away, as did his flawless beauty. For a boy of his age, he had perfect skin and eyes so crystal blue they could mesmerize just about anyone. His usually messy blonde hair was kept neatly under a black hat.

Jorja watched over her daughter from the patio with Leland by her side, and Jade leaned over the side of the railing tearing up. Charles got down on one knee and pulled out a small black box from his coat pocket. As he put the ring on her finger, Rayne's eyes filled up with joy and tears. He kissed her hand softly and stood up.

"I don't like this," Leland said. "I don't like him. There is just something about him; he is not good for her."

"Why do you not like him, Leland, just because he is going to marry our daughter?" Jorja laughed.

Charles was a good boy; his parents owned a pub in town just down the road from Jorja's shop. They had met when the Sullivans had first settled here years earlier. Charles's mother and Jorja had become very good friends over the years.

Charles and Rayne slowly walked arm in hand, back up to the party, where Charles made the announcement. "I would like to thank you all for coming tonight to celebrate with us this very special event, not only is it Rayne's birthday." He paused . . . "But tonight, she has also agreed to be my wife." With a very large smile on his face, he kissed her hand.

Most of the town was at the party dancing and now congratulating the young couple. Therefore, it must have been very easy for the thieves to make their way from shop to shop with little if any notice even though there were about twenty of them. All very large, strong, dark and dirty looking men with the exception of one very well-kept man who stood behind them but not as if he was following, it was as if they were covering him. As they made their way through the businesses almost effortlessly, the pale man would stand in the street. The dirty men never left him to stand alone, half of them would pillage a shop or business, while the others would stay with him. The well-kept man seemed to control the flow of the events that were going on through the small town at that moment.

The thieves carried guns, but the slender man did not; he did not seem to care about the destruction that his companions were creating. When they came upon Jorja's shop, he stopped and turned as if he had felt a ghost.

He motioned to the others, and they dropped everything and hurried to his side. One man held a gun to the air and let two shots fire.

The party stopped to a dead silence as the sound bellowed throughout like a cannon. Then panic flowed through the crowd the guests were scattering to find their loved ones no doubt thinking they were under the attack of war.

Jade found her way to her mother with a look of terror in her eyes. She had a vision of what was to come. "Mother," she cried, "we have to find Rayne, and please do not let Father go." She cried, "Mother, please believe me . . . this will not end well." Jade had always had visions of things to come, although it was never talked about in front of anyone other than her mother and sister. As a mother, it was Jorja's job to protect her family, protect her children and her husband, but Leland was an honorable man and would also do what he thought was right to protect his family. Charles clung to Rayne with all his strength pulling her through the crowd; he would go with Leland as well to prove his worth to Rayne.

"Mother, what's happening?" Rayne yelled from about twenty feet away.

"I don't know, my dear. Are you hurt?" Jorja asked.

"I can't feel my hand, but I think it is because Charles has cut off my blood flow to it," he said, trying to unlock her fingers from his.

"Mr. Sullivan," Charles said as they approached. "I will get my gun and meet with you." The two men went rushing for their pistols.

Just then, a calm stun fell over Jade; she looked at Rayne and her mother. "What did you see, Jade?" Rayne asked in a low voice.

"BLOOD, all over, tell Charles and Father not to go, Mother, please . . . please . . . please!" she cried.

Jade was never wrong with what she saw, although it was never spoken around her father; he did not understand her gift.

The party cleared out quickly; everyone scattered to their homes, to their families. Leland returned within moments. "Come inside, my love," he said, "you and our daughters stay here while Charles and I find out what is going on."

Jorja begged him not to go, but no matter what she tried to tell him, he would not listen; he was very stubborn that way. He thought he was protecting his family. Little did he know this would be the last time he would ever see them.

"Come on, Charles," Leland beckoned, "you can prove to me that you are worthy to marry my daughter."

"It will be an honor, sir," Charles said with a smirk.

They made their way into the main street with a handful of other men. What they saw was beyond strange; there was a quiet street only one man standing in the middle of the road.

"Hello!" Leland yelled, but the man did not answer, but he still stood in front of Jorja's candle shop.

"HELLO!" he yelled louder, but still no response.

Leland and his crowd slowly walked toward the man, still getting no response to their calls.

Against Leland's wishes, Jorja and her daughters crept quietly behind the stores until they got to the back door of the candle shop. As they stepped into the shop, the bellowing of guns and screams of pain rang through the air.

Jade with the look of terror across her face yelled, "Mother, get down, he can see you!" For a brief moment, Jorja's eyes were locked with a pair of glowing red eyes as his image burned into her mind; then in the blink of an eye, everything was dark and quiet again, and a voice faded in the distance. *"Eternity will hold me to you, my love."*

"Did I pass out? Am I dead? Where are my girls?" Panic flowed through Jorja's head, but her body was still.

"It's over." Jorja could hear a voice in her head, but it was not her own.

"She will be okay, Rayne, don't worry," a woman's soft voice said; it was a voice that sounded almost familiar.

Slowly, she opened her eyes. Jorja was surprised at how clear the darkness looked; she sat up looking around the dark room, though she could see everything as if it were daylight. Jorja felt a strange sensation in her throat, a dry burn.

"Leland," she said dryly.

"Mother, can you hear me?" Jade said in a calm voice.

Jorja turned to face Jade who was sitting on the edge of the bed; she could also see Rayne standing with her back to the wall, eyes full of tears.

"Jade?" Jorja's voice cracked.

"Yes, Mother, I'm here," she answered.

"Where am I? What happened? Are you okay? Where is your father?" The questions flowed like water from Jorja's mouth.

"Mother, how do you feel?" Jade interrupted.

Strangely, Jorja felt fine except for the dryness in her throat. Physically better than she had ever felt.

"Where is your father?" she asked again trying to stay calm but feeling that she would break at any moment. Jade looked slowly up toward Rayne who now could hardly stand, tears streaming from her face she ran from the room slamming the door behind her.

"Mother, he did not make it," she said. "His wounds were too bad."

"WHAT?" Jorja began to panic. "What do you mean? What happened? Please tell me."

"When he and Charles went to see the commotion, they were ambushed. A number of men with guns and . . . " she stopped to take a deep breath. "They were shot, he and Charles, several times before they even had a chance to fire back once."

"Charles." Jorja gasped. "Rayne must be—"

"Mother, calm down, she will be fine; she just needs time," Jade said.

"Um, Mom, there is something else," she said unsure how Jorja would react.

Jade looked at her mother without opening her mouth. Jorja could hear Jade's voice in her head say, *You are a vampire. How am I to tell you this without upsetting you?* Jorja laughed . . .

"Vampire, my dear, you have been reading those fiction books again, haven't you?"

Jade stopped and stared as if her mother had just slapped her. "What did you say, Mother?" Her eyes inquisitive.

"I asked if you had been reading those fiction books again, you said I was a . . . vampire."

"Mother, how did you know that? I did not open my mouth?" Jade asked, now intrigued.

"Don't be silly, dear, I heard you say it," Jorja replied, confused.

Jade stared blankly. *"Let's try this again then, can you hear me speaking to you now?"* Her mouth perfectly closed.

Jorja fell back on to her pillow and threw her hands over her face, she wondered, could Jade hear her as well? *"Hello . . . "* No answer. *"HELLO."* still no answer. Slowly, she looked through her fingers at Jade who was sitting there smiling.

"Okay, Mother, I guess it is easier to tell you this way to make you believe." She smiled speaking to her mother through her mind. *"The man who stood outside your shop, well, he saw us come in the back. He looked at you as if he knew who you were, as if he was waiting for you."* Jade continued, *"He came at us so quickly pushing Rayne and I out of the way and pulled you out the back door; we pulled on it to try to get to you, but it were as if it was locked. Then we heard the shots outside again. I thought for sure he had killed you. Everything went silent; all the men who were with him ran back down to the docks and boarded a ship."*

"Stop!" Jorja pleaded aloud as she stood up and walked to the window, opening the curtains wide. The light hit her like a ton of bricks, but it did not hurt. She turned to her daughter. "See, not a vampire, darling; I did not burst into flames." She smiled. "Now, tell me how I got here please."

"I was getting there, Mother, before you interrupted," she said aloud. "Since we could not get out the back door, we went out front, that's when we found . . . " She paused with her eyes down. "Father and Charles lying in the street with the other men who came with them; they were dead . . . all of them. There was so much blood just like in my vision." She brought her head back up to meet her mother's eyes. "Rayne ran over to Charles; he was covered in blood and so was father, but it was too late they were already dead. So I ran around back to find you, you were just lying there like a statue, but your eyes were flickering. Therefore, I knew you were still alive; then I pulled Rayne away from Charles to help me carry you home."

"Okay, that does not explain why you think I am a vampire," Jorja continued, confused with all the details. "What kind of vampire doesn't catch fire in the sunlight?" she asked, still trying to clear her dry throat.

"Mother, I need to speak with Rayne and make sure she is alright. Please stay here until I get back; there is still more to tell you." It was more of a demand.

When the door shut, Jorja walked around the room still trying to figure out what was really happening. Her body felt different, and for some reason, she could hear Jade's thoughts and definitely did not burn up in the sunlight. However, that does not mean she is a vampire, she told herself firmly. Suddenly, the dryness in Jorja's throat was so overbearing she felt as if she would scream, but nothing came out. She reached for the pitcher of water on the bedside table, but when she drank it, she just felt sick to her stomach, as if she'd throw up any minute. The dryness was still there. The only rational thought in Jorja's head was there is no way she was going to drink blood. Nevertheless, she could not get the strange thought out of her head. *"If I really am a vampire like Jade said, why did I not bite her? Is that not what they do? Bite people, kill people."*

Jorja took another deep breath in and realized that she was not really breathing. Air went in but not out like a real breath. She held it in waiting to pass out. Two minutes passed, then five, finally ten, and still nothing, so she let the breath out. *"I guess I really don't need to. I did not feel lightheaded or dizzy."* Jorja walked around the room and started to notice things, things she had not seen before. Her room seemed neither warm nor cold to her now. She could also hear the people outside talking as if they were standing in the room with her. When she looked out the window at them, they walked faster passed the house and tried not to look up. Jorja took another unneeded breath out of habit and walked over to the mirror. She took a good look at herself. "My body is definitely different, much more defined and firmer," she said to herself. Then in a single split second, clarity flooded Jorja . . . Leland was gone; she really was a monster, and her children were not safe with her. She heaved open the window two floors up and jumped. Hitting the ground with a soft step as if she had just walked down a flight of stairs and ran for what seemed to be only a few short moments. When Jorja finally stopped running, she was in a new place that she had never seen before surrounded by trees, a deeply wooded area further north than she had ever been. Jorja's throat burned, dryer than ever, she could not fight it anymore!

In what seemed to be slow motion a large animal came out of the clearing, and before she knew what was happening, Jorja had it gripped below her, her now aching teeth sprang from her mouth and sunk into it with one swift movement. She began to drink from this helpless creature and could not help feeling guilty, but at the same time, she was overflowing with delight, the feeling of the warm fluid flowing into her mouth and down her throat curing the dryness almost instantly. When Jorja finally stood and wiped the little bit of blood that was left on her lip, she realized she suddenly felt stronger, clearer, and more alert . . . if that was even possible.

Jorja sat staring at the now lifeless animal in front of her and began to think of her children, how could she explain this to them? They would be horrified if they were not already their mother, a monster, feeding on poor animals in the woods. Would she ever want to feed on humans? Could she stop herself? How could this all be possible?

Jorja headed back home a little slower this time, but it still seemed to take no time at all to reach the town sign. By this time, it was dark, and no one was out in the streets. All the houses and businesses were closed. *"Do they know?"* she said to herself. "How would they, most people would think vampires cannot come out in the daytime, and when I left, it was early afternoon; the sun still very much in the sky." Jorja realized that she was now talking aloud . . . to herself. When she reached the house, Jade came running out the front door to her.

"Mother, are you okay? I thought I told you to stay upstairs!" she cried. "You scared me to death. I thought you were gone for good."

"Where is your sister, darling? I need to speak with you both," Jorja said in a much calmer voice than when she had left; she assumed her *dinner* helped.

Jorja walked into the house; she could see people, their friends, and neighbors peeking out their windows. She could see they had fear, fear for her, and fear for the safety of her children. Rayne was sitting on the sofa, reading a book that she placed on her lap as if it were on a table. When Jorja walked in the room, Rayne froze, her eyes fixed on her mother; she put her book on the table beside her and stood up.

"Where did you go?" Rayne asked softly. Jorja knew exactly what her daughter was thinking, not doubting that Jade had told her of their *conversation* before she leapt from the window. "I was afraid you would not come back."

"Please, both of you sit down; I need to discuss this with you," Jorja said calmly. She was so happy that she did not have the urge to bite either of them.

Rayne looked at her mother, and she said without opening her mouth, *"Jade said you could hear her thoughts, can you hear mine to?"*

"Yes," Jorja answered aloud.

Rayne's hand covered her mouth as she gasped. Jade laughed under her breath.

"No more cursing to ourselves," she said with a laugh, "she will hear us."

"Rayne, darling, are you okay?" her mother asked in a low, steady voice. "I will understand if you're not."

"Charles," Rayne said in a cracked voice, "they killed Charles . . . and Father. Why?"

"I don't know, my dear." Jorja could see the anger in her eldest daughter's heart she wore it all over her face. "And they...um...well, you." She stopped. "Well, you know."

Jorja did not have to read her daughter's thoughts to know what she intended. Jade sat quietly in the white rocking chair close to them by the fire.

"When we brought you home, you were cold as ice, your body stiff as if you were already dead," Rayne said with tears. "And now you are . . . well, not dead" she pressed her lips together as to stop herself from crying.

"Rayne, I am not sure what he did to me, but I know that I love you, and I will never hurt you, either of you." Jorja turned her head to Jade as her daughter spoke.

"You had to *feed* when you woke up. I could see it in your face," Jade said. "I know you don't want to accept it, but you really are a vampire, maybe those stories I read were wrong? Maybe vampires can come out in the daytime. Maybe they are not monsters."

Jorja put up her hand to stop Jade from speaking anymore. "I don't know what is happening or why, but I do know that I will find out. Even if it means leaving you both, so you will be safe."

"Not a chance, Mother!" Rayne said with a loud bellow. "You are not leaving us. Not now, not ever. I would rather die than lose another person that I love," she said with force. "I will find a way to become like you!"

"No!" Jorja yelled, "Do you know what I just did, where I went when I left?"

"Jade does," Rayne said smugly. "She said you went to *feed.*"

"Do you know what that means?" she asked softer.

"Well, Mother, I have read some of the same books as Jade and I have a pretty good idea what *feeding* is," she answered firmly.

"Rayne, I did not feed on a human," Jorja continued almost embarrassed. "I ran to a wooded area north and drank from a deer."

Jade's eyes went misty, a kind of overglaze for a moment; then a soft smile crossed her face.

"What do you see?" Rayne asked her.

Jorja did not like the thought of them becoming like her since she was very unsure what like her really was.

"Mother, when we brought you back here, you were dead or at least your body was. But you were still talking almost like you were dreaming," Jade whispered. "You told me he bit you."

"I will not bite either of you," Jorja firmly said. "I don't know what I am, but I know I am sure as hell not going to do this to you." She took a deep breath again, mostly out of habit. "It's getting late," Jorja said in a softer voice. "You both should get some sleep."

"Fine, but we *will* talk about this tomorrow," Rayne said as she went upstairs. Jade followed quickly.

Jorja sat in the chair staring into the fire trying to make sense of what was happening. She had read about *vampires* before, and yes, she did seem to have some of the traits, but if she really was one of them, why did the sun not bother her? Curiosity finally got the best of her, and she decided to go into the kitchen and test some of the legends she had read in the books they had.

1) Garlic - very strong smelling, but nope, nothing bad happened to her by smelling it.
2) Crucifix - still nothing.
3) Mirrors - well, she could see herself, and the fiction books said she would not.
4) Wooden stake - well, she did not really want to try that one on herself.

Jorja already knew that the sunlight did not bother her except for a little discomfort in her eyes, and that she can run very fast, the only downfall seemed to be the blood drinking. She tried to eat a piece of bread, and although she felt like throwing up, she was able to eat it.

Jorja walked around the house and looked at a painting of Leland and herself hanging on the wall; she felt like crying, but the tears would not come. Was this another side effect of her *disease*? Was she unable to cry, to show her heart breaking emotion? Of course, she no longer had a beating heart; Jorja could only feel the hardened reminisce of what once pumped the blood beneath her chest. Not pumping, not beating just there.

She tried to compile in her head all the thoughts of her life up to this point, but getting increasingly angry with herself, Jorja decided to go for a walk, but this time, she would keep it a little closer to home. Her senses seemed very sharp she could smell so many new things that she had never noticed before. It seemed so strange for her to see so clear in the dark, but she kind of liked it.

The wind picked up, and a new aroma hit her, sweet almost candylike. It pulled Jorja in like a magnet. She walked what must have been a few short miles to a shallow wooded area where she saw a man sleeping under a large tree.

Jorja had to stop herself! She had the same burning feeling in her throat that had been earlier when she had spotted the deer, but this was a man, a human, she did not *want* to take his life; she did not even know him. The scent was so strong and powerful, and before she knew it, Jorja was standing over him watching him as he slept. The hunger for his scent, for his blood was more than she could stand; and before she could stop, his head was in her hands, and her mouth was on his neck sinking her teeth deep into his pulsing vein. The sleeping man woke and let out a small gasp, but her grip was tight, so much stronger than he was. Now not able to move, the sting of her fangs piercing his tender skin put him into a frozen shock. In her head, Jorja was having a mental argument; she did not want to take this man's life but could not seem to let her grip of his body go. After a few long seconds, his body went limp. His life was over; Jorja had taken the most precious thing... human life. However, with some strange feeling of conquer, it did not upset her for long. She placed his head back on the bag where he had been sleeping. The sweet smell she had followed here was gone.

It was strange, Jorja thought, she did not feel the remorse she thought she would; this for some reason seemed no different from when Leland would bring home fish or meat from the shipping yard.

As she sat in the grass beside the dead man, she heard a voice, a man speaking in her head and the sound of Jade's voice replying to him. He asked her if she was ready, "No, this cannot be happening." Jorja ran as fast as she could back to the house, but she was too late. The house was now dark and quiet. Jorja ran up the stairs to her daughter's bedroom and found them both lying still in their beds... *He* had come back for them.

CHAPTER 2

Present Day

Fast-forwarding through all the brutally hard figuring-out-how-to-survive parts, and that brings us to the present or as Jorja had come to call it the beginning of the end.

It was a beautiful September morning, another first day of school. Jorja and her daughters moved here to start their lives over as their much younger selves . . . again. Too many times, they have had to do this; Jorja had often wondered if one day, it all would end. This time, they picked a small town in rural Canada called Madoc, with a population of fewer than two thousand people. The Sullivan girls had found over the years that they needed to keep interaction with humans even if only in small amounts; it helped them keep control of the urges if they are around the humans more often.

This time, Jorja bought a beautiful century-style farmhouse located on over two hundred acres of deeply wooded forest. The long, winding driveway made the house invisible to the road. The secluded house gave them the privacy they needed to keep their lifestyle hidden but also the closeness to the town where they could interact with the humans on a more frequent basis.

"Come on, girls, you don't want to be late, it's your first day back!" Jorja yelled up the stairs to her daughters.

"Mom, why couldn't we just have stayed in Brazil?" Rayne whined as she walked down the stairs. "I liked it there, no one bothered us, and the scenery was so beautiful."

"Darling, you know we have to keep moving, so we can keep our interaction with the humans every few years. If we don't, then it just gets harder to control ourselves. You remember what happened in Arizona?" Jorja replied.

"Yes."

"And do you want that to happen again?"

"Not really . . . I guess." Rayne sighed.

"I can't wait!" Jade sang as she skipped down the stairs.

She liked it when they started over; it gave her the chance to be a teenager again and get away with doing teenage things. Jorja did not always insist they go to school, especially since they have both graduated high school and university a few times now, but in a town, this small going to high school is the easiest way for them to get interaction with the humans. Not like when they lived in big cities where they could go out and enjoy everything the cities had to offer.

Rayne did not like going to school; she was a very keep-to-herself kind of girl and did not like *mingling* with what is supposed to be the food. Over the years, she had come to the realization that humans are very afraid of the myth of her kind, and that made them very dangerous. In all the myths created about vampires, humans felt they had to kill them by cutting off their heads or stabbing them with wood or silver and burning the bodies. Therefore, even though Rayne was much stronger and faster than the humans were, she really did not want to get close enough to give them the chance to test out those theories.

"Can I at least drive to school this time, Mom?" Rayne asked. "I promise to act like a normal teenage human girl." She rolled her eyes.

"Ohhh . . . if you get to drive, then I want a ride. I am not taking the school bus again; that thing smells funny," Jade said with a giggle. "All those pubescent humans in that tight little space and some of them don't even shower."

Jade, on the other hand, loved to study the humans. She had always been very good at controlling her thirst; she found it fascinating how drastically young girls had changed over the last century and a half. Girls today seemed more interesting, and high school was like her own personal study project. Over the years, Jade had written many books on the study of human nature. None of them published in her name for obvious reasons.

There were, however, advantages that came along with the "*disease*" as the three of them called it. Jorja and Rayne could hear thoughts and see memories in the minds of just about every person they encountered, excusing a very small few. Jade could as well, though she could also see visions of the future this made things a bit easier when it came time to move on to a new place. It also gave them an advantage in economical dealings. Jade knew all the right products and businesses to invest in and all the right places to be, financially, they were very secure.

"Okay, Rayne, but please be careful," Jorja said with a smile. "We just got here. I don't want to have to move again already just because you were showing off *again*."

"Thanks, Mom . . . Love you!" she yelled as she swung Jade around by the arm and pulled her out the door. "We're taking *my* car."

Jorja knew Rayne was not excited about going to school again, but she loved to drive her new car, so she was sure that made her feel a little bit better about being back in civilization.

The house was now silent and very empty, so Jorja decided she needed to do some shopping to make the house look a little more... human. They did not have many human belongings in Brazil; there was no need for them. So she unpacked the little bit of stuff that she did have and decided to go into town. "*If we are going to fit in here,*

I better make it look real," Jorja thought to herself. This was a small town, and no doubt, there would be a welcoming committee out to see them soon enough.

When the three of them arrived back in Canada, Rayne wanted to pick the lifestyle that they would portray, and it really did not surprise anyone that she wanted the rich life. Rayne did not like the thought of being poor; she had grown to like not having to "*work*" in the human world. Jorja had been to university many times and received many degrees over the years while doing research on others like them. She obtained two medical degrees, a science degree, and a degree in parapsychology . . . *that one was fun.* This time, the story was Jorja had been an explorer all over Egypt while her daughters were young and made some big discoveries that made them a lot of money, and now, she was settling down here to write a book about her travels. Rayne loved being creative, and Jorja had to admit she rather liked her stories of them.

Over the years, they had made a few friends in key industries, one man in particular in the law industry. He was a kind man but a very skeptical man until the day Rayne *showed* him exactly why they needed his assistance. He promised never to tell their secret and became very handy whenever they started over since in today's world, people needed IDs and passports to do just about anything. When he was too old to work, he advised Jorja to apply for new birth certificates every ten years or so; that way, they would always have valid identification with pictures that went with the age.

Looking at her new Ontario driver's license, Jorja shook her head. "Most women would love it if their pictures never aged." She let out a sigh, grabbed her keys and went to the garage.

"Oh, I love the smell of new cars," she said aloud to herself; this is one of the advantages as well, she thought.

Jorja sat in her brand-new black *Porsche Cayman*. "What a long stretch from the horse and wagon we left Halifax in!" she said with a giggle.

The house was about a fifteen-minute drive from town; Jorja was always more comfortable living further out in the country where they did not run the risk of neighbors taking notice to their *living habits*. She put the car in gear, backed out of the garage and drove down the long winding driveway to the road. They always try to go unnoticed, but when you move to a small town and pay cash for a house, everyone in town seems to know about it. When she saw the town sign, Jorja slowed down; she could not help but drive fast in this car. It made her laugh a little to herself.

Welcome to the Village of Madoc Population 1350

Jorja drove slowly down the main street looking for a place to do some shopping, but like most small towns, there was not much here. If she wanted to do any major purchasing, she would have to drive to Belleville or maybe Kingston; however, she did find a cute little grocery store. What better way to look like humans than buying food. Of course, this cute little village would no doubt send the welcoming committee over soon, so she thought she had better get something for them to eat. Most humans would question if there were no food in the house since that was the way of human survival.

Jorja parked her car in the small lot and walked into the store. She found it fun to shop for food and see what humans were finding appealing these days. Food had changed so much over the decades, now they eat instant foods, microwaveable dinners, and frozen fruits and vegetables. It was smarter to buy more of the frozen foods because it lasted longer, and it seemed to be what the kids of today liked. Jorja had almost filled her cart when she heard footsteps come up behind her.

"Hello, you must be Mrs. Sullivan," a soft female voice said.

"Yes, I am." Jorja turned around.

"I am Jenny Rivers." She held out her hand.

"Very nice to meet you, Jenny," Jorja answered with a smile, not returning a hand to shake.

"I just wanted to welcome you to town," Jenny said cheerfully. "I understand you bought the old Millers' farm?"

"Yes, that's right," she said, walking toward the checkout.

"Um, so I am told you are an explorer?" Jenny asked following Jorja quickly toward the cashier. "What brings you to Madoc?"

"I'm taking some time off to write a book," she answered hesitantly. "But I really must get going, there is still so much I have to get unpacked."

Jorja did not like to be rude, but she really did not want to answer too many questions, not knowing what Rayne and Jade have already started telling people.

"Oh...um...okay," she said as if Jorja had insulted her. "I'll see you around then."

Through Jenny's mind, Jorja could hear her inner voice. *"I don't really know what to think of her, she seems a little strange and way to pale. I thought she came from Egypt; don't they have sun there? She looks like she has had surgery. There is no way she can have a body like that after two kids!"*

Jorja really hated listening to people's thoughts it seemed so intrusive. She tried to block them out most of the time, but it was funny at times when they would first come to a new place and listened to all the inside thoughts about their *looks*. Jorja paid for the food and walked out to the car; she should have guessed a car like this in a small country town full of big trucks and SUVs people were bound to take notice.

There was a group of teenagers standing behind her car talking about it. Jorja hit the button to unlock the door, and the car beeped startling them. She could not help but laugh to herself as she heard a few of the thoughts that came from them.

"Holy crap! This car belongs to her . . . wow."

"Who is she?"

"Mmm. I love a hot chick with a hot car . . . "

"Excuse me," she said as she opened the door to put the bags of food in the passenger side then walked around the car and got in. Sometimes, it was hard to tone down what people were thinking, and since this was a new place, she guessed it best to take extra care to make sure no one thought anything close to the truth. It did not happen very often, but occasionally, someone would guess "vampires," but when they would tell their friends, they would just get laughed at... Silly humans, vampires do not come out in the daytime...right?

"Hmm, 10:00 a.m.," Jorja said to herself. "Well, I bet I can get some shopping done in Belleville before school is out." She liked to be there when the girls got home on the first day of school no matter how many first days they've had. She knew it could be difficult since they do look a bit different from the other kids; it is sometimes hard for them. Teenagers can be harsh sometimes especially teenage girls. Rayne prides herself on her good looks, and she loved to listen to the boys' thoughts about her. It gave her a bit of warmth knowing that even if she could not have a real boyfriend, at least they wanted her. Jade, on the other hand, always came home with her schoolbooks and got right to work finishing all of the projects for the year with in the first month. Seeing the future had its ups for her too.

After taking the frozen food home and putting it in the freezer, Jorja decided to take a trip into Belleville and see what store she could enjoy there. Belleville was not very far, only about forty minutes; but when other people were on the road, she had to watch her speed. Jorja really hated driving slow, but she hated being pulled over more!

CHAPTER 3

Rayne pulled into the parking lot at Center Hastings Secondary School with Jade in the passenger seat; they looked at each other and sighed.

"Here we go again," Rayne said. "I should get an Oscar for the acting I do around these humans."

"You know the drill." Jade laughed. "Let's go sign in and see how many small towners want to know our entire life story in the first hour. You know these places are all the same; everyone has to know everything." They both laughed.

Everyone saw them pull in and of course stared. Not many teenagers drive brand-new Mitsubishi cars in this town. Comments passed from whisper to whisper, ear to ear. The sisters were not surprised; it happened every time they started a new school. People would comment on how sexy they looked with their pale skin and their deep smoke gray eyes not to mention their flawless beauty and just a hint of mystery.

Rayne and Jade found their way into the main office to sign in and get schedules for the first term. Jorja had already arranged for their registration.

"Good morning," Jade said to the short red-haired woman at the counter who was taken by surprise when she had not heard them walk in.

"Oh! Good morning," the woman answered. "How can I help you?" her voice a bit cracked and startled.

The girls found first reactions to be quite humorous most of the time. No matter how many new schools or new places they lived, subtle fear was usually the first reaction they got. Humans are not a stupid breed; their instincts are usually bang on when it came to possible danger. Even if they tried to hide it, the subtle actions were there.

"My name is Rayne Sullivan, and this is my sister Jade; we are here to sign in and get our schedules," Rayne said softly with a chuckle. She liked that humans felt uneasy around her; it meant they kept their distance. That made things easier for her to deal with.

"Oh yes, Sullivan," the red-haired woman said as she shuffled through papers on her desk. "Here we go, Rayne, here is your schedule, and you are in homeroom 236, that's English with Mr. Cross. You will need to sign in with him. He should assign someone to show you around." She handed Rayne a sheet of paper; on the front was her schedule, and the back was a map of the school.

"Jade, your homeroom will be 104, math with Miss Hart," she said, handing Jade her schedule and a map. "Now you should get to class before the bell rings; you don't want to be late on the first day," she said, her voice still a bit dry and uneasy.

"Come on, Rayne, you can walk me to my class." Jade laughed as they walked out of the office. "Did you see her face? She didn't know what to think."

"Jade, you know they give us the same reaction every time," Rayne said and rolled her eyes as they walked. "Why do you always act surprised?"

Jade ignored the question. "This is my class." She stopped in front of a large door. "I'll see you at lunch; meet me in the cafeteria . . . Okay?"

"Yah, I'll see you there . . . Like always," Rayne mumbled as she walked away.

By the time Rayne found her class, Mr. Cross was already making his welcome back speech to the kids he taught last year. She walked into the room, every one stopped talking, and all eyes were on her.

"Good morning," Mr. Cross said, glancing over to her, "you must be Rayne Sullivan?"

"Yes, good morning," Rayne answered quietly, handing him her paper.

"There is an empty seat at the end of the third row. You can sit there if you like," Mr. Cross told her, pointing to the side of the room.

There was something a little off about him, Rayne thought. As she took her seat, all eyes still following her. He did not seem nervous talking to her. His voice was very calm and understanding. She thought this was a bit weird but did not give it any more thought, guessing it was just because he was a teacher, and it was his job to make the kids feel welcome.

"Jeffery Henderson," Mr. Cross called, "Miss Sullivan has science in room 111 next; I believe you do as well. Would you please show her where it is?" This sounded more like a demand than a question.

"My pleasure, Mr. Cross," Jeffery said with a smile ear to ear.

"Thank you," Mr. Cross said as he turned to the black board and started writing *Welcome to senior English literature.* He handed out the workbooks and began his lesson.

Jade had a bit of an advantage starting in the second year of high school, even though most of the kids knew each other from the younger school grades, it was still new for them. She sat in the back of the room, so she could observe the entire human class without having to turn around. She found that studying them gave her something to do when she finished the work they assigned early. The class lasted just over an hour then she went to her next one; it was history with Mr. Smithfield.

"Good morning, class," Mr. Smithfield said as the students took their seats. "My name is Mr. Smithfield, and this semester, we will travel back in time and learn all about our heritage."

Jade could not help but chuckle; if he only knew that she had done more than just read some book about all the history he would be teaching them this semester. The class dragged on and on as she watched the clock tick slowly forward until the lunch bell finally rang, and all the students got up and walked as fast as they could to their lockers.

Rayne was already in the cafeteria sitting at a table in the back reading a book while she waited for Jade to get there.

"Well," Jade said as she reached the table, "how bad was it?"

"Same old reactions," Rayne answered. "Everyone stared and whispered to each other . . . *Like* I couldn't hear them." She laughed.

The sisters sat there for the lunch hour talking low enough to each other that none of the humans would be able to hear them.

"Everyone is looking at us, aren't they?" Rayne said not taking her eyes off the book in her hands.

"Yup, they sure are," Jade said with a chuckle. "What do you expect? You know this happens every time."

"Yah, well, it doesn't make it any easier," Rayne said with a snarl. "Maybe I should flash them my sexy white smile!" She giggled.

"Oh stop, Rayne, just enjoy the fact that every boy in this room is daydreaming about you," Jade said, laughing with a twinge of jealousy in her voice.

"Whatever," Rayne said, rolling her eyes, "at least I have a class that I like this afternoon. I am in fashion design after lunch then auto shop."

"Must be nice, I have science. You know how hard it is trying to act like I don't know anything, and not giving away answers they haven't taught us yet," Jade said with a hiss.

Laughing, Rayne replied, "Yah, I just had science, what a joke that was."

The sisters sat at the table in the back of the cafeteria for the entire lunch period, talking about the new school, people and area in general. Every few minutes, one of them would look up and take count of the people still staring at them. The loud buzzer rang ending the lunch period, the cafeteria slowly emptied, and the groups of students made their way to their next classes.

"Well, I guess that's our queue," Rayne said. "I'll meet you at the car after school."

They went off to their classes at opposite ends of the school. Jade walked into her science class and quietly sat at the back of the room and got ready to pretend to be learning. The kids slowly piled into the classroom and took their seats. As intrigued as they were with Jade, they still kept their distance. Jade was reading through the science workbook that she picked up on her way into the class, so she did not really notice when this particular girl walked in, picked up her workbook and walked back and sat beside her. This took Jade a bit by surprise, and that did not happen very often.

"Hey," The girl said to Jade, "my name is Ezrabeth Cross." She had a very soft voice; there was no fear in it at all.

"Um...hi," Jade answered, trying to figure out why this girl was sitting there. "I'm Jade Sullivan."

"I know," Ezrabeth said with a giggle. "You just moved here, from Egypt, right?"

Ezrabeth was about five foot three and average build. She had shoulder-length hair with a few different colors streaked throughout it; she looked very much like every other normal human except for her eyes. She had beautiful purple eyes that Jade was sure would mesmerize any human.

"Um...that's right," Jade answered, trying to scan through the mind of this human, but for some reason, it was blank like maybe something was blocking it. This confused Jade, but with all the commotion of the first day, she did not take it to heart, chalking it up to too many things going on at once.

This hour passed as slow as the last class did, but with the exception that Ezrabeth questioned her nonstop about living in Egypt.

What is with this girl? Jade thought, *Why is she trying so hard to make conversation? Is she not afraid of me?* Usually, it is Jade that has to approach the humans to make friends, but she did not usually do that until later in the year once she got a good feeling for the ones she could approach and the ones she couldn't.

"*Maybe I am losing my appeal,*" she thought. "*Maybe there is something wrong with me?*"

The final bell rang, and the halls cleared out. Jade and Rayne reached the car about the same time. Jade had a box of books she put in the backseat.

"Starting already?" Rayne said.

"Yup," Jade replied. "Gotta do something to clear my head."

"What's up with you?" Rayne asked truly concerned.

"Nothing," Jade said quietly. "I just want to go home. I'm hungry."

"I hear ya. I hope Mom got her shipment in from Dr. Scott today," Rayne said hopefully. "I really don't want to have to go hunting."

Rayne's yellow Mitsubishi pulled into the garage not long after her mother did.

"Hey, Mom, how was your day?" she asked.

"Not bad, I did some shopping in Belleville, and I have some furniture being delivered tomorrow," Jorja replied.

"Ohhh...shopping," Jade said with intrigue.

"Well, if the story this time is Rich Explorer from Egypt, now writing a book...," she said, giggling, "I might as well have something to write on."

"But you already have a laptop." Rayne crinkled her nose a bit confused.

"Yes, but I don't really have an office... Don't all human writers have an office somewhere in the house to work in?" Jorja raised one eyebrow.

"Yah," Rayne answered. "I guess you're right."

"So," Jorja paused, "are you going to tell me how school was?"

"I have a ton of work to do," Jade said, pulling a box of books out of the back of the car and walked into the house.

"Why do you do all your work now?" Rayne yelled as Jade walked away. "You will be bored later."

However, Jade was never bored. There was always something for her to do or learn some new gadget to play with or puzzles to solve. Rayne, on the other hand, was not really into the learning end of school. Jorja did not blame her. When you have been to high school a few dozen times there is not much left to learn, it gets boring. Rayne was more into herself than her books. She had to have the latest fashions *usually ones she created.*

"So what else did you get today?" she asked as she helped grab a few bags from her mother's car.

"Well, I got a living room set, a dining room set, and some things to make your bedrooms a little more *lifelike,*" Jorja answered. The story of returning from Egypt made it easier to explain when she was buying *everything* you would need in a livable house. It was always about the appearance of being human rather than the actual lifestyle. People never question them if they appear to be what passed as *normal.*

"What would you like for *dinner* tonight?" Jorja said with a smirk. "It's been a week since we fed, and since we are going to coexist with the humans again, we have to make sure we take extra precautions and feed on a daily basis again."

"Did you get the shipment in today from Dr. Scott?" Rayne's eyes lit up when she asked.

Dr. Scott was a friend they had met while traveling through Europe. He was very helpful and sensitive to their disease. He would regularly send what he called *care packages,* which were blood bags from his clinic in London.

"Yes, he sent a month's worth for each of us," Jorja answered. "Thirty bags each, and he sent a special treat for you."

"Oh, I hope it's young blood," Rayne whispered with a smile.

Dr. Scott had a fondness for Rayne, an infatuation if you will. However, knowing that he could never be with her, he thought it best to keep his distance. Occasionally, he would send his regards and a special treat for her. He knew how much she craved "young blood." She had told him a long time ago that it tasted sweeter.

"Want to take those bags to the kitchen for me?" Jorja asked. "I picked up some extras when I was in Belleville just in case Jade decided to bring anyone over early, you know what she is like."

Jorja went to the kitchen to unload the box from Dr. Scott into the freezer that they built into the counter; they had to lift the entire countertop up to see it. It was a design Jade thought of back in the 1960s when Dr. Scott first started sending them the bagged blood. They built this, so no one would ever accidentally open the freezer. It would be hard to explain to a human. What would they say? "Um, yah, it's great for your skin."

Preparing the blood bag meals was easy now with the technologies that were developed over the years. Now they could heat up the bags of blood in the microwave instead of boiling it in a pot of water on the stove. Warm blood was always more appealing than cold.

"Mmm," Rayne said as she drank her special treat, "remind me to e-mail Dr. Scott tonight and thank him."

"You are such a suck up." Jade laughed.

"Can I help it if he likes me?" Rayne answered with a smirk.

"Ladies."

"Sorry, Mom." They laughed in unison.

The sisters were over a hundred and fifty years old, and yet, they still acted like children at times.

"Well, are you going to tell me how school was today?" Jorja asked.

"It was the same as it was the last first day, and the first day before that and probably last nine hundred first days before that one," Rayne said sarcastically. "I really wish we could have stayed in Brazil. I did not have to go to school there, and I had way more time to work on my next clothing line." Rayne designed hot new clothing lines and sold them to famous designers for them to pass off as their own. The drama it would cause if the humans knew that for the last fifty to sixty years, most of their "designer" clothes came from the mind of a teenage vampire.

"What about you, Jade, how was your day?" with the vibe Jorja instantly got from her, she was almost afraid to hear the answer.

Jade had neglected to answer her mother's previous question by gazing out the kitchen window seemingly lost in another vision. "Doesn't it seem weird to you, guys?" she said out of nowhere while they sat at the table drinking bags of blood like children with juice boxes.

"Does what seem weird, Jade?" her mother asked curiously.

"We are the top of the food chain. We hunt better than any animal out there, and we could feed on anything or anyone we wanted."

She paused. "And yet here we sit at a table drinking bloody bags through a straw."

"Where is this coming from? You know we don't feed on people, Jade," Jorja said harshly. "We have not fed on people in over one hundred years," she continued. "Did something happen at school today? You usually love to study the humans."

"I know we haven't, and I know we don't, but we could." Slowly, she raised her eyes to meet her mother's with a twinge.

"Where is this coming from? Did something happen at school?" Jorja asked again, looking at both of them.

"Nothing happened today at school," Jade said quietly.

She was very good at blocking her thoughts when she wanted to. It was like a child shutting a bedroom door after a fight with her parents.

"Don't look at me. I am quite content not fighting for my food," Rayne said. "Nothing happened today for me; the humans were smart, they kept their distance."

"I just don't see why we can't just do what comes naturally to us and hunt, that's all. I don't want to feed on the humans; I know what *that* does for us," as if she was embarrassed to say it. "But why can't we hunt animals? We did it before we met Dr. Scott."

"Jade, if you want to go hunting, then I will hunt with you. We just need to be cautious; we have kept our secret for too long to let it out like that," her mother answered nervously.

"REALLY?" Jade hollered excitedly, "Can we hunt tonight?"

"Tonight," Jorja answered in shock.

"Yes, please, Mom, there is over two hundred acres behind this house I am sure we can find something back there," she asked as if she were trying to get her mother to let her stay up late or something.

Jorja could tell that this was very important to Jade, although she could not tell why she would want to hunt after they had gone this long. It had been over one hundred years since they hunted humans, and they only hunted animals when it was absolutely necessary. Why all the sudden did she want to do it now?

"Okay, but just so we are clear, you are not going alone. I am coming with you," Jorja said reluctantly. "Rayne, do you want to come with us?"

"And wreck my dress, are you crazy?" Rayne answered. "I have kind of grown to like this civilized thirst-quenching bag. It's much cleaner than running through the woods snagging deer." She chuckled. "Besides I have to put my closet together and do some shopping online. I want to get a jump on the winter line."

"I really wish you would tell me where this is coming from, Jade, it's not like you at all," her mother said in a worried voice. "If there is something bothering you, I really wish you would talk to me."

"Mom, I just feel a little off today. I was sitting in my class with all those kids listening to them whisper to each other." She paused for a moment. "Maybe we should have moved to a bigger place where we can blend in a bit more that's all. You know this town only has like a hundred people in it." Jade never let their remarks bother her before; she would usually take it as a challenge to make friends with them.

"Almost fifteen hundred, sweetheart." Jorja giggled. "But I understand what you're saying; it's hard for me too. We did not ask for this disease, but now we have it, and we will keep on living with it just as we have for the last hundred and fifty years." Jorja hated when her daughters felt out of place. It was bad enough that they had to move so often; they could not keep in touch with the friends that they made. After all, Rayne and Jade were still somewhat teenagers.

They waited until well after dark, even though there were no immediate neighbors, Jorja did not want to chance any mishaps. There is a reason they do not hunt very often, when they hunted, they had to let their animalistic instincts take over, and if a human came into their path, it would be tragic...

"Are you ready, Mom?" Jade asked as she came dancing down the stairs.

"That's quite the outfit, Jade," her mother answered in a disapproving motherly tone. "Are we going to a yoga class?"

Jade had on a tight black shirt and tight black stretch pants—the kind of outfit you would see a human in at the gym to workout in.

"I want to be able to move freely; it's been so long since we've hunted an animal I am sure I will need to be flexible," she said with a smile.

"Are you sure you don't want to come too, Rayne?" Jade asked.

"Nope, not a chance," she replied. "I really have to get to work on this next line if I want to make my deadline."

Rayne was the most civilized out of the three of them. Jorja had her slipups with humans over the years as did Jade, but not once since they left Arizona had Rayne ever touched another human body not even so much as a handshake. It hurt her too much knowing the pain she caused all those years. Too many families lost their loved ones during the first few years while they tried to get a grip on this new life; there was so much to learn, and Rayne hated every minute of it.

"Okay, Mom, let's go," Jade said with excitement in her voice. Jorja had not seen her so intense in many years. However, she still could not unlock the door to her daughter's thoughts tonight to see what brought on this hunger for a hunt.

They left out the back door and ran a few kilometers; it did not seem like much to them since speed was on their side. Jorja had to remind Jade a few times to keep her voice down, or she would scare away all the wildlife.

"If you let down that guard you are holding in your head, you won't need to use your voice, and you won't scare away all the animals," she said softly.

"Okay, Mom, I'm sorry," she said in her mind. *"I just like to have some secrets; I am supposed to be a teenage girl you know. What if I was thinking about boys. Do you really want to listen to that?"*

"Boys, are you crazy? You know you can't—"

"Mom, don't worry. I am not going to, I know I can't, but just once it would be nice to be able to hug a boy or even hold hands," she thought, a twinge of pain in her voice.

"I know, darling, but we can't risk anyone finding out about us, and you know that physically we are a lot colder than them it's not like you can blame your ice-cold touch on the weather in September when we are still in the plus double digits."

"I just wish there was someone else out there like us." She took a deep unneeded breath.

"I know what you mean. Ever since your father passed, it has been lonely for me too. I know there are more of us out there, somewhere. The one who made us has to be somewhere; we just have to keep looking." Jorja tried to push the memory of her deceased husband from her mind.

"I'm tired of looking," Jade continued. *"I want them to look for us."* Even with Jade's ability to see the future, there was something blocking her from finding them; every time she tried to being on a vision or even a memory, it would be nothing but a black abyss.

They stopped running at a clearing where a creek ran alongside the edge of the field. There was a family of deer drinking from the creek.

"Okay, remember your stance," Jorja whispered, although it was through her mind, so there was no real reason to use a quiet inner voice. *"You don't want them to know you're coming for them, use your speed."*

Jorja and Jade both crouched down like two lionesses watching the deer closely, their muscles clinching in anticipation with the scent of the animal blood wafting through the air. Jade kept her stance as still as stone until they were close enough for her to strike. Leaping out of the darkness into the air and catching the deer by the antlers twisting its head and clinging her strong body around it like a snake, overpowering the timid animal quickly and sank her sharp fangs deep into the tissue of its throat. Jorja followed with the same graceful dance, and they fed for a few short seconds until the deer bodies went limp under their tight grasps, dropping the lifeless carcass to the ground, they had made the kill. Jorja had to admit she did miss the power of the hunt. Jade was right, why fight what they were so instinctively good at. She felt much more refreshed after hunting, mostly because when they took blood from a live creature as opposed to a blood bag, they were able to pull the life essence or chi, as some had called it, from the creature. Jorja and her daughter hunted and fed on a few more deer until the thirst had subsided.

They ran back to the house; it had been a very long time since Jorja felt so alive. She really had forgotten how much she enjoyed hunting. However, she knew that if they were going to hunt more often, they would have to find a further place to do it than their backyard. She did not want to bring unnecessary attention to them or their property.

"Did you enjoy yourselves?" Rayne asked as her mother and sister walked through the back door.

"Oh, very much so. I am going to head upstairs and find something to wear to school in the morning," Jade replied with a new smile ear to ear.

"What about you?" Rayne paused waiting for an answer " . . . Mom?"

"Sorry, darling, I was just thinking about a conversation your sister and I had tonight when we were hunting." She shook her head coming back to the present conversation. "Yes, I enjoyed myself very much I forgot how exciting hunting was."

"What did you talk about?" she asked curiously.

"Jade is having an issue again, feeling lonely. You know, interaction with humans, boys, and things like that," she replied. "I told her we all get that feeling, and that I knew where she was coming from. I miss your father very much. That combined with this curse we hold sometimes makes it hard." Jorja sighed. "Anyway, enough about things we can't change . . . How are your designs coming?"

"Great, I have some awesome ideas. I know Kevin and Tammy will, without doubt, end up fighting *again* over who gets to put their name on what." She laughed, then added, "Don't worry about Jade, Mom, she will be okay; you know she goes through this every thirty years or so, I think it's like a midlife crisis or something that just happens over and over again," she said, still chuckling. Rayne continued to click away on her laptop while her mother read from one of her favorite Edgar Allan Poe books.

"Mom," Rayne said after an hour or so.

"Yes, dear?"

"Do you think we will ever find the one that made us? Or any others like us?" she asked in a quiet voice not taking her dark eyes off her laptop.

"I know there is more of our kind out there, baby, and I know when the time is right, we will find them, or they will find us," Jorja answered with as much confidence in her voice as she could muster; after a hundred and fifty years it was a little hard to be optimistic.

"Yah, I guess you're right," she said, still staring at the glowing computer screen.

"Did you remember to e-mail Dr. Scott and thank him tonight?" Her mother reminded.

"Sure did," she said with a half smile. "You know, I kind of miss him. I know he is not the same now as I remember him. I know he is a lot older now, but he was a good friend to me, not many guys would want to stick around after finding out what we are." She sighed then went back to her designs, and Jorja picked up her book again. It was nights like tonight that she really wish they were able to sleep.

Jorja closed her eyes, remembering when she was a human lying in bed at night with Leland, holding each other so tight until they were both lost in dreams. Now all she could do was lie in an empty cold bed and stare at the ceiling, read books that she had collected over the years, do more research on her laptop or just sit there and think. She thought to herself; she would be glad when the furniture arrived at least then she would have something to do putting it all together and rearranging the house a few hundred times. The only downfall to the "She's a writer" story was it meant that she stayed home a lot and did not get a lot of human interaction. It was also very boring; at least in Brazil, they spent a lot of time hiking and exploring the rain forests.

After some time in silence with just the clicking of Rayne's laptop keyboard, Rayne and her mother both got up and went their separate ways in the large house that was still so empty. Jorja spent the rest of the night reading her old books and doing a bit of writing. Jade stayed in her room with the door shut, and Rayne took her laptop and laid down on the large empty floor of her bedroom and continued to work on her designs. This was a common night in the Sullivan home since they did not sleep nor did they need much rest. They got their energy from the blood they drank, and since Jade and her mother had hunted, they had got much more than they had been used to in quite some time. Pulling chi from the animal was something that they did not get from the bag of blood. It gave them a more refreshed view; they could see much clearer and hear sharper than the usual above human senses that they had already.

CHAPTER 4

Knock, knock! The sound bellowed through the empty house, rico-cheting off the woodwork.

"Good morning, you must be Mrs. Sullivan, just point us in the direction that you would like your new furniture set up, and we will take care of everything," the delivery man said with a smile.

"Thank you," Jorja answered, not that it really made a differ-ence where they put any of it; she would only move it again in a day or two anyways.

Jorja could not help but listen to the inner voice of the two deliverymen as they brought in the furniture and set up the elec-tronics; she tried to stay out of their way. To humor them, she tried very hard to act the part of the incompetent woman who did not know how to set up the surround sound to the high-definition sat-ellite receiver and connect it to the seventy-inch flat-screen TV. She defiantly could not show them that they connected both the Xbox 360 and the Wii to the ports on the back of the TV, so they could play both on a split screen, incorrectly, that would just be rude of her. Jorja laughed to herself thinking back to the first video game *Pong* she had purchased to occupy her daughters at night while they did not sleep. She still could not get over how much technology had changed over the last hundred and fifty years! It still aggravated her a little to see that even after a century and a half, most men still thought that women could not even tie their own shoe without help let alone play with electronics, but look out if dinner was not on the table and the laundry not put away.

"Wow! Out here in such a big house and all this new stuff. I wonder what her husband does?" The first deliveryman thought to himself, the second man, however, could only think of how fragile she seemed.

Jorja found it hard not to reply to people when they did not actually speak. She wanted to tell him that her *husband* was not responsible for anything that was in this house including her.

"Have a nice day, ma'am," the second man said once they had finished unloading and hooking up everything. Jorja just shook her head and let it go, if he had any idea how much danger he could have been in from this fragile woman. She could have ended their lives at that very moment, and no one would be the wiser . . .

The delivery truck slowly drove down the winding driveway and on to the road, now out of sight, Jorja let out a sigh . . . alone again. *"Well, I guess I better get to work putting this house together,"* her inner voice sounding much happier now.

Jorja rearranged the living room and re-setup the surround sound to have a better output and then headed to her office to put together the oak desk that the deliverymen forgot about after messing around with the television for so long. "Dammit!" she cursed aloud all the strength she had to do just about anything, and she could not put together a simple desk because there were no screws. Jorja let out a hiss then took a deep breath. *"Maybe Jade was right. We need to release some of our rage and natural instinct in a healthy, hunting way, not a smash to this beautiful piece of furniture to bits way."* For some reason today, she felt aggravated, not a feeling she got very often in this life especially after a hunt the night before. Maybe it was just pent-up from not hunting for so long before that she convinced herself.

Deciding rather than smashing this desk apart she should go in to town, find a hardware store and get some screws . . . Normal humans would do that, wouldn't they?

She picked up the keys, got in her car, squealing out of the driveway and down to the road. The drive into town seemed shorter today, maybe because she was agitated or maybe she was just going a little faster than the last time.

She slowed down when she hit the town sign again, coasting down the street to the stop sign. Jorja knew she had seen a hardware store yesterday by the grocery store. She pulled around the corner and parked in front of the building with the big red and yellow sign and went in.

"Good morning, you must be Mrs. Sullivan," a little voice from behind the counter spoke.

"Ms. Sullivan, thank you," Jorja corrected her, *odd*; she thought to herself she had never ever corrected anyone for calling her Mrs.

"Oh, I'm so sorry, ma'am," the elderly woman said, looking a little concerned when Jorja turned to face her. "*Oh my, I know Jenny had said she was pale, but I didn't think she was this pale; she's kind of creepy,*" she thought to herself, "*but nevertheless, she IS very beautiful—*"

"It's no problem, really," Jorja interrupted the woman's inner monologue in a much softer voice. "Please call me Jorja."

"Okay . . . Jorja. What can I help you with today?" Anne asked, at least that is what her nametag said.

"I am looking for scr . . . " Jorja paused . . . what is that scent? It hit her like a thousand pounds of rock. She had never smelt anything like it before, where was it coming from? It made her throat burn as if she had just drunk a bucket of hot bubbling lava. Jorja couldn't see straight, her head began to spin.

"Jorja . . . ma'am?" Anne, the little woman called to her, "Are you okay?"

Jorja shook her head trying to bring reality back. "Oh, I am very sorry. Yes, I am looking for screws," she answered, still baffled by the aroma that was now infecting every inch of her down to her core.

"I am sure I can help you find that," the man's voice came from behind her. Jorja was not sure if she wanted to turn around for fear. This aroma would seduce her into a feeding rage. The sweet smell surrounded her like a blanket; it took all the strength she had not to attack when she finally had the courage to turn around. Jorja stiffened her body and stopped breathing in the attempt to control her urge and to stop the burning thirst in her throat. As she slowly turned, Jorja saw the face of an angel chiseled in stone. His skin pale, almost as pale as her own. For a brief moment, she could have believed he was a vampire as well, snapping back to reality, she could hear his heart beating; he was very much alive, he was human, he was not like her! The gentleman was about six foot one, his body was firm, his tight T-shirt left no muscular crease hidden on his upper body, and his eyes were a deep purple, mesmerizing.

"Ms. Sullivan, may I help you find the screws you're looking for?" he asked, his head tilted with a half smile causing his dark hair to casually fall over his eye. His voice echoed through her body. Jorja thought that any moment she would attack and end this beautiful man's life. She had not felt the instinct this strong since they had left Arizona so many years ago. "*How could I feel this I do not know this man, I do not want to kill him . . . but that scent, the burn . . .* "

"Ma'am . . . " His long dark lashes taunting Jorja; every wave was like a fan pushing his aroma at her.

"Yes, I'm sorry, please do," she said, shaking her head.

"Hold your breath, Jorja, you don't need to breathe, you're not human. If you don't breath him in, you will be okay."

"Okay, Ms. Sulli . . . I mean Jorja, that will be $4.50," Anne, the lady behind the counter said, now feeling very uneasy at the sight of Jorja's eyes turning from smoke gray to deep black. Jorja put her sunglasses on quickly.

"Keep the change," she said, throwing the woman $20 and quickly exiting out the door to her car. Jorja got in and locked the doors keeping the windows up locking that sweet aroma out. "What is wrong with me?" she said aloud. "He is a human, but humans don't smell like that," she continued to argue with herself. "What is he? He is not like me, his heart was beating, but he was so pale, and those eyes . . . " Jorja stopped herself and tried to think rationally. "Maybe he is ill, maybe that is the aroma I sensed?" The weak always have a different scent. Oh, but that is not it, the weak had never made her throat burn like this before. She sat there a bit longer trying to put her thoughts together before she would try to drive through town and end up running some poor innocent person over.

Tap, tap! On the window.

This can't be happening, she said to herself. Jorja opened her eyes and looked out the driver's side window. She locked into a pair of the deepest, most seductive, purple eyes she had ever seen. He signaled to her to put the window down. Reluctantly, Jorja started the car and hit the electric window button and opened the window about four inches. His scent rolled in and hit her like a ton of bricks. *Control yourself, Jorja,* she told herself, *the girls do not want to move again yet.*

"Can I help you?" Jorja asked in a broken voice trying not to breathe him in.

"I wanted to introduce myself," he said. "You ran out so fast I did not get a chance to—"

I ran out, so I didn't kill you. Why are you still standing here? Jorja said in her head. *You still have a chance to run. I promise I won't watch what direction you go, not like that would make a difference I could track your smell anywhere.*

"My name is Adrian Cross, I teach over at the high school," he said with a soft smile. "You are Jorja Sullivan, right? Rayne's mother."

"Yes, I am. Nice to meet you," she said aloud still thinking. *You still have a chance to live, run, run as fast as you can. I will lock myself in the car, so I don't run after you, just run . . . run . . . RUN . . .*

They locked eyes, and for a brief moment, Jorja heard his thoughts. "*I don't hear her heart . . . But she can't be . . . it's not possible. Could she really be, no that is crazy. Adrian, get a grip on yourself . . . walk away before you do something incredibly stupid. Don't blow it here.*"

He was arguing with himself just as she had been doing. Did he really say he could not hear her heart beating? The thought of that made Jorja laugh; her heart has not beaten in over one hundred and fifty years, but how could he know that? How could this human with a beating heart notice that hers was not?

"I am sorry for the intrusion, Ms. Sullivan," Adrian said in a low, broken voice as he took off back down the road toward the high school.

"*You're sorry, I want to jump out of the car and drain you where you stand, and you are sorry! Oh my god, Jorja, get a hold of yourself. You have the control. You fed last night. For crying out loud, you don't need to hurt him, right now, you just need to go home; there is no one there that you can hurt.*" She pleaded with herself as she put the car in gear and backed out of the parking spot. Jorja pushed in the clutch and put the car in first gear. Before she hit the town sign, she was already in fifth. "*Just make it home,*" was all she could think, "*don't stop, just get there.*" His aroma still lingering in the car; she put down the windows and let the fresh air flow through, and his scent was gone almost instantly. She came up to her road and flew around the corner not slowing down. "Almost there," she mumbled in the car as she hit the driveway almost taking out the cedar fence that lined up the sides to the house. Stopping just short of hitting the garage door as it opened a lot slower than she wanted; Jorja pulled into the garage and closed the door behind her. She was home; he was safe . . . for now.

Jorja walked into the large living room now full of boxes from everything that had been delivered earlier. She sat down on the large white leather L-shaped sofa and put her feet up on the ottoman. *"Okay, Jorja, now let's be realistic about this. This Adrian Cross, IS a human, all the life signs are there. He has a pulse to start with, that is a huge giveaway, and his scent well that sweet intoxicating blood aroma has to be human. Wow! Pull yourself together, there is no other answer; maybe I just need to hunt again tonight and get this out of my system."*

CHAPTER 5

Ezrabeth sat with Jade again today in science class, talking for almost an hour straight.

"I don't mean to sound rude," Jade said in a soft low voice, "but shouldn't we be listening to what is being taught?"

"This stuff is so boring to me, I just thought, maybe, you felt the same," Ezrabeth replied, sounding almost shocked at Jade's statement.

Ezrabeth stared at Jade for a few seconds, not saying anything. The look on her round face was so concentrated. It was as if she was trying to read Jade but couldn't.

Jade sat there for a few more seconds trying to figure why this girl thought this was boring to her. Did she look bored? Did she act bored? Did anyone else seem to notice her lack of interest in the human version of science? Jade tried to read Ezrabeth again but still got nothing, not a peep from that mind that was as black as the midnight sky.

"I'm sorry if I insulted you," Ezrabeth said under her breath. "You just seemed . . . different to me."

Different, what did she mean by different? Could she possibly know?

"Different?" Jade replied with one eyebrow raised and half a smile.

"Yes," Ezrabeth said, looking at Jade's eyes that were now turning a darker black, "like . . . well, never mind. I'm sorry I bothered you," Ezrabeth said in a disappointed low voice.

Jade knew how important it was for them to keep their secret from the humans, and Ezrabeth was clearly a human. She had a heartbeat, she was breathing, and she had the distinct aroma of human blood flowing through her veins. Jade was very confused, was this girl just one of those kids that were a little off, a little unstable or just one of those lonely kids that looked for friendship in other lonely kids?

"I'm just not really sure what you are talking about Ezrabeth," Jade replied in a friendly calming voice.

"It's okay . . . I have work to do, so I better get to it," Ezrabeth replied sounding a little embarrassed.

The sound of the bell was music to Jade's ears. She had never been more thrilled to hear the bell ring; she grabbed her books and headed out to the car as quick as she could without bringing attention to herself. She threw her books in the back and got in. "*What's with this girl, there is no way she could know anything,*" Jade thought as she tried to scan through the pages in her head, but she could not see this girl anywhere in the future; she could not even see her in the very near future. "*There must be something wrong with me!*" She was so focused on Ezrabeth that she had not noticed Rayne get in and start the car. The sound of the radio startled her.

"What's with you?" Rayne asked.

"Nothing. Can we just go home?" Jade hissed. "I really need to talk to Mom."

"If you say so, but you are going to have to let that wall down if you are going to talk to her," Rayne said concerned. "I sat here for five minutes before I turned the car on, and I could not hear your thoughts at all, and I *know* you were thinking; it was written all over your face."

"I know, I know . . . can we just go please. I don't want to sit here anymore," Jade said in a shaky voice as she stared out the window at the kids walking to their cars and getting on the busses. A very vivid vision came into Jade's head; the thought of it terrified her. She fought very hard not to let Rayne see this sudden change. As they sat in the parking lot waiting for the students to clear the way for Rayne to pull out, Jade gasped. "NO."

"What is it, Jade?" Rayne, knowing full well now that her sister had seen a vision.

"Nothing. Let's just get out of here," Jade mumbled.

"You're going to have to open up soon, Jade, you're starting to scare the hell out of me," Rayne said, shaking her head.

They waited in silence for the kids to clear out of the way and then pulled out of the driveway, stopping at the stop sign letting a car past them. Jade's body tensed, her eyes now glowing bright orange. Her hands gripped the seat as she locked her eyes on the car passing them.

"What's your issue Jade?" Rayne hissed. "It's just Mr. Cross, my homeroom teacher."

"Not him," Jade growled through her clinched teeth and venom filling her mouth.

"Then who?" Rayne said surprised. "His daughter?"

"NO! Can we just go home now? Please?" Jade said still clinching her teeth. She hadn't actually been looking at the car or the people in it; she was trying to cover up the vision she was having.

"Sure . . . I guess," Rayne said, wishing she knew what was going on.

"Put your sunglasses on," Rayne said in a worried voice as she sped through town. "Your eyes are turning."

It was a very quick ride home in silence as Jade stared out the window watching the trees fly by along the side of the highway. She seemed to be in a coma the entire way home, staring blankly, obviously lost in a vision that she was not sure about. They pulled into the garage, and Jade jumped out almost before the car came to a complete stop. She left her books in the backseat and ran into the house and up to her room slamming her door behind her and turned on her stereo. Rayne knew something was up; the only time she acted this way was when she was upset and trying to calm down. Rayne grabbed Jade's books for her and brought them into the living room where Jorja was still sitting on the couch now reading a book to clear her head.

"Okay on the weird crap-O-meter," Rayne said as she walked in. "This would have to be off the charts."

Jorja put her book down and looked at her daughter with her eyebrows pushed together. "What are you talking about?" *Did she see what happened with Adrian today?*

"Just an FYI, Mom, Jade is weirding me out, more than usual today," she replied. "She said she wants to talk to you, but I warned her to take down her wall before she even tried."

"Okay, what happened today to make you say that?" Jorja asked, confused.

"Well, after school, I came out to the car, and she was already sitting there waiting for me. I got in and sat there for almost five minutes. I tried to read her, and I got nothing. She did not even notice I was there until I turned on the radio," she said as she pulled some books out of her bag to start on her homework. "Then when we pulled out of the parking lot, Mr. Cross and his daughter, passed us at the stop sign, and Jade started freaking out. Her eyes turned bright orange; she was grinding her teeth, and I think she even broke my seat."

"She freaked out when she seen Adrian and his daughter. She must know what happened today. She must have seen my reaction to Adrian at the hardware store?" Jorja panicked but cloaked her mind, so Rayne could not see in.

"Okay, well, I'll give her some time to herself. Whatever it is when she is ready to talk to me, she will come down," Jorja said as calm as she could but still very worried.

A few hours passed and Jorja had retreated to her office and was reading through some old poetry that she had collected. Rayne finished her homework and decided to go for a drive. She wanted to go and check out Belleville and see what the clothing stores here were selling. She always liked to see her designs in the displays. No sooner did she pull out of the garage, and Jade came down the stairs.

"Mom," she said softly, "do you have a minute?"

"I have all the time in the world . . . remember?" she answered with a sigh. "What's on your mind? I really wish you would let me in."

"I need to leave," Jade said in a crackly voice.

"Your sister just left for Belleville. You could have caught a ride with her," Jorja said, still trying to read her.

"No, Mom." She paused. "I need to leave on my own for a while."

Jorja knew she was not talking about going out for a bit. "Where are you going to go?" she asked. "Is there anything I can do? I know you are well old enough to be on your own, but that doesn't mean I won't worry about you," she said sadly. "I am still your mother."

Jorja knew something had been bothering her daughter for a while now; she did not usually block her out so long. Jorja did not want her to leave, but she knew she could take care of herself, and Jorja knew Jade was strong enough to fight her urges. She was a good hunter, and her ability to see the future would guide her where she needed to be.

"When are you leaving?" Jorja asked, feeling her unbeating heart breaking.

"Tonight, Mom, I don't want to make this any harder than it already is," Jade said, staring at the floor.

"Be careful, baby," Jorja requested as she watched her bring a few bags down the stairs and put them in the back of her Mercedes SUV. Jorja knew Jade had her reasons for going. She just wished she would tell her what they were.

"Does Rayne know or do you want me to tell her?"

"I left a letter in her room," Jade said as she hugged her mother tightly and got into her SUV. "I have my cell if you need me. I love you, Mom."

Jade pulled out of the garage, and Jorja watched her drive away. She hoped she would be okay. Even though Jade was over a century and a half old and this was not the first time she had taken time to herself, it was still very hard for Jorja to watch her youngest daughter go out on her own. She decided to go back up to her office and start writing to help clear her head. Jorja enjoyed writing about her eternal life, and it was a great outlet to help her through some of the lonelier times without her deceased husband.

A few hours later, Rayne arrived back at home. Jorja heard her pull into the garage from her office above it. She did not go to meet her; she wanted to give her daughter a chance to read the letter Jade had left for her. Jorja hoped Rayne was not too upset that her sister had decided to leave. Jorja heard Rayne walk into the house and up the stairs.

"Mom, are you home?" she asked in her mind already noticing that Jade's SUV was not parked in the garage.

"Yes. I'm in my office. Jade left something on your bed you need to read," Jorja answered back.

Rayne walked up the stairs and into her room carrying some bags of new clothes. She picked up the letter on the bed and started to read. Jorja couldn't help but read it through Rayne's mind.

Dear Rayne,

I am sorry to leave on such short notice, but I don't know how to handle this vision I've had. I know you will understand. I was trying to see into the future this afternoon to figure out Ezrabeth Cross, but what I could see was far beyond anything I wanted to ever see. There was nothing but darkness when I thought of her, and then all the sudden, another vision came, and I saw a boy. He looked like he was in pain; he was standing at a bridge looking over as if he was going to jump. Normally, I wouldn't even bother worrying about what the humans do, but he seemed different it was like he was calling for me. I don't understand any of it, and it did not come to me until I spent the afternoon blocking out Ezrabeth talking. When we seen her after school at the stop sign, his face flashed through my mind, he was calling for my help. Then, I had a horrible vision that I cannot share with you just yet. I have to see what this means. I have no idea how any of it has to do with Ezrabeth or even if it does at all. I know you will understand soon enough. Please take care of Mom; she will need all of us very soon. I have my cell if you need me, but please just give me some time to figure this out.

Your loving sister for eternity,

Jade Sullivan

Rayne sat on her bed for a few minutes staring out the window. "*Take care, little sister, I will miss you. I hope you find what you're look-*

ing for," she whispered to herself as she stood up and walked toward her mother's office.

"Mom, did you see the letter?" she asked through her mind.

"Yes, I did, are you okay?" Jorja answered back.

"I guess. I just hope she'll be safe. I couldn't handle losing her for good. I am going to go for a walk; I'll be back in a bit."

That night was one of the longest nights of Jorja's life; she was so worried about her daughter, both of her daughters—Jade for taking this trip alone, and Rayne because now she would be so alone at school. She tried not to worry about what Jade meant when she had said that Jorja would need them all soon enough; then she started to wonder about the boy on the bridge Jade had seen. Jorja wondered who he was. Jade had never really bothered with the lives of humans that way before, why would it matter to her if he jumped off the bridge. Jade had been the last one of the three to be turned into a vampire. She knew how he did it but would never tell her mother or sister for fear that Rayne would try to create another for her companion. Jade would never allow anyone to have the same eternal fate as they did. After they left Arizona, Jade could not handle the thought of taking a human life even if it meant they would live forever in our eternal world. She had slipped up a few times over the years but only when a human would cross her path while hunting for animals; she never turned them should had let them die, and it almost destroyed her. So many times, in the early years, she had been so overwhelmed with the death of the innocent people they had killed that she tried to end her timeless life, but she soon realized that what killed normal humans had no bearing on her. Their hardened bodies withstood the sands of time, no knife nor gun nor any other human killing device made the slightest impact on them. She gave up after a few years of searching for a way to die and decided to research the humans and a way to help heal their pains.

Rayne, on the other hand, would now be completely alone at her school, suddenly lost in a world surrounded by the things she hated the most, mortal teenagers! These creatures would grow up to get married, have children, have careers and grow old. The very things Rayne could never do. This had been a very long night for her as well, so she did the only thing she could think of to ease her pain.

"Mom," she asked as she walked toward Jorja's office after returning from her walk, where her mother was still writing trying to keep her mind busy.

"Yes, Rayne, I'm in here," Jorja answered through the half-open door to her office.

"Take me hunting," Rayne asked, though the tone in her voice would suggest it was not a question but more of an "I'm going even if you don't" statement.

"What?" Jorja was more than a little shocked. "You want me to take you hunting?"

"Yes," Rayne sounded almost confident in her answer. "I've put it off for too long, and well, I've been thinking I guess, about us and our kind, and maybe Jade was right." She sighed. "Maybe we shouldn't try to fight what we are anymore. Maybe we should just accept it with honor and live this endless life as it is intended?"

"Okay, now you're scaring me," Jorja said, not sure how she should react. "Are you going to leave too?"

"No, Mom, that's not what I am saying." Rayne reassured her mother. "I just think that I have treated this like a disease for too long, maybe it's time I embrace what we have as a gift."

Was she really saying this, was she really having this massive change in heart? Jorja was happy to see that she was being so positive, but at the same time, it did frighten her that Rayne had done a complete three-hundred-and-sixty-degree turn in her outlook in a matter of hours.

"Darling, if you want to go hunting, I will take you, but I would prefer to go somewhere a little farther away than our backyard if it's okay with you?" Jorja offered. "If you like, we can go to Algonquin this weekend and do some hunting. I don't want you to miss school; it would look too suspicious if you both didn't go."

"Okay, well, I guess it is Wednesday already, so we can leave Friday after school? Maybe do some hiking like we did in Brazil?" she asked with a smile. It was nice to see Rayne positive, Jorja thought. "I would love that."

The following morning, Rayne drove her Mitsubishi to school alone; she was not very excited about sitting alone at lunch, or worse, the questions about her sister not being there. Jorja drove in not long after her daughter; she thought it would be better if she went to the school herself to explain her daughter's absence. Jorja decided to make some human story about Jade going to live with her father in Alberta for a while; that would keep them from questioning Rayne. Split parents had become somewhat of a normal thing in the human world. Did no one believe in the sacredness of marriage anymore? Jorja parked her car in front of the school; there were kids standing out there waiting for the bell to ring. She ignored the perverse comments they said to each other and walked into the main office.

"Good morning," Jorja said softly to the red-haired woman behind the desk that apparently did not hear her come in.

"Oh, I'm sorry you startled me," the woman said as she looked up. "How may I help you?" Her voice calmed as she met Jorja's softened gray eyes.

"I am here about my daughter," Jorja replied, "Jade Sullivan."

"Oh yes, Jade. Would you like me to page her down for you? She should be in homeroom," the woman said as she opened her book to find the pager number to that room.

"No, that won't be necessary," Jorja's soft voice was hypnotic, just as her daughters had been when they picked up their schedules.

"She is not here. I wanted to come in and pick up her school records. She has decided to spend some time with her father in Alberta, so I will need her records to send to him."

"Oh, I'm sorry to hear that, Mrs. Sullivan," said the red-haired woman. "I hope everything is okay," she sounded genuinely concerned.

"Yes, she just needed her space," Jorja replied with a smile. "You know teenage girls."

"All too well," the woman added with a chuckle. "Here is her file, Mrs. Sullivan. I hope she enjoys herself in Alberta."

"Thank you, I am sure she will," Jorja answered calmly and turned to walk out of the office. In the hall, Rayne waited for her mother. She looked so lost and alone. "*It will be okay.*" Jorja reassured her with her mind. "*She is strong, and she seems to have a plan for this boy she is going to find.*"

"*I know, but that doesn't make it any easier,*" she replied blinking her eyes. "*I have to go to homeroom now; I don't want to keep Mr. Cross waiting,*" Rayne continued without opening her mouth.

"*Mr. Cross, Adrian Cross is your teacher?*" Jorja asked, trying not to let her daughter see her other thoughts.

"*Yah, he is a bit weird though, he doesn't act like the rest of these weird humans,*" she said, "*I have to get going, Mom, I'll see you at home.*"

"*Okay, darling, see you this afternoon,*" Jorja replied, still blocking her thoughts of the encounter she had with Adrian earlier.

Jorja walked back out to her car in the empty lot at the front of the school; all the students had disappeared to their morning classes. She sat there for a minute thinking about everything that was going on with Jade, and to top it off, Adrian was Rayne's teacher, go figure! She put the car in gear, backed out of the parking spot and decided instead of going right home, she would take a little drive around the area. Jorja like to know her surroundings and what better way to know them than to explore them.

Jorja did not know what made her pick this place on this day, but she turned off the highway down a dirt road. Jorja drove for a bit until she came across a beautiful conservation area. She parked her car and took a long walk through the wooded area around the water. It was clear that the town took pride in this little conservation area; there had been a lot of work done on the old buildings to restore them as well as keeping the land around it natural. Jorja found a quiet little spot next to a beautiful clear blue spring and sat on the rocks. She could hear the birds, crickets, and all the other little creatures that were too afraid to come too close. Sitting there for a few hours watching the water gave her, more than enough clarity to think about what was going on around her. Jade had left; Rayne felt lost, and yet, Jorja could not help thinking about Adrian. What was it about this human? The same thought kept running through her head; it was his subconscious comment about her nonexistent heartbeat. Jorja had many thoughts about Adrian Cross that afternoon, would it make a difference if he was a vampire? Would she be willing to ask Jade how to make him that way? Could she be so selfish? Jorja's life had gone on for over a hundred and fifty years empty and lonely. The more she thought about Adrian, the more she began to think it was possible she could develop feelings for this human, but that was ridiculous!

CHAPTER 6

Snapping back into reality and out of the sea of thoughts that had flooded her head, Jorja was surrounded in darkness. She was so lost in thoughts that she did not hear the footsteps behind her...if there were any.

"Jorja."

A man's voice said in a soft low tone. She did not have to turn around; she knew it was him. It was Adrian. What was he doing out here? Did he not know how dangerous the woods could be at night and out here? Being alone with her really did not help his odds.

"Adrian." Jorja breathed his name, still keeping her back to him. "What are you doing out here? It's late. Don't you know how dangerous the woods are at night? You could be attacked by an animal or something."

"I would be more worried about your safety, Jorja, the woods at night are no place for a lady," he replied, stepping closer to her.

"Please stop there. I don't think you should come any closer," she pleaded. Jorja really did not want to hurt him, and the closer he came to her, the stronger his scent was, and the more her throat burned for his blood.

"You won't hurt me, Jorja," he said calmly. "I have no fear of that."

"How can you be so sure?" She chuckled, still staring at the water in the stream that had turned black. "You don't know me, Adrian." *Why is he so calm?* she thought to herself, and then it dawned on her, *why was he all the way out here?* He took another step closer, now less than ten feet from Jorja. It would take her only seconds to turn and attack, but even with the burn in her body and the hunger for his sweet blood, Jorja stayed frozen where she sat, her body clinched solid as a rock; she did not *want* to hurt him.

"I know more about you than you care to tell me," he said, taking another step. "But why are you here all alone tonight?"

"I took a walk this afternoon to clear my head, my youngest daughter moved out today to go and live with her father in Alberta," she said, hoping he would believe her, but something told her he would not, "and then I found this beautiful spot. Why are you out here?" It occurred to her that she could not hear his thoughts right now, could he have found a way to block them.

"You and I both know that is not the truth about your daughter, don't we, Jorja?" He paused, "And I'm out here because I have been looking for you for many years," he said, taking yet another step closer. "I did not know when I would find you, but I knew you would be out here."

What did he think he had found? Jorja stood up from the rock she had been perched on. "Exactly what do you think you have found?" she asked as she turned and looked at him. Jorja was stunned; to her revelation, his eyes were the same glowing shade of fiery orange that hers were at that moment. She took a step closer and stared at him for a brief moment entranced by the very sight of him, his pale face was glowing in the moonlight. Was this even possible? Could he be like her? Was he a vampire? No, there was no way; she could hear his heart beating.

"How?" Jorja stared into his eyes. "I can hear your heartbeat; I can smell the blood flowing through your veins."

"I know it is hard for you to understand being that you are a full blood," he said so calmly now standing less than two feet from her.

"They call us Dhampir, my daughter and I, half human half vampire; well, she is less than half I guess."

"But how did you know what I am?" Jorja asked again with intrigue. Could this really be happening?

"It was three little things that gave you away," he said with a smile. "The sound your heart did *not* make, then your eyes that day in the hardware store and most of all . . . your scent."

"*My* scent . . . What about you?" she said almost lost in the depths of his eyes, forgetting all about the burn in her throat. "You have the sweetest-smelling blood I have come into contact with in a very long time; it was all I could do that day at the hardware store to control myself I have never wanted to feed on a human that bad before."

"Should I take that as a compliment?" he asked with a chuckle.

"No, I don't think you should; I am having a very hard time controlling myself... right now." Jorja looked away ashamed.

"Jorja, you can't hurt me." He reassured her. "Even if you did bite me, remember I *am* half vampire."

"Then it's the other half I am worried about," she said as he took the last step; he was now standing inches from her. She could feel the heat of his body flowing to her like waves from the ocean hitting the shores.

"Don't be worried," he said, as he put his warm hand on her icy hip pulling her closer to him. "I told you, I have been waiting for you."

The feeling of his warm human hands sent chills down Jorja's already icy body. She knew she should want to pull away; she did not even know this person, but she could not bring herself to do it. Why now, after all these years did he have to find her? Jorja's head was spinning in so many directions she did not know what to think. All the sudden, his hand moved from her hip and wrapped around her pulling her closer to his burring body. The feeling of his warm body melting into her icy core was mesmerizing, for a moment, she had forgotten the burning in her throat craving his blood.

"Jorja, I have waited so long for you," he said in a low sensual voice. "Don't be afraid."

"I'm not afraid for me, Adrian," she said, now trying to pull back. "I am afraid for you. I have never met anything like you."

"We could always play a little game of see what hurts?" he said, raising one eyebrow with a smirk. "I have never been hurt by humans; I have yet to break a bone or catch a cold."

"Adrian, if I was to hold you too tight and injure you or worse bite you, I . . . I just . . . " Jorja stared into his eyes, and for some strange reason felt, as if she had known him for years, as if they had always been together, but that was not possible she had been alone for so long. "I have taken too many human lives in my time, I refuse to risk another."

Before Jorja could say another word, he pressed his burning lips to hers. She had not felt passion like this in over a hundred and fifty years; she fought him a little at first, but his hold was stronger than she had expected. Jorja knew if she really tried that, she could break away from him, but it had been so long since she felt the strong arms of a man around her; she quickly gave in and kissed him back. Jorja tried so hard not to let her monster out; she could feel the venom start to flow to her razor sharp teeth and froze trying to control herself. She did not want to hurt Adrian. He pulled his head back when he felt her freeze and put his hand on her cheek.

"The same venom flows in me," he said softly. "You can't hurt me, Jorja."

"How can you be so sure that I won't hurt you or worse kill you?" she said, staring into his still fiery eyes. "You are only a half vampire."

"I have lived sixty-seven years now, Jorja," he said in a very soft calm voice, "and every day, I have prayed for happiness, and now I have found you. There has to be a reason for that."

He kissed her again then slowly moved his lips down her throat; before Jorja could stop him, he sank his sharp teeth into her skin, the skin until that very moment she had believed to be impenetrable. It did not hurt but rather it felt warm as if he had injected her with his heat. He took very little blood and then softly kissed the area he had bitten. He slowly raised his eyes back to hers. Within seconds, the abrasions he had made were completely gone.

"Did that hurt you?" he asked softly.

"No," she whispered, still in the trance of his embrace. "It was warm; I could feel your venom but no pain."

"Your turn," he said, "I promise it will be alright."

Reluctantly, Jorja placed her mouth to his neck, would she be able to stop as he did? He squeezed her closer, and without another thought, her fangs sprang from her mouth, and she bit into him trying to be as soft as he had been, but when she tasted his blood, she could not control herself. She squeezed him as close as she could and drank the blood that was flowing into her mouth; instantly, the burn in her throat was gone, and she let her grip go pulling her mouth back.

"I'm so sorry, Adrian, are you okay?" she asked, as he adjusted his stance.

"Oh, Jorja, my love, I am better than okay," he replied with a laugh as he caught his breath. "I have finally found you."

"I did not . . . hurt you?" Jorja asked nervously.

"Oh, no, my dear, far from it. I can feel the burn from the bite but not pain, and I heal very quickly. That was the best feeling I have had in many, many years." His eyes tracing her face.

Adrian and Jorja sat on the rocks overlooking the running water; he held her for hours as they talked about the past, how they had become damned to this life and the search for the one that made her and her daughters what they are. Jorja told him about her daughters and where Jade had really gone. He asked many questions about her travels and the extra senses they had. Jorja asked him about his past, how he became a half vampire and if it was possible for him to be turned into a full vampire like her.

"My father was a vampire, my mother was a very beautiful woman from England; he enslaved her with his charm. She fell in love with him and left her family behind to come here to Canada with him." Adrian's voice was low and monotone. "I do believe he loved her; my aunt would tell me many stories about him and how he worshipped my mother. He knew that physical love was not possible with a human because he was much stronger than her but after time he gave into her needs." His voice now sounding stale. "A close friend of my mother's found her almost dead when she arrived for a morning tea visit. My father was gone."

"I'm sorry," Jorja said in a low calm voice.

"She knew by the bruises on my mother exactly what had happened. She nursed my mother barely keeping her alive until the day I was born. Feeding her the blood of the small animals she would catch around her house to help me grow inside of her." His eyes lowered as he paused before going on with his story. "My birth caused her death; she was not strong enough to live through the horrific ordeal, and after all, she *was* human. My mother's friend, little did my mother know then that the woman I call my aunt was a witch, was a wonderful woman as well with a great deal of patience for my difficult journey. She taught me how to hunt and how to use my instincts."

They sat on the large rock in each other's arms. Jorja was mesmerized by his voice as he spoke more about his younger years and his aging process as it was very different from the humans. For about seventeen years, he seemed to age twice as fast as humans do; then all the sudden, it stopped, and for the last fifty years, he had not aged at all.

"Why did you come out here tonight?" Jorja whispered. "How did you know I was here?"

"I come out here every night, looking for you," he said slowly looking in to her eyes again that had returned to their usual smoky gray. "I dreamt you would be here. I know that may sound strange to you, but up until I dreamt of you, I was positive that I would be alone forever."

"But I am not like you," she said ashamed.

"I know," he said with a laugh. "I can't hear your heartbeat, and today, when your daughter came to class, I listened for hers too and nothing. I guess I did not notice it before since there was so many other beats in the room."

"Rayne, does she know about you?" Jorja immediately began to panic.

"No, once I realized what you and your girls really were, I went to my aunt's spell book and conjured a blanket spell for my thoughts until I could figure if it was safe or not," he replied. "So Rayne would not have been able to read my thoughts."

"How did you know that we could read thoughts?" Jorja asked. "Can other vampires do that?"

"I am not sure, but my aunt used to tell me that my father could read my mother's thoughts," he said. "But I have not met any other full blood or half-blood vampires to ask them."

"But your father," Jorja looked hurt, "has he never come back for you?"

"I assume he would think I was dead like my mother; he was so angry with himself for hurting her," he replied. "He left a note for my aunt telling her he was sorry, and that he could not live with himself for what he did to her, and that he knew if he turned her that I would die anyway." He sighed. "I guess he would rather us both die than have her live his immortal hell."

"Adrian, I still don't understand how all this is possible. My daughters and I have searched the world for over a century and a half looking for our kind," Jorja said, "and we have found nothing, not even the one who made us."

"I know this is hard to believe, Jorja," Adrian said, kissing her cheek. "I promise that with time, you will come to see that this is for real. Now it's almost dawn I have to get ready for work," he said, still holding her tightly in his strong arms. "I am sure Ezrabeth will be wondering what happened to me, sometimes I think she is the parent, and I am the child."

"Almost dawn," panic rode up in Jorja's throat, "I have to get home; Rayne must be so worried. Please don't say anything to her just yet," she asked him. "I need some time to process all this."

"Okay, my love, now you should get home before the search party comes out." He chuckled. "I will see you soon." He kissed her lips one last passionate time then he was gone, flying through the forest and out of sight. Jorja quickly got back to her car and drove home, trying to figure out what she would tell Rayne since she had promised her that they would go hunting this weekend. Jorja thought she could tell her daughter that she had been checking out places that she knew would be safe for them to hunt.

Jorja pulled into the garage and found Rayne working on her car. She had picked up some new parts to make it more *her*. "Hey, Mom." Rayne looked up from under the hood. "Where have you been all night? I was worried about you after you left the school yesterday."

"I'm fine, dear; I was exploring some places for us to go this weekend for our hunt," Jorja said, still a bit dazed, "that is, if you still want to go?"

"Oh yah, wild horses couldn't keep me from this trip." Rayne's smile went ear to ear. "I have been thinking about it all night."

"Alright, darling, we will leave right after school," Jorja said as she headed in to the house.

CHAPTER 7

Jorja spent most of the day online mapping out the trip since she had told Rayne that is where she had been the night before. Jorja hated lying to her daughter, but before she could tell her the truth she needed to make sure, they were safe. It didn't take Jorja long to find a nice area in northern Algonquin that seemed to be having an issue with bear attacks, what better way to help the humans and satisfy their lust to hunt at the same time. Jorja had never hunted bear before; the thought of it rather excited her since everything else they had ever hunted was such easy prey. She had no fear of getting hurt by this animal, but its sheer size and strength seemed so much more appealing. Knowing that it could not hurt them but still giving them a bit of a fight sounded like a good way to get out some of her frustration.

Jorja could not help but think of Adrian and what he told her about his father, how he just left his mother, a woman that Adrian was made to believe he was so deeply in love with, yet this vampire just walked away. As she thought about the previous night, she could not help wondering if Adrian was half human, why it did not affect him when she bit him. She had felt her venom entering his flesh and could feel his body tensing as she slowly fed on him, but when she stopped he was okay, a little shaky but still okay.

Jorja decided since she had never found any realistic information on the Internet about her own kind, maybe she should do some research on "Dhampir," but all she could find was a few movies and some fictional books on these so-called children of Count Dracula. What an absurd thought, Count Dracula, a shape-shifting cloud of smoke that could enslave the minds of women everywhere. It is hard to believe that the humans actually like this monster, but there were Internet-based fan sites and forums everywhere, the humans adored him. *"I bet their attitude would change very quickly if they ever ran into a real vampire."* She spent the rest of the day in her office writing in her journal about the previous night and trying to rationalize how she felt regarding Adrian. The connection she had felt to him was something she had never felt before not even with her beloved Leland; Jorja briefly felt guilty for her feelings.

Jorja heard Rayne's car pull in the driveway, and before she could turn around, Rayne was in the doorway to the office.

"Are you ready to go?" she said with a smile.

"Yes, dear," Jorja closed her journal and cleared her thoughts quickly.

Jorja wanted to ask Rayne if Adrian had said anything to her at school, but then, she just assumed if he had, Rayne would have told her. Something like that would be very hard for Rayne to keep to herself.

"So what are we hunting this weekend, Mom?" Rayne asked after about ten minutes of silence in the car.

"Bear." Jorja smirked.

"BEAR." Rayne's eyes lit up like a human child at Christmas. "Seriously, we are going to hunt bear?"

"That's the plan," she said, keeping her eyes on the road in front of them. "Algonquin is having an infestation with them, so I thought we could sort of, help out."

"Wow, bear." Jorja could see the pondering look on her daughters' face. "Can we really do that? I mean they are so big."

"Why couldn't we?" she replied. "What is the worst that will happen? They'll scratch us." Both of them laughed at the thought of a bear clawing at their stone bodies.

"Yah, I guess you're right, wow this is going to be fun," she said, now more excited than ever. "This means I can finally put some of this strength to use."

Jorja could see how excited her daughter was about the thought of fighting with a bear; to be honest, it excited her too. They never just let themselves let loose and just be vampires; maybe this could become an ongoing event for them.

The drive did not take very long; only about two hours, there were no other cars on the road, so that made it easier to navigate faster. They pulled into a campground and registered for the cabin Jorja had reserved. She figured they could make it look real instead of leaving the car on the side of the road somewhere, and this way, they could get some pictures during the day to make the house look human again. Family pictures were not something they had very much have on display for the obvious reason. Rayne sat in the car while Jorja registered and picked up the key. The cabin she chose was not accessible by car; they had to park at the main building then canoe to where the cabin was located.

"You'll like this, darling," Jorja said to Rayne as she walked back to the car with the keys in hand.

"What will I like?" she asked, her curiosity spiking.

"See that canoe by the beach there?" Jorja pointed.

"Yes."

"That is how we reach the cabin."

"Oh, I can't wait to see it." Rayne was more excited than ever.

"Let's go, they say it takes six hours to canoe to the cabin." Jorja laughed, knowing they would be there within the hour. Jorja and Rayne got in the canoe and began to paddle slowly until they could no longer see the main building then sped up reaching the cabin about forty-five minutes later. The cute little one-room cabin was cloaked in acres and acres of forest. Jorja was impressed by its simplicity; Rayne fell in love with a small wooden porch facing the water where she knew she could spend the daylight hours sketching the scenery.

"Oh, by the way, Rayne." Jorja leaned in closely to her daughter as if to tell a secret as they stepped out of the canoe. "The man at the main house said to watch ourselves; there have been a few bear attacks this month."

"That's too funny." Rayne laughed. "If he only knew, it's the bears he should be worried about."

It started to get late, and Rayne was getting anxious; they put their things in the cabin, got changed, and headed out into the forest. The women walked slowly for a bit speaking only in their heads; they talked about school and how Rayne was adapting to the new town. Rayne spoke very highly of Adrian; he did not treat her as the other humans did. Jorja wanted to tell her why, but she knew it was not the right time for that.

After a short walk, they came upon a very large male bear pawing at a tree stump; he had not heard them come up, as they were much lighter on their feet than humans were.

Do you want him, Rayne?

I think I would rather you take the first one, Mom.

Okay, dear, stay back. I might need some room for this one; he is pretty big.

As Jorja came into his view, he stood up and growled. He stood almost seven feet up right and must have weighed about six hundred and fifty pounds. It would have seemed very wrong to any human if they had seen the events unfolding, a five-foot-one woman wrestling with this enormous beast. Rayne watched with amazement while the bear and her mother played back and forth for a bit. Jorja felt very exhilarated to take on such a large beast. After about five minutes of letting him think, he could eat her; Jorja took her kill. She drained the bear until his lifeless remains dropped to the ground; she had never felt so much energy from a kill before.

"Wow, Mom, that looked beautiful, how do you feel?"

"Amazing! Now your turn."

They did not have to walk very far until coming upon another bear, but this one was smaller, a female. Rayne wasted no time; she crept up on the beast from behind, leapt forward and wrapped her body around it like a snake squeezing just enough that the bear could not get free. She sank her fangs into the beast and began to feed. This lasted only seconds, and the bear was dead. Not a mark on her, she was so graceful.

"How do you feel, darling?"

"Mom, I have never felt better. I am so glad we decided to come here."

"Well, my dear, you wanted to hunt. I am glad you enjoyed it. Let's head back to the cabin; it will be dawn soon. We do not want to run into any hikers out here, though I do not think I could drink another drop if I tried."

Just before dawn, Jorja and Rayne reached the cabin and sat on the wooden porch; with sunglasses on, they watched the sun come up across the water. What a beautiful sight, this is perfection.

"I think we have found our new retreat," Rayne said as she lay back in the lounge chair on the porch. "Do we have to leave so soon?"

"I could tell the school you are taking some time off to deal with your sister leaving," Jorja answered. "We can always build a cabin of our own out here." She smiled.

"Really? You and me building a cabin," she said, staring out over the water, "that would mean the world to me, Mom."

They stayed on the porch for most of the day relaxing from the night's hunt, what a feeling to have taken on such a large beast. It was the biggest kill either of them had ever done. Sitting there watching the ripples in the water as the fish came up to tease the cranes, Jorja could not help but think about Adrian. How was he doing since their encounter?

"Mom," Rayne said, "why are you thinking about Mr. Cross?"

"It's a long story," she replied, trying to clear her head again.

"I'm sure I have time to hear it," Rayne said, taking off her glasses and looking at her mother with a crooked smirk.

With a little hesitation, Jorja decided it was probably best to tell her daughter what happened. She would find out eventually, so Jorja told her how Adrian had found her sitting by the water and how he explained what he was and how he came to be that way. She even told her daughter about the biting experiment. Rayne was fascinated with the information her mother was giving her but even more than that, now there was even more hope for her to find others like them. Although she was curious why her mother's venom did not harm Adrian, after all he is only a half vampire.

"I guess that would explain why he was in such a good mood Friday at school and did not give out any homework," Rayne said with a laugh. "But why did you not tell me this yesterday?"

"I was worried about how you would react, with your sister leaving, and now this. It's a lot to take in all at once," Jorja replied.

"Does he feed like us?" Rayne asked curiously.

"I think he does," Jorja answered.

"You should have asked them to come, Mr. Cross and his daughter." Rayne paused. "I wonder if she knows about us. Jade seemed to have an issue with her at school before she left. I wonder if that's why."

Jorja and her daughter sat overlooking the water almost the entire day talking about the possibilities. Jorja could see that her daughter was finally starting to be happy. Rayne suggested in the late afternoon that they take a walk down the beach and see where a good spot would be to build their cabin. During the walk, they came across an area completely covered with trees; it would be a nice area to build. Rayne suggested that they clear some of the larger trees and use them to build the cabin.

"After all, we are going to need at least three bedrooms in our new getaway," Rayne said to herself with a laugh.

"Three bedrooms, how many people do you plan on bringing out here?" her mother asked as if she could not figure that one out for herself.

"Well, you and Mr. Cross will need a room, then one for me and one for Ezrabeth." She paused. *"Then when Jade and her new friend come home, we will build another room on for them."*

"You are very sure of how this is going to work out, aren't you?" Jorja chuckled.

"Come on, Mom, you know as well as I do that things happen for a reason. We have all been alone for too long," she replied in the most sincere voice.

Jorja knew her daughter meant well, and she was right. This all happened for a reason. Rayne mapped out the area in her head and started drawing up the blueprints in her sketchbook. She was a very determined girl when she wanted to be.

They stayed there for almost a month only going into the main building once to pay for the extension to the *vacation*, call the school and find a town to get Rayne some books and some supplies to help with the build. Jorja spoke with the landowners about purchasing that piece of land they had found, not very many people could say no to her when she persuaded them to give her the answer she wanted. They agreed to let her purchase a larger portion than she had originally requested although it did not surprise Jorja.

Rayne and her mother spent the first week clearing an area large enough to build the small home and shaping down the trees to begin building. Their strength and skills came in very handy in a place where you could not get normal building equipment in. By the beginning of week four, the retreat was nearly completed; they even built some of the furnishings to give it that *homey* touch.

* * *

The drive was long; Jade did not know exactly where she was going or even the full reason why. She just knew she needed to find this boy; she hated vague visions. Jade knew that his strength would help save her mother's life . . . and her own, but she did not know when or how. She hated to leave without telling her mother and sister what was going on, but she knew they would have tried to stop her or at least go with her. Jade saw images flashing through her head of landmarks that she had remembered when she was traveling with her mother. The faster she drove, the more vivid the visions became. Jade passed from state to state stopping only to put fuel in her vehicle and hunt where she could, knowing she would need all her strength for this. Five days passed then seven; Jade thought she would never find the bridge in time. She stopped in Georgia to hunt again, and as she finished feeding, she could see the bridge as clear as day in her mind. She was not far from it.

Only a few miles from where she had been hunting, she found him. Holden Lynch, a twenty-year-old man who had just lost both his parents and his young wife, the only family he had, in a horrible plane crash and was ready to end his own life.

"Holden," Jade said slowly walking toward him on the bridge. "Holden Lynch."

He turned to face her in shock, "Who are you, how do you know my name?" he answered, his face wet with tears.

"I know who you are, Holden, and that's all that really matters right now," she said in a low calm voice.

"Are you an angel?" he asked.

"No," she laughed a little, "but I promise you I can help."

Jade could hear his thoughts; he was thinking she was here to collect his dead remains from the rocky bottom. She took a step closer to him and touched his face. He did not pull away at her touch.

"Holden, please trust me. I am here to save you." She didn't want to tell him just yet that as much as she was here to save him, he would do his part to save her and her family.

"I can't be saved, I have nothing left," he said as the tears filled his eyes again. "They were all I had."

"You have me now...," Jade said, holding her hand to his.

"What is your name, angel?"

"Jade." She smiled, hiding her fangs. "But I am far from an angel."

"You look like an angel to me, you're here, aren't you?"

"Holden, I want to help you, but in order for me to do that, you have to want my help," Jade said in a firm voice.

Holden did not put up much of a protest; he was thinking to himself, *"What's the worst that can happen? She kills me... well, that's no different than I was going to do anyway."* He stepped down off the ledge of the bridge, stopping briefly to look in wonder as he realized that she was actually standing up there with him. They got into her Mercedes with no second thoughts and drove to a motel close by. It did not take Holden long to start opening up to Jade; he truly thought she was an angel coming to take him to heaven. They talked for hours; he told her about his parents, his young wife and his life with them, and of course, how they had died in a plane accident. They were beginning a vacation, and he was supposed to be with them, but his commanding officer delayed his leave, so he sent them ahead and was to fly out in a day or two. Holden's parents had been in the military; he told Jade that he had spent most of his life on an army base, once he came of age, he had enlisted himself. Holden had been training to fight in the military for the last two years, and before that, he had the training that his schools offered on the base. As for his wife, they had met on base where she lived with her family and attended school with him. Jade could see his pain, in not only the words he spoke; but more in the ones he kept inside. After a few hours of spilling his life story to Jade, he finally asked how she planned to help him. Confidently, Jade told him, "I am a vampire," knowing that he would not believe her.

Holden looked at her with his head tilted a bit. Jade knew by the thoughts in Holden's head that he clearly thought he may have already died, and this was all in his imagination.

"Okay, turn into mist or a bat or something." He laughed. "Wait, shouldn't you be bursting into flames right about now or something? It's like three in the afternoon."

"You watch too much TV." Jade laughed, louder than she had planned.

"I take that as a no?" he said, raising one eyebrow. "So how am I going to know for sure that you really are a vampire if you can't do any tricks," he asked with a bit of sarcasm.

"Oh, I have tricks." Jade smiled, still holding back her fangs. "But I'm not sure you want to see them."

She almost felt guilty now, should she really be changing him? He has such a great character, but Jade knew if she didn't change him and just let him leave, he would end up killing himself over his deceased parents and wife anyhow.

"Holden."

"Ya."

"I told you I could help you, but only if you really wanted it?" Jade asked in a low voice when the conversation had dwindled to him staring out the window wondering why heaven or maybe it was hell had motels.

"Well, I'm enjoying talking to you, and it's been really nice to not feel so alone for a little while, if that's what you mean," he said, looking at her a bit confused.

"No, I mean if I leave now, are you still going to kill yourself?" she asked, trying to justify to herself that this was okay to do.

"Well, yah… I mean it's been nice talking to you and all, but let's be real, you and I both know I am already dead," he said so calmly.

"Holden, I know you don't believe me, but I *am* here to help you," Jade said as she gently guided his body to lie down on the motel bed. "Do you trust me?"

"You are one strange little angel." Holden crinkled his forehead closed his eyes and put his head down on the pillow.

"Please don't hate me when you wake up," Jade said softly as she leaned and kissed his neck gently before she sank her razor fangs into the dark pulsing vein. His arms instinctively wrapped around her and squeezed, but it only took seconds to drain his body of life; as Holden took his last breath, Jade began the process to change him.

CHAPTER 8

Rayne and her mother continued to hunt bear in the area and fed very well over the course of the month. One evening, when they got back to the cabin from hunting, there was a note on the door. Rayne looked a little confused; Jorja took the note off the door and read it.

> *My dearest Jorja,*
>
> *I can no longer run from my feelings. I have searched the world to find you again, and now here you are! I will be waiting for you when you return from your trip.*
>
> > *Eternity will forever hold me to you, my love!*
> > *Eternally yours!*

"*How did Adrian know where to find us, surely he cannot track my scent this far even I could not do that,*" Jorja's inner voice spoke out. Rayne was upset that he did not stay. As Jorja held the letter in her hand, a harsh realization hit her. It was not Adrian's scent on the paper. This was a different aroma, but what or who was this? Flashes of memories suddenly ran through Jorja's head as she held on to the note, of the night she was born to this endless life, and the voice she heard before her heart beat one last time. "Eternity will forever hold me to you, my love," the voice rang; then it was gone. Was this possible, could he have found her after all these years they have searched, could the one who gave them this never-ending life have returned?

"Mom, are you okay?" Rayne asked in a now worried tone. "Do you want to go home tonight? I will understand if you do," she said, hearing her mother's internal conversation with herself.

"No, dear, we still have work to do here," Jorja replied.

"We have all the time in the world to finish the house, besides it is almost done now we just have some small things to do inside." Rayne paused. "And I really want to go home now. I think I have missed enough school; they will start to think I dropped out or something."

Jorja could tell Rayne was worried about the reaction to the letter; they packed up the clothes they had brought with them and loaded the canoe. Jorja and Rayne paddled back to the main house; it was closed for the night, and they left the keys to the rented cabin in a drop box with a note thanking them for the use of it then got in Jorja's car and sped home.

To both Jorja and Rayne's surprise, Adrian was waiting for them when they pulled in the driveway. Jorja could tell by the look on his face that something was wrong. Rayne said hello to him then went straight into the house to give her mother some privacy.

Adrian flew over to Jorja as fast as he could, throwing his arms around her. "I'm so glad you are safe, my love," he said in a shaken voice. "You were gone for so long."

"Of course I am safe, Adrian, I was only hunting," Jorja replied, a little confused.

"I know you can hunt, I have no fear of that," he said before he kissed her softly. "I really wish you would stay away from bear though." Adrian laughed.

"If you know I can hunt then why do you seem so shaken? And how did you know about the bear?" Jorja pulled her face back from Adrian's.

"I can smell it on you." He paused staring into her eyes with pain on his face.

"Adrian, what is it?" Jorja asked confused.

"It's my...father."

"Your father." She was even more confused now. "But I thought that—"

"He's here," Adrian said, cutting Jorja off.

"But that's good, is it not?" She crinkled her forehead a little bit as she did most of the time when she was trying to figure out things. "You have waited so long for him to return to you. Where is he now?" Jorja was starting to get a bad feeling in her core.

"I don't know right at the moment, but he is close by, he . . . " pausing again, Adrian held Jorja closer to his warm skin, "he remembers you."

"What is he talking about, remembers me? The only vampires I have ever known is the one who...Oh," it hit Jorja like a truck. The note on the cabin door she was now sure did not come from Adrian. This was all too much for her to deal with. Could it be possible, the one who damned her to this endless life was Adrian's father? Could the universe be so cruel?

Jorja took Adrian's hand and led him into the house. "Please sit down, Adrian," she said, pointing to the leather sofa trying to make sense of the events.

"I shouldn't stay, Jorja, I just had to make sure you were safe," Adrian said, pulling her to him again. "I am afraid if I stay, you will do something you regret."

"Adrian, I could never have regrets with you." Jorja touched his face. "You have given me so much hope for over a century and a half. I thought my daughters and I were the only ones."

Adrian pulled her tight to his warm body and kissed her lips, soft at first then harder. Jorja froze for a brief moment, she knew what he wanted, was she able? Would she hurt him? It had been so long since Jorja had felt this way. Adrian picked her up and cradled her in his arms.

"Jorja," he said softly, "will you hate me in the morning?"

"Never," without a second thought, Jorja's mind clouded over, unable to stop herself.

He carried Jorja up the stairs to her bedroom, pausing every few feet to kiss her again. He laid her down gently on the soft king-size bed covered in a light beige feather duvet. Gripping her body in his arms and kissing her lips slightly harder than before. Jorja could feel his body tensing as hers did on a hunt. She could taste his venom start to flow into her mouth.

"Could you ever love me, Jorja?" Adrian said in a low sensual voice.

"Adrian," Jorja replied in a daze, "I don't want to hurt you," she whispered. Jorja knew this was a bad idea. She had not been with a man since her husband had been killed, and she had been turned into this monster, but she could not help herself; she was being drawn into Adrian by something out of her control.

"Shhh," he moaned between kisses as he continued to press his body against her.

Jorja battled internally; she could not stand to hurt him. She felt they had such a deep connection as if she had known him forever, but was it because she truly thought she could love him, or was it because he was the first nonhuman man she had not since she had been turned. The inner battle continued in Jorja's mind as Adrian continued to kiss her slowly moving from her mouth to her neck and trailing lower. She had never had a connection like this with anyone or anything before. *"I could not be able to live with myself if I hurt him."* Jorja did not have much time to ponder how this would work before she realized that Adrian did not care if she hurt him; he had taken total control over her body. The feeling was so strong, so intense that she could not control herself any longer... Her monster took over.

* * *

Adrian lay asleep in the bed for hours; Jorja sat with her back to the large wooden pillar at the base of her bed and stared at him, amazed that she had not killed him. Jorja could see the wounds all over his body, wounds that she had caused. Although they were healing very quickly as he slept, Jorja knew he must be in pain, but to her surprise by the time he woke, all of the wounds had healed completely. Adrian rolled over and stared at Jorja in the sunlight with a warm orange glow in his eyes.

"Good morning, my love," he said as he sat up to kiss her.

"Adrian, I hurt you," Jorja's voice broke, and she pulled back from him, pinning herself against the bed pillar.

"No, I told you I heal quickly." He laughed. "Are you alright, my dear? You look terrified."

"I was terrified for you, I...I lost control," she answered ashamed. "I thought—" He put his finger to her mouth.

"I told you it would be alright, you can't hurt me, Jorja...well in a pain that I don't enjoy anyway." He chuckled; his voice was soft and low.

He took Jorja's hand and pulled her down to him until they were both lying parallel across the fluffy blankets, which were strung radically on the bed. He wrapped his arms around her, to help her calm down. *How could he stand to have my icy body against his extremely warm torso.* The thought entered Jorja's mind to pull away, but it quickly disappeared as he kissed her forehead. Her inner debate ceased for the time being as they stayed in each other's arms for most of the day, talking more about their past and how he felt about his father being so close. Until he mentioned his father, Jorja had forgotten all about the letter. She did not want to tell him about it; she knew that would upset him. Jorja knew she had to deal with that on her own!

The doorbell rang. Jorja could hear Rayne talking with a female; it was Ezrabeth, and she had tracked her father to the house. Ezrabeth was not quite like him since her father was only half vampire, and her mother was one hundred percent human. She was almost all human she had very little of the vampire's blood in her but did receive some of the extra traits. Jorja listened to Ezrabeth and Rayne in the living room talking; Ezrabeth sounded excited and told Rayne that she needed to talk to her father. Rayne knocked on her mother's bedroom door, but before she had a chance to speak, Jorja was up and to the door opening it slowly.

"Ezrabeth would like to speak with her father," Rayne said in an apprehensive voice. She knew what had happened between Adrian and her mother that night. She could smell his blood, but she was also worried about the letter and who had left it knowing that it had not been Adrian.

"Thank you," Jorja said, "we will be right down."

Adrian was standing behind Jorja when she shut the door. He held her tightly and kissed the back of her neck; Jorja could tell he was still very weak, the night's events had taken most of his energy. As strong as his vampire's side was, he was still half human. He told her not to worry again, but how could she not he could hardly walk; Jorja had not noticed how much this affected him since he had not tried to stand until now. They walked down the stairs to the main living room where Ezrabeth was waiting for him. The expression on her face was unreadable. Jorja left them in the living room and joined Rayne in the dining room where she was setting up the chessboard; it always relaxed them to play. Jorja sat down with her daughter at the large wooden table and began the game. They had not been playing for very long when Adrian and Ezrabeth joined them in the dining room. He was still very weak looking, but he was getting better.

"My love, I want to properly introduce you to my daughter," he said. "This is my Ezrabeth."

"Very nice to meet you, my dear," Jorja replied, unsure if she should shake her hand or give her a hug.

Ezrabeth reached out and shook Jorja's hand, not the least bit bothered by her temperature. "It's nice to finally meet you too." She laughed. "I have been hearing so much about you for the last five years ever since my dad had that dream." They both chuckled.

"This is my daughter, Rayne," Jorja said as she waved her hand toward Rayne. "I'm sorry that Jade is not here to meet you as well."

"That's okay," Ezrabeth said. "I've met her at school, I hope she is okay."

Jorja thanked her for her concern and invited them both to stay. Rayne asked Ezrabeth if she wanted to come upstairs and see some of her designs. Ezrabeth was very excited; she did not have many friends and even less that invited her to hang out with them. Adrian was thrilled that they had hit it off; he felt very guilty that his lifestyle had cause his daughter so much loneliness.

Ezrabeth had never encountered full-blood vampires before, and when her father did not come home last night, she began to worry that something very terrible had happened to him. She knew he was upset with the return of his father although she could not understand why he was not happy about it, but she also did not know of Adrian's conversation with his father regarding Jorja. Adrian sat at the large wooden table and continued the chess game with Jorja that Rayne had started while he was talking to Ezrabeth. He was a very good chess player; Jorja guessed much like herself years of loneliness gave much time for mastering things like this. They played for what seemed like hours, talked more about his feeding habits and how they were much the same as Jorja and her daughters. He told Jorja that he could eat human food as well, but it did not give him the strength or the energy that blood did, so for the most part, he hunted at night while Ezrabeth slept. As well he did not usually need much sleep himself unless he was very drained. *"I guess that would explain him sleeping this morning,"* Jorja thought to herself. He explained that because Ezrabeth was almost all human; she did not drink blood at all. She survived on normal human food and had to sleep just like a normal human to recharge her energy. She did, however, have Adrian's strength as well as speed, and his tracking senses; she can find him just about anywhere. Jorja offered him one of the blood bags that Dr. Scott had sent. Adrian was pleasantly surprised that there was such a large selection of blood types in the collection. Jorja explained that Dr. Scott would send these for them usually every month or two, and that between the three of them they had different taste preferences for human blood. She heated a bag and gave it to him to help him recharge his energy.

Rayne and Ezrabeth came down the stairs just before dusk; Jorja figured that Ezrabeth would no doubt be getting hungry. Rayne, on the other had, was still very full from the hunting trip as was she. Rayne took Ezrabeth into the kitchen and offered her pick of the frozen meals her mother had purchased in town. They had no doubt had a lengthy discussion about both of their eating habits as well. Adrian seemed quite surprised that she had human food in the house given that none of them ate it. Jorja laughed as she explained about Jade and her human study projects; how she would often bring them to the house so to appear human themselves, they would have the human food in the freezer. Jorja and her daughters were able to eat human food; she explained to him, they were just not able to digest it like normal humans would. Once the humans left, the house they would have to regurgitate it much like a human would throw up it was very awkward and a bit painful to do. "I'm sure any human would find it comical watching us," Jorja added.

The girls came into the dining room after Rayne had prepared the premade frozen meal for Ezrabeth; she found it rather fun to prepare food. They sat at the other end of the large wooden table and continued to talk and question each other while Ezrabeth ate her pasta. Jorja was very curious about Ezrabeth as well and about her mother although she would not ask unless Adrian or Ezrabeth brought it up.

When Ezrabeth finished her meal, she excused herself from the table and advised her father that it was getting late, and since she had school in the morning, she should be getting home. Adrian agreed, he had to be in class as well in the morning; and if he were going to be able to teach his class, he would have to recharge himself a bit more. Rayne offered to give them a ride since her mother's car only had two seats; they agreed.

"C'mon, Ezzy," Rayne said with a smile ear to ear. "I'll show you my car."

Rayne and Ezrabeth went to the garage, and Adrian turned to Jorja; holding her face in his hands, he kissed her softly and whispered, "I love you, Jorja Sullivan. I have never been more sure of anything in my entire life, never forget that." He held her for a few more moments then she walked him to the door. Rayne and Ezrabeth were waiting in the car outside. Jorja felt a pang in her chest where her heart lay dormant. *"How can he say he loves me?"* she said to herself.

The house was now empty, and Jorja's mind was free to wonder. She thought about Jade and how she was doing and where she was it had been a month since she had left. Jorja pulled her cell phone from her pocket and sent her daughter a text message.

Hey, darling, just checking in making sure you are okay. I miss you.

Love, Mom

The message she received back was a little odd but nevertheless, Jorja was happy to hear from her.

*I am okay, but I cannot come home just yet, I know
you will understand...Miss you & love you too!*

Many thoughts were running through Jorja's head as she cleaned up her bedroom. It looked as if it had been turned upside down. She pulled the blankets up to fix the sheets and stopped dead staring at the bed. The sheets were covered in blood from the night before; as half vampire as Adrian was it was the human side of him that now soaked her bed.

"What have I done to him, no wonder he was so weak. There is no way he can tell me that he's okay."

Jorja quickly removed the bedding, took it into the backyard and burned it in the fire pit. She could not look at it never mind try to clean it. She stood staring into the flames of the small fire that was now destroying the evidence of the monster in her praying that Adrian would realize this was a bad idea for both of them and stay away.

"Jorja," a deep male voice with a strong Irish accent whispered behind the trees.

Jorja spun around to see who it was. It was not very often people could creep up on her, but lately, it seemed to happen more and more, a pair of glowing red eyes peered through the trees.

"Who are you?" Jorja asked in a rather demanding voice as she walked toward the trees, unsure if that is a wise move or not, but at this point in her over one hundred and fifty years, what difference would it make if it were a bad idea.

"Please don't come any closer yet," the voice said, still behind the tree line in the shadow of the forest. "Your family is not safe, Jorja."

"What do you mean they are not safe? Who are you?" Jorja demanded, her defenses clearly rising. "Let me see your face," she said in a calmer voice this time. She did not want him to leave; she wanted answers.

"They know about you, I am sorry I have failed you," he said, still not showing himself.

"Who knows about me? What are you talking about?" Very confused, Jorja stepped closer to the tree line. "Come out here and talk to me." She took another step toward the trees.

"I can't come out there, the sun is still up."

"The sun is still up, what difference does that make? If he's a vampire like me, the sun would not affect him, is this some kind of prank?"

"I don't understand," Jorja said, now stepping into the tree line and into the shade. "Please, let me see you."

A man stepped out from behind the trees but still kept in the shade. He was a tall and slender man, very pale as well. She knew instantly who he was... the face from so many years ago that had burned into her mind.

"I know you," she said in a low steady voice as she walked closer to him.

"Yes, Jorja, you do. I was worried that you would not remember me after all these years," he replied softly.

How could she ever forget the face of the man that doomed her and her family to an empty eternal existence, it was not possible. Even though Jorja had so much rage building up inside her regarding that subject, she still wanted to know why he was here and why he thought they were in danger.

"What is your name?" she asked him, suppressing any signs of hatred that may show.

"Cavan...My name is Lord Cavan Lear."

"Alright, Lord Cavan Lear, you said my family was in danger, from what?" Jorja replied, trying not to sound sarcastic. "What could we possibly be in danger from?"

"They are looking for you," he said in a low shaky voice, "the Guardians."

"The Guardians, who are they?" Now she was intrigued; they had searched for so many years and found nothing. Now he wanted her to believe there are Vampires *Guardians*, and they want to meet her . . .

Jorja stood in the shade of the trees as Cavan explained to her that the Guardians were the oldest vampires clan in the world. They were kind of like the royals to the vampire's world and not much happened without them knowing about it. They had heard about Jorja and her daughters and how they could be exposed to sunlight with little difficulty; their eyes were the only part of them that seemed to be affected. Cavan told Jorja that the Guardians had always known she existed, but it was not until recently they found out about her apparent rare condition so naturally they wanted to know why they are able to withstand the sun's rays. He told her that he had been sent to find her since he was the one that created her his link was strong. His orders were to find Jorja and bring her back to Ireland where the Guardians convened. Jorja could tell by his hesitation when he spoke that they did not just want to talk . . .

"What can they possibly want with me? It is not like I could do anything special; going out in the sunlight hardly seemed a crime worth punishment especially since we do not draw attention to ourselves."

"Why do I need to go there?" Jorja asked Cavan hoping he would not give her the answers that she really did not want to hear.

"You are special, Jorja, you, Rayne and Jade," he said. "Your blood can change the way all vampires live.

"We have searched for so long, why have they not come to us earlier?" she asked very confused. Jorja tried to read Cavan's thoughts, but as she suspected, they were blocked.

"I've done a very good job of keeping you a secret from them. Until just recently, they did not know you were a day walker. You have caused no trouble to bring attention to yourselves, except for the little incident in Arizona; but then, they expected that since you were what they call *newborn* or *infants* to our breed, and coincidently, you killed only at night." As he spoke, Jorja watched him very curiously, his posture, his muscle structure, even as he spoke, Jorja could see ever so slightly a twinge when he said her name. "I had kept a close watch over you, Jorja, until about sixty-eight years ago since you clearly learned to control your thirst as did your daughters. I had no fear that you would not expose your vampirism in the daylight."

"But why did you just leave us to die then?" Jorja asked in an almost angry voice. "When I woke, the sun was beating in on me; surely you knew that would kill us then. How am I supposed to believe you are looking out for our best interest after leaving me to die?"

"I did not want you to die!" he yelled, shocked by the statement. "The full transformation takes approximately five days for your body to completely change. I left you under a crate in that ally behind that shop. I did not know your daughters would find you under there, then when I came back to change your children, I made sure all the windows were closed, and the curtains drawn when I left."

"But why did you leave us?" Jorja tried not to sound defeated. "I knew nothing of what to expect and how to survive." She could feel her anger growing again but swallowed hard to keep calm, after all, it had been over a hundred and fifty years, and she wanted answers.

"I wanted to stay, but I knew that once you had *turned,* I would be able to find you easily enough." His voice sounded almost magical when he spoke, "but when I came back to get you, you had already left and were making your way south with your daughters." He paused and stared at Jorja intensely. "When I found you in Arizona, you had seemed to have already come to terms with what you were. I thought it best to keep my distance and let you try to live a normal human life."

"But we searched for so long and found nothing." Jorja's face hardened.

"That's because what you were searching for did not exist," he replied calmly. "You were searching for vampires like yourself, and my love, they just do . . . not . . . exist."

"Adrian . . . what about him? He has no reaction to the sun either," Jorja spoke, still trying to convince herself that attacking Cavan would not be the best idea right now.

"Since his mother was human, she passed on her share of the genes to him. His human side makes him immune to sunlight," Cavan said, looking ashamed of the thought of Adrian.

As Cavan had been talking, Jorja had hardly noticed that he had been walking her through the deeply wooded area that was her back-yard. It was now past nightfall; the world around them was black. The only time she had ever been back there was to hunt with Jade one evening. Jorja stopped for a moment; it was nice to just take in the beautiful scenery that was now lit only by the moon. They came across a small rock quarry that was almost beachlike. Jorja sat on the rocks that lined the water with her back against a dead tree stump; Cavan came and sat beside her.

"It was you that left the letter for me," more of a statement than a question. "At the cabin . . . it was you?"

"Yes," he said, staring out over the all-too-still black water. "I have been watching you since I found you again a few months ago here."

"Watching me . . . "

"I was going to confront you sooner, but I found you and Adrian together in the forest before you left." His eyes still staring straight out over the water. "I was in shock to see him. I . . . I thought he was dead, but when he told you about his life, I knew instantly that he was my son."

Cavan paused for a few moments staring into the calm black water then turned to Jorja and took her hand. His touch was very different from Adrian's; his hand seemed a more natural temperature.

"Jorja, I have waited so long to tell you why I came to you that night." He paused now looking in her eyes. His eyes were burning bright scarlet.

He dropped his eyes down to the stones beneath them. "When I found you that night, something inside me woke up; when I saw how scared you were, I felt I had no other choice. Those men would have killed you if they found you, just as they killed the men that confronted us." His eyes met hers again. "Over these years, I have tried many things to keep my distance while I watched over you. I was so ashamed that I had condemned you to this eternal existence. I could not bring unnecessary attention to you and your unique condition."

"But Adrian's mother," Jorja interrupted, her voice was broken, "you loved her; she was human, and you did not do this to her."

"I saved you!" he said, pulling her chin up with his hand and looking into her eyes. "As for Adrian's mother, I met her while following you through England. She was almost my dinner. She was not like the other humans I had encountered. She was not afraid of me; she actually welcomed my cold touch. So when you came back to Canada, I brought her with me." His hand dropped to Jorja's lap where he held both of her hands tightly together. "She begged me to allow her physical love, and I resisted for as long as I could until the day I could not resist any longer." His grip tightened on Jorja's hands. "The Guardians found out about her and ordered my return to Ireland. I knew that she would not survive the birth of a vampire's child, and with her death, the child would certainly die as well."

Cavan and Jorja sat on the rocks until it was almost dawn; he told her stories of his fifty-year punishment from the Guardians for being with a human and not changing her. Once his fifty-year imprisonment had ended, he began his journey to find her again.

"I must go my sweet," he said, tracing Jorja's face with his hand. "The sun will soon rise. You could never know the joy I now feel having found you again. I will come for you tomorrow evening, and we will go to the Guardians; it is better that we go to them rather than they come here . . . It is safer for your family; the Guardians will not harm them if you go to them. I will meet with you here at dusk."

"No, I can't leave yet. Please give me some time here with my children to say good-bye . . . I am sure the Guardians are not going anywhere anytime soon," Jorja pleaded in surprise.

Cavan sighed. "I really shouldn't allow this, but I know what your family means to you." He paused and looked her face over. "Okay, my love. I will go back to Ireland myself and explain that I have found you and request your time. I will return soon."

"Thank you," Jorja said, trying to figure out if he was being genuine or not. There was just something not sitting right with her about his story. "Will I know when you are coming back?"

"I'll call you, please keep your reasons for the leave from your children . . . Adrian as well, we don't want any unnecessary issues," Cavan said as he kissed her hand and disappeared into the trees.

Jorja sat on the bank for a bit longer thinking about everything Cavan had told her. *"I will not let the Guardians hurt my family, and once they come here, I know that they will also have an issue with Adrian. I'm not going to let them hurt him either."* Jorja did not want to admit it to herself, but she may be falling in love with him. As she walked back to the house, Jorja thought about how she would tell him she had to leave without him being worried; then another thought crossed her mind . . . *"Do I even have to tell him? I could just leave him a letter telling him I've gone hunting again or something, if I don't have to face him, it would be much easier to lie to him . . . "*

CHAPTER 9

"Where were you all night again?" Rayne asked as she packed her bag for school.

"I went for a walk out back; there is some beautiful scenery back there," Jorja answered as she walled up her thoughts. She was not about to tell Rayne about Cavan and risk her telling Adrian; he would lose his mind if he knew what she had to do. Jorja was sure he would find out soon enough.

It was not long after Rayne left for school, and Jorja was puttering around the house putting new bedding on the now bleached mattress, then she heard the doorbell.

"Shouldn't you be at school?" she said with a chuckle when she opened the door to see Adrian standing in front of her.

"Taking the day off, I needed to see you again...I think I'm addicted to you," he said, laughing and wrapping his arms around her waist.

Jorja pulled back from him quickly; the vision of her bloody bed flashed through her head. She was not going to let that happen again.

"Jorja, what's wrong?" he asked, confused. "Are you alright?"

"I'm fine, Adrian," Jorja said, coming a little closer to him again. "I'm sorry, I just . . . Oh, never mind." She sighed, what was she supposed to say? *Hey, Adrian, I am leaving for Ireland with your dad soon to go see some Guardians who may or may not want me dead . . . so don't wait up.* He would never understand.

"Jorja, my love, what is it?" His eyes were locked on Jorja's. "Whatever it is you can tell me."

"It's nothing, Adrian," she said, pulling away and sitting down on the large white leather L- shaped sofa.

"Okay, now you are scaring me," he said as he sat beside her and took her hand. "Did I do something wrong?"

"Him do something wrong, not possible, I'm the one in the wrong; I know I had hurt him physically, and I know that I will hurt him emotionally if I let this continue not to mention I have no idea what is going to happen when I meet the Guardians."

"No, Adrian, you have done nothing wrong," Jorja tried to sound positive. *"How am I going to tell him I have to leave, and I might not return; how could I tell him not to worry about me?"* Jorja's internal monologue continued.

"Then what is it, my love?" he said, putting his arms around her again, then whispered, "Please tell me, Jorja, whatever it is we can make it better."

Jorja hated to lie to him; she was so thankful to have found him. He had already given her so much to live for in a life she had thought to be doomed alone for eternity, just by being what he was.

"Adrian, I can't tell you what's going on, but I promise that as soon as it's over, I will explain everything," Jorja tried to reassure him. "It's just, I have to leave soon, Adrian, but only for a little while," she added in a low voice as she turned her head away from him.

"LEAVE?" Adrian's voice reached a panic. "What do you mean you have to leave? You just got back from hunting."

"I'm not going hunting, please, Adrian, you have to trust me. It's best for everyone right now." If Jorja could cry at this moment, she would. She could feel his grip tightened on her.

"It's Cavan, isn't it?" The expression in his eyes was devastating as he said the name. "You are leaving with him."

"Adrian, please don't make this harder than it has to be. I told you I would explain everything when I return. Please, you just have to trust me." Jorja tried to rationalize what she had to do, but it really did not help.

"Do you love him?" Adrian asked, staring into Jorja's eyes.

"No, Adrian, how could you even ask me that?" she replied, placing her icy hand on his face. "That's not why I have to go, please don't ever think that."

"I love you, Jorja Sullivan, more than you will ever understand. I could not stand to lose you." He took her face in his hands and kissed her lips. "I would not survive it," he added harshly.

"He said he loved me...the thought of hurting him is just too much, but what can I do? I know that if I do not go to Ireland, the Guardians will come here, and that would be tragic to everyone. I have no other choice."

"Please don't talk like that. I won't be gone long. You have to trust me. Please it's best for everyone," Jorja said, trying to reassure him that everything will be fine. She had no idea what was going to happen, but she didn't want him to know that.

"I owe you more than I could ever give back, Jorja, you are literally my dream come true," he said as he pulled her over and onto his lap so that she had a leg on each side of him, and they were face to face. Jorja put her arms around his neck and stared deep into his eyes that were now glowing fiery orange. His warm hands began rubbing up and down her stiffened spine, tracing every bony bump. With an open hand, he caressed her entire back and neck; pulling her into him, he kissed her lips.

"Adrian . . . .what are you doing?" Jorja asked softly, as if she did not know what he wanted.

"You know very well what I'm doing," he said with a smile as he jumped up off the sofa, picking her up with him and flew up the stairs before she could even open her mouth.

"Adrian, we can't," Jorja whispered as they hit the foot of her bed. "You don't understand, I don't want to hurt you."

"I'll survive, my love, I promise you that." He laughed, staring into her eyes, no doubt trying to hypnotize her again. Jorja tried to be firm; she could not let this happen again. She was too strong for him, and she knew she did not have the self-control to keep from shedding his blood...again.

"Adrian, please don't do this," she uttered as his lips covered her again "I . . . I . . . " It was too late her monster had once again taken over.

Adrian woke a few hours later it did not take his body as long to heal this time. *How could I do this to him again? I have to find a way to make him understand that until I find a way to control myself, we cannot do this anymore.*

"Good afternoon," he said, peeking out from under a blanket of feathers.

Jorja could not even find the strength to greet him back. She was so ashamed of herself how could she do this to him again, how could she keep hurting him. She looked up to meet his eyes and gave him a faint smile then turned away.

"Jorja, it will get easier for you," Adrian said as he pulled himself up, so he was leaning against the headboard. "I promise we can figure this out."

Jorja could not stop her tongue and lips from moving as she blurted out. "Don't you understand...It's because I love you, I don't want to hurt you." As fast as she said it, her hand came over her mouth. *What did I just say? Did I honestly just tell Adrian that I love him? How is this even possible? How can I ever love anyone I am a monster?*

Adrian's eyes widened as he looked at Jorja. He slid his body across the bed and took her face in his hands. "You said it." He gleamed as he kissed her. "You told me you love me too."

Jorja could see the excitement all over him; to Adrian, it did not seem to matter what else was going on around them, not his father, not Jorja leaving, not anything. "Do you really mean it, Jorja?" he asked, staring deeply into her eyes. "Do you really *love* me?"

"More than I could tell you, but this isn't right. I am not going to keep hurting you," Jorja said, trying to be realistic with him, but he was not listening anymore; he was too excited.

"Jorja, I have to go home for a bit, but I will be back. Please don't go anywhere. This is very important," he said as he threw his clothes on and staggered toward the door.

"Adrian, wait!" Jorja yelled as she caught up with him in the hallway. "You should feed before you go."

"See, there you go already trying to take care of me," he said with a smile. "Okay, Jorja, but let's make it a quick one. I really need to talk to Ezrabeth when she gets home from school."

Jorja got Adrian a warmed blood bag, and he drank it quickly. He was anxious to get home, so she made him up a second bag to take with him and then watched his silver SUV drive away down the winding driveway.

Jorja heard Rayne's Mitsubishi rumbling in the garage when she got home from school. She did not come in the house right away, but she called to her mother in her mind just to make sure she was home.

"Mom, are you here?"

"Yes, dear, I'm in my office, how was school today?"

"Not bad, how was the day with Mr. Cross . . . "

"Rayne . . . "

"Haha! I'm sorry, Mom, I'm gonna work on my car for a bit."

"Alright, I'll be up here if you need me."

Rayne had taken a liking to working on her car when she was having what she called a *"fashion block."* That meant she could not think of what to design next. Therefore, she would work on her car, tuning it up to make it faster than it should be.

It was almost midnight when Rayne came into the house and up the stairs.

"Hey, Mom, there is a race this weekend some of the local kids are going to put on," she started. "I am goanna play it cool for a bit then leave them all in my dust," she continued, laughing. "It sounds cool, they clear the track if there is any snow and race to see who handles better."

"Be careful, Rayne, the last time you raced was such a mess." Jorja reminded her, the last race she did, one of the local kids cut her off trying to be funny as they were going over 150 km/h she flipped her car. The car was totaled, but thank goodness for seat belts . . . that one took a while to blow over. How could a car roll five times then catch on fire and not put a scratch on the driver. She convinced them that she had on her five-point racing harness, and once the car stopped rolling, she took it off and jumped out just before it burst into flames. Needless to say, they moved not too long after that. Using the excuse, that street racing was too dangerous; and to punish her daughter, Jorja moved them out of the area. Rayne was not too happy with that one; she actually enjoyed living in Nevada that time.

"I'll be fine, Mom; these are just handling timed races, only one car at a time on the track," she retorted. "They have some race track up by Belleville that the kids go to."

"Up by Belleville?" Jorja was curious.

"Yah, a reservation or something I think," she replied. "I don't know I wasn't really listening, but I'll get the details tomorrow now that I have made a few adjustments." She laughed.

"Just be careful this time, Rayne," her mother said.

Rayne went to the dining room and began to set up a chess game. Not ever sleeping definitely had its disadvantages . . . it gets really boring at night.

"Come on, Mom!" Rayne yelled up the stairs. "I'm all ready for ya."

Jorja headed down the stairs for another long game of chess. It is rather relaxing and helped keep her mind off all of the other things she was trying to hide. *"What would Rayne say if she knew about Cavan? If she knew, I would have to leave soon to protect them from whatever the Guardians had planned."*

The sun came up through the Victorian windows of the dining room as Jorja and Rayne continued to play their game in silence, both of them concentrating very hard on hiding the thoughts of their next moves. All of a sudden, Jorja's cell phone vibrated in her pocket, and Rayne jumped up.

"Crap, it's 8:00 a.m. already." She hissed. "I am going to be late." Neither of them were used to paying much attention to the time anymore since they were in the rainforest in Brazil for about five years they had no need for human time. It took a bit of getting used to again.

Jorja pulled her phone from her pocket seeing a message from Jade.

I am so happy for you, Mom; we will be home soon.

"Why is she happy for me? Did she not see what was going to happen with the Guardians?" Her phone went off again.

Oh yah, say YES . . .

Yes, to what? Okay, now, Jorja was confused, but she felt that way a lot with Jade since she could read the future and most of the time blocked everyone out from seeing her thoughts. Jorja knew there was no point for her to text her daughter back. Jade never liked to give away a surprise.

Rayne flew into town trying to make it in time for her first class. As she ran into the long hallway to her class, the bell rang; she slowed down and walked into her homeroom. Mr. Cross chuckled as Rayne took her seat.

"In a hurry this morning, Miss Sullivan?" He smiled.

"Yah, I guess I . . . um . . . overslept," she answered with a sarcastic giggle.

The rest of the class looked at her like she was crushing on Mr. Cross the way she had looked at him when she spoke and the way he seemed to favor her even though she had missed a month. Rayne could hear the whispers and thoughts of the other kids in her class.

"*What a joke,*" she thought to herself, "*won't they be surprised when they find out he is dating my mother?*"

"Rayne," Adrian said as the end of class bell rang, "could you stay after for a few minutes? I need to go over something with you."

Rayne could hear the kids talking on the way out the door.

"*I guess she is going to pass this class...*"

"*Yah, tell me about it. I mean look at her she is so hot no wonder he wants to talk to her.*"

"*I bet they have something going on.*"

Rayne waited at her desk until the room cleared out; she gave Adrian a disgruntled look as the last student left.

"I hope you're happy," she said in a sharp voice. "They think I am into you now."

"Aren't you?" Adrian laughed, trying to act shocked. "I'm sorry, Rayne," he continued with a chuckle as he walked back to her desk and sat in the chair in front of her. "I have to ask you something, and I want your honest answer."

"Well, go ahead then, but make it quick. I have another class to be late for you know," she said, looking at her watch.

"Rayne, I am going to ask your mother to marry me tonight, and I wanted to know how you felt about that?"

"You're going to what?" Rayne answered shocked.

"I am going to ask her to marry me!"

"Oh, you are crazy, she *will* end up killing you. You know that, right?" Rayne seemed genuinely concerned for Adrian's safety.

"You let me worry about that, Rayne," he said with a smile. "I love her, and that's all that matters."

"How are you going to have a wedding? I mean it's not like we are going to go to a church and go all religious?" Rayne asked. A legitimate question she thought.

"Well, I know a pagan priestess," he began. "She could perform a wedding ritual for us."

"You are serious about this, aren't you?" Rayne asked, raising her eyebrows.

"Yes, I love your mother very much," he said with so much sincerity. Rayne almost felt her icy heart warm a little.

"Okay, crazy one," Rayne said with a laugh. "If you love her that much and you are willing to let her shred you apart, then you have my blessing," she said as she leaned over to hug him then thought better of it and stopped herself.

"Thanks, now get to class before you're late," Adrian said, chuckling. "I'll see you tonight."

CHAPTER 10

Jorja hopped into her car and drove into Belleville. Shopping was about the best thing she could do right now, besides she needed to get new bedding she was quickly running out. *"Who knew I would go through sheets so fast?"* There was a large department store by the mall; it seemed to be the easiest place to get everything she needed. Jorja picked up a few more sheet sets and pillows as well as two more duvets. She walked around the store watching all of the humans do their shopping, reading their minds was easy. Most human thoughts were the same, *sex . . . money . . . is my husband cheating . . . man, that woman has a nice butt . . .* Nothing out of the ordinary for human thoughts, she put the bedding in the car and headed home.

"There, that looks better," Jorja said aloud after putting the bedding on the oversized bed.

"Sure does," Rayne said, walking in behind her. "So what's the plan for tonight?"

"What do you mean plan for tonight?" Jorja asked.

"Well, I was thinking maybe I could invite Ezrabeth over."

"I don't see why not, as long as Adrian is okay with it," Jorja answered, happy that Rayne had taken so well to Ezrabeth.

"I don't think he will have a problem with it," Rayne said in her head walking back out of the room giggling.

"What was that about?" Jorja asked quickly, but her daughter was already down the hall and on the phone.

"Hey, Ezzy, what are you up to tonight?" Rayne asked. "Cool, are you coming over?"

"Great, see you soon. I'll be out back . . . tanning" she laughed and hung up the phone. Tanning outside at the end of October, only a vampire would find that funny in the chilly Ontario weather.

Adrian's SUV pulled up the driveway and parked in front of the garage. Ezrabeth got out and ran around to the back of the house to meet Rayne. Jorja was so happy that they got along so well; she was worried about Rayne with Jade being gone. Rayne does not befriend humans easily, but Ezrabeth does have a little vampire in her, so maybe, that makes all the difference. Well, Rayne was happy, and Ezrabeth had someone she can relate to, so Jorja guessed that was the only thing that mattered.

Adrian knocked on the front door and walked in.

"Jorja, are you here?" he called.

"I'll be down in a minute," Jorja called back down the stairs; she wanted to finish putting the rest of the bedding away that she had picked up.

Jorja walked down the stairs to find Adrian standing in the living room with his back to her staring out the large window. Looking stunning dressed in black dress pants with a black dress shirt. He turned to greet her as she hit the last step coming down the stairs.

"I feel a little underdressed." Jorja laughed, in a pair of dark jeans and black hooded sweater. "What's the occasion?"

Adrian did not say a word; he just turned his body to face Jorja and walked close. He put his warm hands on her icy hips; she could feel his touch burning into her through her jeans. As he pulled her closer to him, he gently kissed her forehead then kissed her cheek, then he pulled back and walked them both over to the white leather sofa, and Jorja sat down. Adrian knelt in front of her and pulled a small velvet box out of his pocket, still not saying anything, he opened the box. Inside was the most beautiful rare vintage black diamond stone, set in a 24ct white gold band. Jorja could feel her body tensing but was it excitement . . . or was it fear?

"Jorja Sullivan," he said as he held her hand in his.

"Will you give me the honor of being my wife for the rest of our everlasting lives?"

Jorja was speechless; she could see Rayne and Ezrabeth out of the corner of her eye peeking in through the kitchen. *"Is this really happening? How can I say yes to him knowing that I have to leave, and I may not return?"*

"Adrian," Jorja said in a breathless whisper, "is this really what you want? I mean you know I have to . . . " Adrian put his finger to her lips.

"Shhh," he said, holding his hand firmly to her mouth, "we will worry about that later . . . *together*, I love you, and that's all that matters."

Jorja pulled her head back and leaned back on to the large leather cushion; she curled her lips in to cover her teeth. *"Okay, let's think about this for a minute; you love him, Jorja, and you can't deny that, but is love enough?"* Jorja sat there for a few seconds longer. She could hear Rayne and Ezrabeth in the other room.

"Say yes, Mom," Rayne said in her mind, *"you have waited way too long alone; you deserve this chance to be happy."*

"Oh please, oh please, oh please say yes, Miss Sullivan." Ezrabeth was thinking. *"He loves you so much, oh please say yes."*

Adrian stared in silence while the thoughts ran through Jorja's head until finally, she stopped thinking, and a smile crossed her face. Everyone was holding their breath waiting for the response.

"Adrian," Jorja said, leaning back toward him and kissing his lips. "Of course I'll marry you," she said with a large smile.

"Oh yes, yes, yes." Flew from Ezrabeth's thoughts. *"I am so excited."*

"Thank you, Mom, this is the right choice," Rayne thought as she and Ezrabeth flew out of the kitchen into the living room.

"Oh, Jorja, I love you," Adrian said as he put the ring on her finger.

The world started spinning around; Rayne and Ezrabeth were making plans for the ceremony. Adrian wanted to invite the entire town. Plans were being made, people were being called, and yet Jorja felt frozen, unable to slow down the world that was now spinning around her. Adrian had spent most of Ezrabeth's life in this little town where he had made friends . . . well, as close of friends as he could get without giving away his secret. No matter what Jorja tried to do or say at this point, everything seemed out of her hands.

Finally after about a week of total body and mind shock, Jorja told Rayne she had to go up to the cottage and hunt, but this time, she wanted to go on her own. With everything going on here, she needed the time away to think about things rationally. "*I mean come on, I have to deal with the fact that I have to leave everyone soon. Adrian did not seem to understand that when I leave to deal with this issue that I would be doing it on my own without him, and there was a strong chance that I might not return.*"

Rayne understood why her mother had to go on her own this time; Jorja promised her that she would take her the next time. Jorja left late Wednesday night after Adrian went home with Ezrabeth; they both had to be at school early. Rayne told her mother she would let Adrian know Thursday in her homeroom class, that she would only be a day or two.

The view sitting on the beach watching the sun come up across the icy November water was like watching a fire spread across a still black wheat field. It was beautiful, peaceful...empty.

Jorja spent the better part of the day just lying on the frost-covered beach watching out over the ice-coated water. The seclusion giving her the space she needed to think things through.

"You know you love him, and you know he loves you. But then, there is Cavan; he seems to have other thoughts for how I will spend the rest of eternity, but that doesn't mean I can't talk to the Guardians and come to some arrangement with them to keep them away from my family. Whatever they want from me, I am sure they can be rash."

Jorja heard rustling in the trees behind the cabin; she held still listening for human thought or otherwise but could hear nothing. There was an all-too-familiar scent. Oh, she knew this scent, taking her stance, Jorja waited for her black bear to come out from behind the trees. He emerged into the open beach area and caught sight of her; he was immediately in defensive mode. Jorja struck at him but not in a manner to feed off him just yet; the game of back and forth was entertaining and a great way for her to get some built up emotion out. He struck at her with his large claws tearing her vest; Jorja swatted back at him more to agitate than to hurt. He took another good swipe scraping his black claws across her arm; the sounds were hilarious, like running fingernails down a chalkboard. Jorja had never heard such an amusing sound come from her body before. This was more exciting than when she and Rayne had hunted. After about fifteen minutes of wrestling with the oversized play toy, Jorja took her kill and fed. Once his enormous body was drained, and his remains went limp, she released her grip and let the carcass fall to the ground. Jorja knew she could not just leave it there, so she decided to make use of the remains; Jorja skinned his Hyde to make a cover for the floor in the cottage then cut up the meat and spread it throughout the woods behind her for the wildlife to eat. *"I guess even in my most carnivorous form, I can still help the other smaller predators since food this time of the year was scarce for most of them."*

Now feeling very full and recharged, Jorja puttered around the cabin putting some final additions in where she could. She could not help her mind from wandering back to the idea of marrying Adrian. She wondered when he wanted this to take place and the people he wanted to be there, where they were going to hold it. The thought of getting a wedding dress made her giggle just a bit. Human traditions that she had not thought about in over a hundred and fifty years now seemed so important.

"Well, I guess I could always have Rayne design one and have it made. I'm sure that would just make Rayne's day."

"Stop! Jorja, what are you thinking? You know that Cavan will be back soon, and you probably won't even make it to the wedding alive." Jorja couldn't help thinking like this, but it was true; at any time, Cavan would be back to take her to the Guardians, and she would have to leave without even saying good-bye. *"Okay, that's it. When I get home, I'll tell Adrian that this can't happen. Yup, that's what I'll do I'll tell him we simply can't get married."* So sure of herself, now stronger from the bear, Jorja knew she had the strength to break it to Adrian, so she packed up and went home.

* * *

"Are you crazy?" Rayne yelled; she had never raised her voice to her mother like that before.

"Rayne, this is not your choice to make," Jorja replied firmly.

"You don't know what you're doing; he is great for you," Rayne said, her voice still above normal.

"Rayne, think about this logically. He is only a half vampire," Jorja said in a very serious voice. "Eventually, I *will* kill him."

"There has to be a way." Her daughter's voice now so sincere. "He loves you so much, and you both deserve to be happy." She paused. "Wait a minute . . . Jade . . . Jade knows how to turn them;

she can turn him fully." She had so much enthusiasm in her voice now; she almost sounded like she was singing.

"I don't even know if that is possible," Jorja replied, "and I am not going to ask her to do that."

"Mom, please don't run from him," she pleaded, "he loves you so much. There has to be a way for this to work, there just has to be. It's time to stop running."

Jorja had never seen Rayne like this, how could she let her down. Maybe Cavan would come back after the wedding or if she was lucky not at all. She could not let Rayne down or Adrian for that matter. Even if Cavan came after the wedding, Adrian would still have to let her go with him to protect her family.

Saturday morning, Adrian came over to see if Jorja was back yet and start making the wedding plans, the four of them sat at the dining room table—Rayne, Ezrabeth, Adrian, and Jorja. Rayne had her laptop out beginning to design the dress while Adrian and Ezrabeth went through the Pagan calendar to find the perfect date. Since before her death, Ezrabeth's mother was a very spiritual Pagan woman much like Adrian's mother and aunt. Ezrabeth wanted to choose a date for them that had great spiritual meaning. Jorja read the thoughts running through Ezrabeth's mind; she was thinking that her mother would be so happy Adrian found love again. Ezrabeth's mother had passed away when Ezzy was only five years old; she had been diagnosed with cancer, and it tore Adrian apart that he could not save her life. He could not turn her because he was only a half vampire, and the venom he carried was not strong enough to change her; it would only kill her. Her death came quickly once diagnosed she lived only three short months. The thoughts ran through Ezrabeth's mind, as she was looking through the calendar; suddenly, she gasped looking up at Jorja. She had remembered that they could read thoughts. Her eyes met Jorja's, and she threw her hands over her mouth.

"It's okay, dear," Jorja said softly.

"Miss Sullivan, I'm sorry I forgot you could—" Jorja cut her off before she could say the rest.

"Ezrabeth dear, it's okay. I did not mean to hear it," she replied. "But I am truly sorry."

Up until that point, neither Adrian nor Ezrabeth spoke much of her mother or what happened to her. Jorja felt like she had violated Ezrabeth's privacy. Adrian was now staring at both of them trying to figure out what just happened.

"It's okay," Ezrabeth said with a sigh slowly taking her hands away from her mouth. "I just miss her, that's all."

"Sweetheart, I understand missing a loved one, believe me I do understand that." Jorja reassured her. "There is nothing wrong with missing them."

Adrian now knew exactly what was going on. "Jorja, I'm so sorry. I guess we should have talked about this earlier," he said with his head hung down.

"It's okay, Adrian. We all have our past. It's something we live with forever," Jorja replied as calmly as she could, trying not to think about Leland.

Ezrabeth continued to flip through her calendar while Adrian and Jorja sat in silence watching her and Rayne. Finally, Rayne popped her head out from behind the laptop screen.

"Ezzy, have you picked a date yet?" she asked. "I have the dress almost done, but I need to know what season, so I can finish the top of it."

"Um . . . well, if it's okay with you dad," she said, looking at Adrian. "I was thinking maybe June for the summer solstice?"

"I think that is a wonderful idea," he answered, smiling at Jorja. "That will give us around six months to get everything together, which should be plenty of time. What do you think, Jorja?" he said, touching her hand.

"*Six months,*" she thought to herself, "*would Cavan be back by then? Is it really enough time?*"

"Jorja," Adrian said again, "are you okay?"

"Yes, I'm sorry. June is fine," Jorja answered, shaking herself out of a daze, "will that be enough time to put it together, Rayne?"

"Yup, the dress is done." She laughed. "I already had it made for a summer wedding I was just making sure I did not have to add a cloak."

Adrian tried to peak his head around to see her design. "Nope, not a chance," she said, turning the screen away. "You don't get to see it until the wedding day, Mister." They both laughed.

That night while Adrian and Jorja were lying in bed, she listened to him ramble on about plans, the future and all sorts of other things that she could not focus on. He could obviously tell she was distracted because he stopped talking and started kissing her.

"Adrian, wait," Jorja said, putting her hand up to his smooth bare chest. "I need a favor from you."

He looked a little confused but replied, "Anything, baby. Anything you want, just name it."

"I don't think we should, anymore . . . until after the wedding," she said, trying not to make eye contact with him.

"Ugh...anything but that." He sighed.

"I'm serious, Adrian; I think it's for the best." This time making eye contact with him, so he would know how serious she really was.

"You are really serious?" he asked.

Jorja nodded.

"Well, my love, if that is what you really want, then how can I argue with that?" he said with a sigh. "But that doesn't mean I can't still hold you at night... right?"

"I would really love it if you *would* still hold me," Jorja said, smiling at him. The safe feeling in his arms was what she really needed to help clear her head of all the thoughts that were racing through.

CHAPTER 11

The last few months seemed to fly by as Jade taught Holden to hunt, how to live in his new life, and helped him deal with his urges to feed on the humans. He was her perfect match in every way. So eager to learn everything she could teach him, they just clicked.

"Jade," he said one night before they hunted, "how did you know where to find me?"

"I just knew, Holden, I knew you were there waiting for me," she replied. "We were meant to be together."

"I have kind of a silly question, but it's one that I have been thinking about a lot the past few months," Holden said as he watched her reaction.

"Yes, vampires can have sex just like humans, Holden." Jade laughed.

"How did you know I was going to ask that, you always know what I'm thinking?"

"My mother, sister and I can read thoughts. I was hoping that you would be able to as well, but it doesn't seem that way," she replied. "I can also see into people's future, that's how I knew to come and find you, you are my future."

"I don't get any special power...that sucks," he said, making a clicking sound with his tongue off his teeth.

"Who knows, maybe your powers will show up later." She giggled. "Or maybe they are just so far beyond what I know that we just can't see them yet." Jade smiled at Holden and winked.

"Come on, let's hunt. I sense there is a pack of wolves out tonight." She smiled.

"Wolves." He raised his eyebrow. "Hey, I used to watch movies and read books about werewolves and vampires...any of that true?" he questioned.

"Not that I know of, but then until my mom met Adrian, we were sure we were the only vampires left out there," Jade said with a sigh. "So who knows anymore, there could be an entire world we don't even know about." Her eyes widened sarcastically as she let out a low laugh.

Jade took Holden's hand and brought him closer. She had been so focused on teaching him how to control his hunger that she had never really shown him emotional or physical attention partly because he was much stronger than she was, and she was a bit worried that he would not know his own strength and partly because she wanted to give him time to mourn his wife. They had only been married a short time, but that did not mean he loved her any less.

"Holden, do you believe in fate?" Jade asked.

"I'm here, with you, as a vampire." He chuckled. "That ought to pretty much sum it up right there."

"You were ready to end your life that day on the bridge," she continued, but he put his soft yet strong finger over her mouth.

"Jade, you have given me a new life, one where I will never be lonely...I have you...forever," he said softly then kissed her cheek as delicate as he could, trying very hard not to hurt her.

"Come on, Holden, we have to hunt now," she said, pulling away from his hold. She had not thought this far ahead. Jade had never been with a boy before. Over a hundred and fifty years, both mortal and immortal and no physical contact not even so much as a kiss. She had to admit for the first time in her long life she was unsure, maybe even a little scared.

After feeding, they made their way back to the hotel to clean up. Holden was still working on the graceful part of hunting, but he was getting better. When he was done in the shower, he came out of the bathroom in just a towel. Not really out of the ordinary, he usually came out of the bathroom to get dressed while Jade had her shower and clean up. However, this time, when she came out of the bathroom, he was still in his towel sitting with his back against the headboard of the bed, and his feet crossed out in front of him. Jade's nerves fluttered around in her stone body like butterflies trapped in a glass jar; she was definitely not sure she was ready for what he had in mind.

"Come...sit here, Jade," he said aloud, but his thoughts were speaking louder than his voice.

Jade sat on the edge of the bed beside him; Holden took her hand and kissed it softly. "Am I strong enough now to control myself?" he asked, "Can you see?"

"Holden," her fingers still intertwined in his tight grip, "I know you are strong enough to control yourself, but I don't know if I am ready for what you are looking for just yet."

"I think I love you, Jade," Holden whispered as he pulled her closer and kissed her softly. "If you are not ready, then that's okay, we have all of eternity. I promise you I'm a very patient man." He pulled her in again and gently kissed her lips just long enough to make her mind reel; then he pulled himself back and smiled.

"Holden, how did I get so lucky with you?" Jade asked. "Even for a new vampire, you're so understanding and gentle. I know human men that don't have a fraction of the strength you do, and they would not be so patient."

"Well, that, babe, is because they don't love...they just lust." He laughed.

Jade leaned toward him on the bed and slowly put her lips to his. She wanted him to know she loved him too. He pulled her down so that she was lying beside him, his arms now wrapped around her tiny body. For a moment, Jade almost felt frightened of the hold he had on her as they kissed; after all, he was still in just a bath towel.

"Holden." Jade inhaled.

"Shhh, Jade, I know, and I promise I won't hurt you. I just want to kiss you that's all, I promise." He breathed softly, a habit he had not wanted to break.

She could not say no; she was being hypnotized. Jade thought it might be too soon, but she did not want it to end. His strong arms holding her, his lips pressing against hers, she could taste the venom flowing through his fangs, as his grip got tighter.

"Holden," Jade whispered as her body froze stiff, and she pulled her head back from his.

"I'm so sorry, Jade," he said, letting go at once, "did I hurt you?"

"No, babe, you did not hurt me, it's just," she paused and let out a sigh, "it's just we need to slow down."

"I'm sorry, Jade, I thought I could control myself better," he said, ashamed.

"Holden, you did nothing wrong; you stopped when I asked." Jade locked eyes with his as she held his chin up. "You're amazing at controlling yourself. Don't ever be sorry."

* * *

February 14 Engagement Party!

The *hall was slowly filling up with people from the little town where Adrian had spent the last ten years; even some of the kids in Rayne* and Ezrabeth's classes had come out to celebrate. People that Jorja had never met before were coming up hugging and congratulating her; Jorja found it all a bit overwhelming and could not help but remember the last party that she attended. Rayne's eighteenth birthday so many years ago. Jorja tried to keep the thoughts out of her head and enjoy the evening with the people of this little community that Adrian had come to love so much. Nevertheless, no matter how hard she tried to keep it out, the memories of that dreadful night filled her head.

"It's okay, Mom, I can't stop thinking about it either," Rayne said, coming up behind Jorja, handing her a prefilled glass of *red wine*. "Here, have a drink; you look like you need it."

"Where did you get this?" Jorja asked, shock that her daughter just handed her a glass of blood in a hall full of humans.

"Ezzy," she said plainly, "she thought that being in a room with this many humans and all the attention focused on you and Adrian, it would look kind of funny if you did not have anything to drink all night; she figured that people would be toasting you guys."

"You two amaze me." Jorja couldn't help but smile as she felt a warmth rise up through her body. "I am glad that you two have hit it off so well; you have no idea how that makes me feel."

"I have a pretty good idea, Mom; almost as good as I feel now that you have found Adrian, and that you're finally happy again. It's been too long for all of us."

"Rayne was right; it has been way too long for all of us. Just because we are damned to this life, forever does not mean we should not have happiness. Even if it is only temporary!"

"How are you holding up in here?" Adrian asked as he found his way out of a crowd of people and wrapped his strong arms around Jorja, squeezing her just enough to let her know it was going to be okay.

"I'm doing alright; thanks to Ezrabeth." She laughed. "She is a very smart girl, thinks of everything."

"I know; when she poured me a glass of wine, I couldn't believe it. She really did think of everything."

The DJ stopped playing the music as Rayne and Ezrabeth stood on the stage together at the microphone and thanked everyone for the great turnout. They opened up the stage for anyone that wanted to say a few words or just give their congratulations. For the next forty-five minutes, people flooded the stage, making speeches and giving thanks for being invited to the engagement celebration. After everyone was done, the DJ started the music back up, and guests were dancing and mingling again. Even Rayne was dancing with one of the boys from her science class; everyone looked like they were having a good time.

When the party was over and the hall had cleared out, Jorja sent Rayne and Ezrabeth home, so Ezzy could get some sleep; it had been such a long night for her. Adrian and Jorja stayed to finish cleaning up; they loaded everything in the back of his SUV then took one last look around the empty hall to make sure there was nothing left. As Jorja made her way across the floor to the exit, she heard music playing faintly behind her. Jorja turned around to see Adrian leaning against the stage beside a little CD player.

"What are you doing?" she asked softly as she walked back over to him.

"May I have this dance?" He took Jorja by the hand and spun her around, pulling her close to him. "Now this is more like it, just the two of us."

They danced around the entire hall until the music stopped.

"Thank you, Adrian."

"You don't need to thank me," he said, kissing Jorja softly.

"Yes, I do, you have made me feel alive again. For so long, I just went day to day thinking I would never be happy again, and you have changed that, you've opened my eyes...and my heart."

"We both have loved and lost in our lives, Jorja, but that doesn't mean that we don't deserve to be happy with each other now."

The drive home was slow, well, Jorja thought it was slower; but Adrian says he was doing the speed limit. "*I guess we still have a different opinion of the speed limit.*" Adrian pulled into the garage where

Jade used to park her Mercedes beside Rayne's car and started to unload the back of his SUV.

Ezrabeth was sleeping by the time they got home; Rayne was in the living room playing tennis on the Wii.

"I think I finally get this game," she said, laughing as they came through the door. "Oh, by the way, Ezzy is passed out in Jade's room if you are looking for her. I was kind of thinking, maybe we could set up the empty room beside your office as another bedroom." Rayne paused her game and looked at Adrian as if she was waiting for approval. "Well, since Jade will eventually be home and I was not really sure what the living plans are going to be after the wedding, I assumed that we would all be living here."

Adrian and Jorja both looked at each other and smiled, neither of them had really thought about the living arrangements. Leave it to Rayne to think of all the details.

"I think I just assumed that we would live here in this house since we had the room, what do you think, Adrian?" Jorja asked, looking at him.

"I actually hadn't given it much thought, but that does make sense since there will be six of us if Jade brings home that boy, but ultimately, this is your house, my love, and you make the final call."

"Well, Mom, what do you think? Can we put together that room for Ezzy?"

"I think it would be a great idea." Jorja smiled.

"Great then. Ezzy and I are heading to the city when she wakes up to do some shopping and pick out some cool stuff for her new room." Rayne was thrilled.

Adrian and Jorja headed to her room for some quality "*us*" time; before the sun came up, they were going hunting up at the cottage later, and he wanted to relax a bit before they went wrestling with the wildlife.

CHAPTER 12

The next few months flew by faster than Jorja could count; it was now almost to the end of April, only a little over a month now until the wedding and still no word from Cavan. Maybe he was not coming back; it had been almost six months since he left to speak with the Guardians. *"Could I be so lucky, did they decide to just leave us alone?"*

Rayne and Ezrabeth did most of the planning while Jorja seem to let everything go flying by at warp speed. The plans were set, her dress was almost ready, everyone seemed to be excited... everyone except Jorja. *"I really need Jade right now; I need her to tell me what is ahead, to tell me that everything will be all right."* Jorja tried to reach her youngest daughter on her cell phone, but she did not answer or return any text message. Jorja knew Jade has her way of working, but this was not helping; she wanted her here and hoped she could at least see that and come home soon.

Rayne flew in the door after school. Her arms were waving as if they were on fire.

"It's ready, it's ready, it's ready!" she yelled. "Come on, Mom, let's go. We have to get to Toronto tonight by seven to pick it up. Ezzy is in the car waiting...come on."

"Whoa, slow down," Jorja said as Rayne was pulling her out of her chair. "What's in Toronto?"

"Um, let's see...only the best wedding dress of all time," she answered. "Now come on, we have to go."

Jorja had to admit she was a little excited to see it; Rayne hadn't even let Jorja see the drawings of it before it was sent to be made. Ezrabeth sat in the back jabbering the entire two-hour drive there; she was excited to see the dress as more than just a drawing.

They pulled up in front of a quaint little dress shop where a woman was standing at the window watching for them. Jorja walked in, and the woman immediately took her to the dressing room at the back of the store.

"Close your eyes, Mom, I don't want you to see until it's on you," Rayne said with confidence.

Jorja closed her eyes while Rayne pulled the dress over her head and laced it up the back. The lace felt silky on her arms she wanted so badly to open her eyes but with restraint, Jorja kept them closed until Rayne said she was done and walked her out to the main room where Ezrabeth and the shop owner were waiting.

Ezrabeth gasped.

"Open your eyes," Rayne said as she bit her lip.

Jorja opened her eyes and stared into the full-length three-fold mirror. It was the most beautiful dress she had ever seen. Long white gown, corset-style back with laced silk sleeves that did not cover her shoulders but instead started at her chest line, beading covered the top half of the dress a unique wavy vine pattern with flecks of red shimmering in some of the beads. The base of the dress was floor length and was capped with the same wavy vine pattern lace that flowed outward from under her breast.

"Rayne," Jorja said, taking in a deep breath, "it's beautiful."

"Miss Sullivan," Ezrabeth said, "you look amazing."

"Please, Ezrabeth, I've told you before call me Jorja," Jorja said, chuckling.

Rayne and Ezrabeth fluttered around the store for the next few hours putting together jewelry, shoes, and accessories. Jorja felt like a doll standing there just staring at herself as the girls tried on all kinds of different shoes on her. Finally, they found a pair of vintage-style boots that matched the dress along with a veil. Time seemed to stand still for those few hours; Jorja stood there watching herself in the mirror while the world sped up around her. This was really happening; she was really going to marry Adrian Cross.

After hours in the dress shop, Jorja was finally able to take the gown off and have it packaged up, so they could take it home with the other items Rayne and Ezrabeth had picked up. The drive home did not take long at all since now it was after midnight, Ezrabeth fell asleep in the backseat, and there were no other cars on the road, so Rayne turned off her headlights and sped back to Madoc.

Adrian was waiting at the house when they returned; he carried Ezrabeth up to her bedroom and put her to bed without waking her. Rayne took the dress and other bags into her room where Adrian would not see them; she was so proud of her design that she thought maybe she would start her own wedding line.

The morning sun peeked in through the window where Jade and Holden were laying in each other's arms. Jade had kept to her morals and had only let Holden get as far as kissing her while they shared a single motel room. She believed that even though she had kept her virginity for a hundred and fifty years, she did not have to give it up just because they had spent the last few months together. She wanted it to be special, and call her old fashioned, but she wanted to be married first.

"Holden, we have to go home today," Jade said, lurching upright.

"Home," he said intrigued.

"Yes, my mother needs us." The blurred vision she had before leaving Madoc was now coming through crystal clear.

"I get to meet the parents...wow, even as a vampire that's kind of scary." They loaded up Jade's SUV then started back to Canada. Jade explained everything to Holden as she was seeing it. She told him her mother thought she had to leave; she thought it would save them all. However, she was wrong. It was all Cavan's way of getting her away from them. He knew that she would do anything to protect her family... No matter what! Holden just sat staring at Jade most of the drive home, listening to her babble on and on about Cavan and the Guardians. Yes, they knew about Jorja, and yes, they did want her blood and venom for testing. Jade could see her mother lying on a steel table with tubes coming out of both arms and Cavan watching her being drained until she was almost dead just to find the answer to her endurance to the sun. Holden was amazed Jade could see so much detail from a vision; she explained to him it was like watching a movie in her head. The more vivid the visions were, the faster Jade drove.

The phone rang around six thirty Saturday morning; Jorja recognized the Irish accented voice on the other end immediately.

"Jorja, you must meet me at the riverbank at dusk," Cavan said in a very stern voice. "We have to leave at once." Then he hung up the phone. No explanation. No struggle. Just dead air on the line. Jorja had no other option she would do whatever it took to keep her family safe; she needed to find a way to leave without anyone knowing. Jorja stood dazed trying to think of what she was going to do, what she was going to say, nothing! She was not going to say anything. She just had to go . . .

When Ezrabeth woke up later that morning, she and Rayne decided to drive into Toronto for some shopping. *"Now, how am I going to get away from Adrian?"* There was no way to do it. She did not even hunt alone anymore; he hunted with her, so she could not use that as an excuse. There was no way he would understand that she had to leave tonight. The thoughts passed through Jorja's head on how to make it seem not so suspicious. This was the weekend; he always stayed on weekends how could she explain. Then it dawned on her, but could she really bring herself to do that to him again, to cause him that pain? Jorja had been so good at controlling herself, but she knew this would make him sleep. It seemed to be the *only* way she could make him sleep . . . take all his energy away again. Jorja hated herself for needing to do this to him, but it was the only way. She loved him too much; she knew what she had to do!

Jorja stared at Adrian now sleeping under what not so long ago was her duvet. *"How could I do this to him? How could I allow myself to do this to him again?"* She couldn't stand to stay and look at what she had done to him any longer. She packed her bag for the trip not sure how long she was going or if she was even coming back. Jorja did not know how Cavan planned on getting there, but she assumed that they would have to drive to the airport at dusk. Once her suitcase was in the car, she came back into the house and went right to her office to write Rayne a letter and try to explain what was happening without making her worry. Jorja wrote one to Adrian as well. She really wished Jade was here; she would be able to tell her if she was coming home, but Jorja couldn't call her either, deep down, she knew exactly what Jade would tell her.

She finished Rayne's letter then checked in on Adrian; he was still asleep, she was thankful for that. Good-byes were not exactly her expertise she had never got close enough to anyone to require a good-bye. Jorja placed Rayne's letter on her bed and the note for Adrian on the nightstand beside him. She gently kissed his forehead and whispered, *"I love you. I hope you understand why I had to do this."* Then she shut the door.

Finally, it was almost dusk. Jorja knew Jade was home; she could hear the SUV coming up the dirt road. Jorja knew she didn't know exactly what to expect, but she knew what the outcome was going to be; she would not be coming back home. Cavan walked up behind her silently. "*I really have to get used to listening for the light feet of vampires. I have grown too accustomed to the heavy human foot.*"

"It's time to go, my love," Cavan said, placing his hand on Jorja's hip.

"This doesn't feel right." She turned pushing his hand off her.

"Do not fret, Jorja, you are saving your family by coming with me, and the Guardians will respect you for that," he said, gripping her hand tightly and pulling her toward where she had left the car. "Our flight leaves first thing in the morning." He smiled. "We have a direct flight in a first-class cabin where I can close off all the windows from the sunlight."

"Where are we going tonight?" Jorja asked confused, she was getting rather frustrated not being able to read his thoughts.

"Tonight, we just need to get away from here; your daughters will surely be out looking for you soon enough," he said, "and we can't have them in danger now, can we?" His sarcastic smug smile made Jorja want to slap him, but she knew he was right, she did not want them to get hurt; Jorja turned and got in the car.

Jade and Holden reached the Sullivan house at dusk, but it was too late Jorja's car was already gone. Jade took Holden's hand and went inside. Rayne was coming down the stairs holding a letter.

"It's from Mom," Jade said to her sister waving her hand. "I don't need to read it. I know she is in trouble."

"Jade, help me out here, tell me what to do. I already took Ezrabeth home; I don't want her to know what's going on," Rayne said in a panic. "Mom would never just leave us like this."

"Cavan told her it was the only way to save us, but he is full of crap; the Guardians don't even know where we are."

"What Guardians? Please slow down," Rayne pleaded. "Remember I don't see the future like you can." Rayne stopped for a moment and stared at Holden, a little shocked that he was intertwined in her sister's arm so tightly.

"Oh, I'm so sorry, Rayne, this is Holden; and Holden, this is my sister Rayne," she introduced.

"Um, nice to meet you," Rayne replied, still very upset.

"Is Adrian still here?" Jade asked, her voice gone from her normal light and chipper to something of authority.

"Yah...in Mom's room, but I would not take the newbie in there..." Rayne warned. "There is a lot of blood."

"Oh," Jade said, suddenly realizing what she meant. "Holden, babe, I need you to wait here for me please, there is going to be a lot of fresh blood around, and I don't want you to be overwhelmed."

"Alright, I'll be right here," he said, kissing her hand.

Jade went to the kitchen and got a blood bag and heated it up for Adrian; she knew he would need it and then flew upstairs to her mother's room. On the way up the stairs, Jade got another vividly horrifying vision... it was too much for her to handle.

"Adrian," Jade bellowed, running into the bedroom, "wake up."

Adrian slowly opened his eyes still a little weak from his blood loss. Jade flew over to the bed and tossed him the scarlet bag.

"Drink this, I need your help," she said in a terrifying voice.

"Slow down, what's wrong, Jade," Adrian said, pulling himself to an upright position on the bed, refocusing his eyes.

"It's... It's my mom." It was hard for Jade when she saw the visions to remember that others do not see them as she did; it was hard enough to see them once never mind having to replay them in words for the others.

"Where is she?" Adrian hissed, as if just realizing why Jade was back. "Please, tell me she hasn't left yet."

"It's so much worse than her just leaving early, Adrian, please drink up." Jade grabbed her cell phone and dialed her mother's number. "She is not answering. I know she has her phone." She looked at Adrian. "Tell me everything you know about Cavan." Then she grabbed the phone and typed, *Mom, I know you are there, and I know what you are doing, you have to come home.*

Jade hit send with a trembling finger.

Rayne walked into the room and stared at Adrian; she had read Jade's thoughts. "You knew she was going to leave, why didn't you stop her?" She hissed through her teeth.

"Rayne, it's not his fault. Cavan convinced Mom that it would be safer for us if she went with him; you know she would do anything to make sure we were safe," Jade snapped back at Rayne. "She *thinks* she is protecting us."

Rayne pulled out her cell phone and typed, *Jade is home, Mom, she has seen what is about to happen to you. PLEASE do not go with Cavan tonight.*

"Holden, are you okay?" Jade called.

"I think so," Holden said from the hallway.

"You will be okay, babe, just stay out there please."

"Um...could you, ladies, give me a second here, so I can get up. I'm uh..." Adrian said, looking down at the blankets.

"Oh, sorry, yes, we will be downstairs," Jade said, suddenly realizing that his clothes were on the floor beside the bed.

Adrian got up and dressed with a little difficulty; he looked over to the nightstand where a folded piece of paper was laying addressed to him, and he opened the paper and read.

My dear Adrian,

I wanted to say good-bye, but I am no good at that stuff. I will be back before you know it. Please do not worry about anything, darling, everything will be all right. I love you with all my heart.

Jorja

Still drinking the blood bag, Adrian made his way down the stairs to the living room. Rayne was sitting in the wooden rocking chair facing the window. Holden and Jade were on the sofa; she had her hands woven into Holden's for safety, as he was still very new to this life. Jade knew how hard it was for him to be around humans still.

"Okay, Jade, tell me everything you saw," Adrian said as he sat in the large white leather chair.

"Where do I start?" Jade said with a sigh. "Cavan, the one who made us, has convinced my mother that the Guardians need to see her because we are not affected by the sun as other vampires are." Jade paused to look at Holden for a moment. "There is something in our blood, and apparently, our venom too that they can use to make other vampires into *"day walkers"* like us."

"What are they going to do to her?" Adrian hissed angrily through his teeth.

"They are going to take blood and venom from her to study to see what is different in her compared to them and try to duplicate it for the others." She paused. "I can see her very weak. She is strapped down to a table. The tests are showing them that the reason why we are able to be exposed to the sun is our DNA in the blood and venom, but they can't duplicate it, so they just keep draining her." Jade began to shake; Holden put his hand to her face.

"Baby, please don't break down on me; I won't be able to control myself if you break down, you know that, and I don't want to hurt anyone," his voice was deep and sincere.

"I'm sorry, I just can't help it. She is in so much pain, and she can't seem to move. Cavan is just watching them." Jade wished she could cry.

Adrian was beside himself thinking of what was going to happen. He pulled a phone out of his pants pocket and dialed.

"Jorja, turn the car around, NOW!" he demanded.

"Adrian, please don't do this, you just have to trust me...please I am doing this for all of you," Jorja pleaded,

"No, Jorja. You don't understand. Jade told me everything... please turn around and come home." Adrian begged.

Cavan took the phone and spoke, "Adrian, it's better this way."

"You listen to me, you sick son of a bitch; I will hunt you down and kill you with my bare hands," he growled into the phone. "If she feels one ounce of pain..."

The phone disconnected, and Adrian dialed back just as fast. "Dammit, he turned the bloody phone off."

"She left me a letter, Adrian, but I don't know if you should read it; she asked me not to let you," Rayne said, unsure if she should really be telling him.

"Please, Rayne, just bring it to me," Adrian demanded.

Reluctantly, Rayne went and got the letter; she handed it to him. "I'm warning you, you don't want to read it," she said, not letting the paper go.

"Rayne," Adrian said in a painful voice.

She let the paper go, and he read the letter aloud.

Rayne,

I have to leave for a while and go to Ireland; I have found the one who created us, but there is a large complication that I need to take care of for all of your safety. The man who made us is Cavan Lear; he is also Adrian's father. There is so much wrong

*with every aspect of this situation. I cannot even
begin to explain it to you. I have to leave tonight.
Please contact Jade if you do not hear from me. I am
sure she will know what to do if I don't return...I
don't have time to explain anymore. Please make
sure Adrian is well; he was very wounded when I
left him, and please do not tell him what's going
on; I don't want him to worry. I will do whatever it
takes to keep you all safe even if that means I cannot
return. I love you ALL more than you could know.
Please take care of Adrian and Ezrabeth; they are
part of our family now. I hope you understand why
I could not stay to say good-bye.*

Your loving mother.

Adrian stared at the paper in his hand; Jade could see the rage
and pain in his face, his fiery eyes now brighter than ever. "I'll kill
him," he said. "I warned him, and now, I am going to do it."

"Hold on, Adrian," Jade said, snapping her fingers in front of
his face to get his attention. "They aren't going to Ireland . . . "

"What? Where are they going then?" he asked, confused.

"They are going to see other vampires, but they are not in
Ireland. Cavan just made her think that, so she wouldn't know where
she was when...*if* she woke up," she replied, cringing at the thought
of her mother being so helpless; Cavan knew Jorja would fight him
off if she knew they were still safe.

"Wait, what do you mean woke up? But she doesn't sleep."
Adrian's eyes widened. "Do I even want to know how he knocks her
out?"

"Vodka," Jade said with one eyebrow raised.

"Vodka, like alcohol vodka." The expression on his face was
sheer confusion.

"Well, since we don't have functioning inner body parts to absorb the alcohol, it is funneled directly into our bloodstream, just like when we drink blood, making it almost a thousand times stronger to us than to a human," Jade explained.

"He gets her drunk." Adrian hissed. "What kind of bullshit is this?"

"He knows it will knock her out long enough for him to drive to his compound," she told him. Adrian now vibrating at the thought of what was happening.

Jorja drove down the highway into Toronto where they were to board the plane for Ireland in the morning. Cavan spoke very little as they drove and even less once, they reached the city. This made Jorja unbelievably uncomfortable.

"Cavan, be honest with me," Jorja whispered.

"Jorja, relax," Cavan's voice was low and guarded. "The Guardians requested some tests from you, that's all. Don't be worried, Adrian is just upset that you're gone." His voice changed to a softer, more sensual tone. "Pull over, I'll drive from here."

Thoughts danced throughout Jorja's head as she tried to figure out what was really going on. Cavan knew that she would do anything to protect her family, more and more she knew that he just used that to draw her away from them.

"Where are we going tonight?" she asked again.

"You'll see, my love," he replied in his low Irish accent. "Now... no more questions. Drink this." He handed her a bottle of clear liquid.

"Water." Jorja laughed.

"Please, Jorja, just drink it, trust me it will help you relax."

Trust is not something she had right at that moment, but nothing she had drank thus far had killed her, so she tipped the bottle up and swallowed the clear liquid, it tasted nothing like water!

"What the hell was that?" Jorja asked, scrunching her face up after consuming the entire bottle; it made her throat burn, but not the same burn she got when she needed to feed. It was more of an irritated scratch.

"Vodka." Cavan laughed. "It will help you relax."

"What the hell did he say? Vodka, as in human alcohol vodka, how the hell will that help me?" All the sudden, Jorja felt very dizzy, she soon realized the effect of alcohol on her; she had never felt like this before even as a human. Her eyes became blurry, the lights of the city were now flashing by at superspeed. Jorja could feel her head getting to heavy to lift as she leaned back in her seat.

"What did you do to me, Cavan?" she asked . . . or at least she thought she asked.

For the first time in over one hundred and fifty years, Jorja was asleep or at least what felt like sleep.

Rayne sat in the rocking chair staring out the window trying to think of what they could possibly do to save her mother.

"I've got it," she said, spinning around.

"What, Rayne?" Jade answered a bit shocked.

"We have to go there; you can find her, Jade. I know you can," Rayne's voice carried hope.

"And what can we do once we get there? Reason with them... they are too strong for us to fight," Jade said and then paused; her face changed instantly as the vision hit her. She knew exactly what she had to do. "That's it, Rayne, you are a genius."

"I know, but what did I *not* say this time that was my idea," she replied, a little shocked at her sister's reaction.

Jade jumped off the sofa pulling Holden with her, and they flew up the stairs. Adrian looked at Rayne and scrunched his forehead.

"No idea," she said to him.

Holden and Jade were upstairs for over an hour. She had to make sure he would be okay before she could attempt to change Adrian to a full blood since Jade had to take him to the point of death and let his heart stop for just a few seconds before his body would allow her venom to convert him. Once Holden was ready, she locked her bedroom door.

Downstairs, Rayne got Adrian another bag to help bring back his strength faster.

"Why do you let yourself get like this?" she asked him.

"I love your mother, she is an amazing woman," he replied.

"Yah, but there has to be an easier way for you to show her you love her though." She chuckled. "Can't she turn you into a full blood or something? It would be much easier on you, don't you think?"

Jade ran back down the stairs. "Rayne, I told you, you were a genius."

"What did I do now?" Rayne said, rolling her eyes.

"Adrian, we need all the help we can get to save her," Jade said, taking his hand. "How much do you love my mother?"

"Do you even have to ask?"

"Yes, I do. I have to be sure."

"There are no words to describe how I feel about Jorja."

Jade paused and stared at him for a very long minute then listened for Holden; he was upstairs locked in her room for . . . safety reasons.

"If I told you that if you were a full-blood vampire, you could save her life, would you do it?" Her eyes were fixed on him.

"Jade, I would give up my life to save her," he replied with no hint regret whatsoever.

"Come with me." Jade took Adrian's hand and walked up the stairs.

"Jade, what are you doing?" Rayne yelled.

"Trust me, this was your idea," she said, shutting and locking the door to her mother's bedroom behind her.

I'm sorry, Adrian. This might hurt a bit."

CHAPTER 13

Jade walked out of the bedroom locking the door behind her and called out to Rayne to pack some clothes then went to her room where Holden was. She took his hand; Jade could tell he was having a hard time adjusting to the restrictions in his new life.

"We need to hunt; we are leaving in three days," she told Holden, hoping it would help.

Holden was sitting on the edge of the bed; he reached out and wrapped his arms around Jade tightly.

"How do you do it?" he asked. "How can you handle the blood without going nuts."

"A century and a half of practice," she said with a smile. "Don't worry, babe, you are doing great. We need to hunt soon though, so we are all strong enough when we find Cavan."

The next two days went by painfully slow. Rayne tried to occupy herself with her clothing line, but that was not working very well for her. Holden and Jade continued to bond, talking about their pasts... well, mostly Jade's. Holden was very intrigued with her history he found it very interesting to hear about historical events in the first person. Rayne called Ezrabeth; they did not want to frighten her, and she had befriended Rayne. She explained a little bit to her about having to go and get their mother, and that she would not see her father for a little bit but for her not to worry. They would all be home soon. Rayne hated to lie to Ezzy, but it was for her own safety. She told her that Adrian had already left; no one wanted her to come to the house and see him before he was ready.

Adrian knocked on the bedroom door just loud enough for Jade to hear him . . . He was ready. It did not take long, only two days, for the change to happen since he was already a half vampire. She unlocked the door and walked in closing it behind her.

"How do you feel, Adrian?" Jade asked him.

"Thirsty," he replied, "I thought this was going to make me stronger."

"It will, but you have to feed." Jade handed him a blood bag. "This will get you started, but we still have to hunt."

"I don't feel any different than I did," Adrian told her as he looked down at his body that really did not look any different either. He still had a very muscular tone to him, and his color was still the same pale cream shade it had been. There was only one minor change to his eyes; they were no longer the deep purple they had once been, now they were the same misty smoke that Jade's were.

"You will have to take it easy for a bit; you are going to have new urges now," she told him. Adrian grew up on animal blood; he had never craved human blood before, but now, his senses were heightened, and his instincts would gear him toward that. Being half human himself before he did not have any desire to feed off them, but now with the human half of him gone, it's a brand-new world for him to adjust to.

"I will be alright; I am doing this for Jorja," he said with a crooked smile. "But maybe you should keep an eye on me, just for a bit."

"Well, there is no humans in this house, so you should be okay for a little while, but I would suggest keeping your distance from Ezrabeth for a little bit." Jade advised. It would devastate him if he ever hurt her.

"Oh...I did not think of how this would affect her. I guess I thought there would not be much of a change," Adrian said with a bit of sadness.

"Rayne and I talked to her yesterday; we didn't tell her about you. I thought it would be best to wait," Jade said as she sat down beside him. "She thinks you went to pick up my mom, so you would be gone for a bit; we didn't want her coming over here and having any incidences . . ."

"Thank you, Jade, your mother will be so proud of you," Adrian said as he gave her a hug.

"Whoa...easy there." Jade caught herself from falling off the bed. "You have a whole new set of muscles now; you're a lot stronger than you were."

"Sorry, Jade, I guess this will take some getting used to," he replied, still pondering in his head all the new possibilities for himself. "And your mother . . ."

"You are a lot stronger than her too, Adrian, be careful not to hurt her." Jade laughed, knowing full well, what he was thinking.

She patted Adrian's shoulder and stood up. "We have a lot to do; it won't be easy getting to her."

"And Cavan . . ." Adrian growled through his teeth.

"He's with her. I don't know how much time we have; she will be very weak." Jade pointed to his clean clothes in the armchair in the corner of the room. "We are going to go up to the cabin in Algonquin for a few days to hunt; it will be better up there, more to feed on. We need all our strength to get her out of there," Jade said, walking out of the room. "Come down when you are ready, and we will get going."

It did not take Adrian long to finish the blood bag and get dressed. "I'm ready," he said in a very calm tone as he reached the bottom of the stairs; he knew he would have to fight, and he was ready for anything. He loved Jorja very much that was clearer to him now more than ever before.

"Okay, let's hit the road," Jade said, reaching for Holden who was standing by the window looking out. Rayne had already packed the SUV with their bags, and she was waiting in the garage. "I told you there had to be an easier way." She giggled looking at the newly turned Adrian. "How do you feel?"

"I'm surprised." His eyebrows crinkled. "I don't really *feel* any different except this burning in my throat."

"That will go away after you hunt," Jade added as she got in the driver's seat and started the ignition.

The cabin Jorja and Rayne had built was beautiful; it was easy for Jade to find the trail to the cabin without having to use the canoe she drove along a path and came in behind the house. Jade had seen the cabin in her vision, but it was nothing compared to seeing it firsthand. The thought that her mother and sister built this beautiful building with their own hands was overwhelming. Holden could not believe his eyes either.

"Where were you when my parents needed their kitchen remodeled?" Holden said with amazement to Rayne. "This looks amazing, you two really did this all yourselves?"

"I designed it, but my mother showed me how to build it," Rayne replied. "She is really unbelievably talented." Rayne had so much pride in her voice when she spoke of her mother.

"Every day, that woman just makes me love her more," Adrian added. "How many men can say their better half built a house with their own hands and actually have it look good?" He laughed.

Adrian and Holden took the bags inside while Rayne and Jade went down to the water.

"Your Holden seems nice," Rayne said with a hint of jealously in her voice. "He seems to really care about you."

"Don't worry, Rayne, your time is coming," Jade assured her. "I promise you."

"Don't tease me, Jade, I have been alone for far too long."

"I'm not teasing," she said, "remember I can see it...you can't."

"Whatever, I don't have the patience for that right now," Rayne snarled. "Men only complicate things, remember...Charles and then Dr. Scott."

"Yes, they loved you very much, Rayne, Dr. Scott still does," her sister told her, but Jade knew that no matter what she said, it would not help right now. The chance would come again, Jade could see that, but unfortunately, for Rayne, that time was not today.

"Wow, Rayne, the architecture on the inside is more beautiful than I would ever have imagined," Holden said as he walked down to the beachfront where Rayne and her sister were standing.

"Thanks," she said sharply then spun around and headed back up to the house.

"Something I said?" Holden asked, confused.

"No, she just has a lot to deal with right now, babe; don't worry about her, she will be alright," Jade countered wrapping her arms around him. "We will wait until dark to hunt; I don't want to run into any hikers out here."

"That works for me; I think I am doing pretty good so far. I don't want to disappoint you," Holden said half smugly with a laugh. Jade knew he would eventually kill a human; she could see that in his future, but that will not make her love him any less. It will be an accident; unfortunately, an accident that she would have to let happen.

Holden and Jade sat on the beach in two handcrafted wooden chairs that her mother had made. He held Jade's hand as they looked over the still water. Neither of them spoke much for the next few hours, Jade thought that it was just nice to be here with him. *I could really handle living out here not having to worry about humans or any other issues that we seem to encounter in the human world.* Jade thought to herself. All her studies of the humans over the years has just made it harder to deal with the fact that no matter what she did, their life would come and go, and she would always be there in the shadows watching it happen. Jade tried to clear her head, so she could clearly see her mother again, but every vision she had was the same stone-cold motionless body lying on a table surrounded by the very creatures that call themselves their species.

Jade watched the sun setting across the water, and for the first time in hours, Holden spoke, "How many vampires can see such a beautiful view?" He rubbed his hand up and down Jade's arm.

"None . . . That's the problem," she snapped, then immediately recoiled. "I'm sorry, babe; I'm just really worried about my mom." Calmer, she reached for his hand and squeezed it.

"I know." His eyes met Jade's softly. "I didn't mean anything by it; it's just this is all so new for me," he said, trying to recover his words.

Adrian walked down the beach behind them. "Rayne is getting anxious," he said, "it's getting dark, and she wants to start hunting soon."

"Okay, just a few more hours. I want to make sure there are no hikers to run into." They all went back up to the house; Rayne was waiting by the window. "Just a bit longer, Rayne, we have to be safe," Jade said. She knew her sister was in a hurry to get back on the road, but it would do them no justice to be sloppy at this point.

Finally, it was late enough. Jade stared off into the trees scanning the pictures in her mind for any human activity, and she found none it was safe to hunt. Rayne ran off in her own direction impatient to hunt and get back. Holden stayed close to Jade, as he always did when they hunted out of fear that he may come across a human. The thought of killing a human for food was not a happy thought for him. Adrian followed Holden's lead still unsure of his new self. Not too far from the cabin, they came across a pack of wolves. In an instant, Jade knew feeding on these wolves would not be such a great idea. The vision came seconds too late, no sooner did Jade pause to inform the others not to attack; Holden was already leaping through the trees.

The snarls coming from all directions were enough to shake the forest. Adrian ran into the beast that was now on top of Holden knocking it backward while Jade reached for Holden trying to pull him away. The now very angry beasts were circling them, growling, snarling teeth exposed ready to attack. For the first time, they were not the hunters; they were the prey. All the sudden, Jade could hear a faint voice speaking. *"I can hear one of the wolves' voice."* The voice was in shock that Holden had attacked. He was conversing with the other wolves in the pack on how to deal with this situation.

"Really...shifters!" Could this even be possible? Jade thought.

"STOP!" She shouted aloud and stood straight up out of her fighting crouch. Then she could hear nothing but silence from either side.

"What are you doing, Jade?" Holden hissed. "I will not hold back if those dogs try to attack you."

"Don't worry, I don't think we are in danger here," Jade said calmly. "Who is in charge of your pack?" she asked, looking for the biggest of the beasts.

"I am," Jade heard the voice clearly in her mind, but no mouths opened.

Holden and Adrian stood and stared. Jade could hear the confusion in their thoughts but could not take the time to explain; she had to stop this before it got worse.

"What is your name, wolf?" she asked, turning toward the beast that spoke through his thoughts to her.

"You can hear me?" he replied in his mind.

"Yes, I can." Jade smiled softly. "What is your name?"

The other wolves still circled around them while the largest of the beasts stopped in front of Jade. She could see through his green eyes, he did not want to hurt them.

"My name is Justin," he answered as he stood up on his hind legs and shifted from a beastly dog to a beautifully sculpted man. Jade was in awe, before her stood a beautiful six-foot man with shoulders that made him look like he should be a football quarterback; his eyes were a deep emerald green. Surprisingly enough in his human form, his chest was bare and completely smooth; he looked no older than twenty.

"Now we can talk properly," he said, as he gave the others permission to take their human forms as well.

Holden and Adrian stood silent in amazement. "It's okay," Jade said, turning to them. "I see no harm."

"Speak for yourself!" a female voice came from behind Justin, the male leader, as she stepped out holding her bleeding arm. This must have been the wolf that Holden attacked. "You keep that, that, whatever the hell he is away from me," she growled. "What kind of stupid people attack *wolves* anyway?"

"The kind that thought you were a wolf and not a person," Holden replied with remorse. "You don't smell human," he added, crinkling his nose.

"What are you doing out here this late at night, and why are you attacking us?" Justin asked.

"I am sorry I did not see you out here when I searched for humans; we came out here to hunt, that's all," Jade answered politely.

"You hunt with your hands?" Justin raised his eyebrow. "Or do you just get some thrill out of wrestling wolves?" He laughed.

"How do I put this lightly?" Jade paused. "We don't really hunt with our hands..." a half smile crept from her lips exposing a small hint of her fangs.

"Oh, dammit," one of the other males barked. "They are frigging vamps!"

"How do you know what the hell we are?" Adrian hissed as he stepped in front of the male.

"Because you vamps are all the same, you waltz in to a place and think you can just push us around," the male snarled.

Both men now standing face to face, the male wolf waiting for his leader to give him the permission he needed to rip Adrian apart, and Adrian holding as still as stone waiting for his opponent to make the slightest advancement.

"Push you around?" Jade questioned looking at Justin.

"Yah, we've had quite a few bad run in's with vamps in the past." He sighed. "But I get the feeling that surprises you."

Holden was now at Jade's side with his arms locked around her waist. She could feel every muscle in him tensing, but she did not want to break eye contact with this leader for fear that it would spark the others to attack.

"Up until very recently, we believed that our family was the only ones of our kinds left." Jade sighed. "We have searched for over a hundred and fifty years and not found anything."

"Okay? I don't understand," Justin said, confused. "You said you were hunting, but you weren't looking for humans?"

"No," Jade was abrupt "my family doesn't drink from humans; we feed on animals, or we can sometimes get blood from a blood bank."

"Um," Adrian interrupted, "I don't mean to be rude, but I'm... um...you know...so could we maybe speed this up a bit."

"Oh crap, I'm so sorry, Adrian." Jade turned to him for a moment breaking eye contact with Justin. "Please just hang on a few minutes longer." As she turned back to Justin, the others in his pack began snarling behind him.

"Enough!" he barked at them.

"Justin, I am truly sorry, but we have to leave now unless you intend on eating us; we would like to be on our way," Jade said flatly.

"You are a very brave little one." He chuckled as he moved toward Jade, now standing merely a few feet away from her. Holden's grip on Jade tightened, as Justin got closer, he hissed behind her stepping to the side and pulling Jade away from Justin.

"Your mate seems very protective." Justin winked at Jade. "But something tells me you don't need his protection, do you?"

"I see no harm here," Jade replied calmly, stepping back in front of Holden who was very uneasy with the thought that this beast was getting so close to her.

"You seem very sure of that." Justin was getting cocky, taking yet another step closer to Jade.

"I am very sure, and no, we don't want to fight," she said firmly without thinking twice.

"Okay then, if you are not here to cause us issues, then I have no problem with you, sweetheart, and neither will my pack." Justin turned to the rest of his pack giving them a harsh look.

"We will be on our way then, but we will see you again," Jade said with a smirk seeing a very clear vision in her mind.

"You did not tell me your name, sweetheart," Justin added.

"Jade!"

He smiled and took one final step closer to her. "Hmm, Jade." He touched her cheek gently. "I will see you again," and then he was gone. Justin and his pack took off through the trees, almost as fast as Jade could run with her vampire's speed. Holden spun Jade around and held her to his chest with a loud sigh of relief.

Adrian came and put his hand on her shoulder. "Mind explaining what the hell just happened there?"

"Well, I think we just made some new friends," Jade said with a chuckle. "Come on, we need to feed Adrian."

"I guess at this point, nothing should surprise me!" Adrian said sarcastically as they ran off in the other direction to feed.

By the time they got back to the cabin, Rayne was already sitting on the beach. It was almost dawn; she had called to Jade in her mind earlier letting her sister know she had returned. They would have to stay a few more days and feed before Adrian would be strong enough for the trip, but after his display with the wolves, Jade knew it would not take him long, maybe a day or two. The four of them sat on the beach watching the sun catch fire over the water as it topped the edge of the lake. What a beautiful sight, "*I cannot imagine any creature, vampire or otherwise not being able to enjoy such a beauty.*"

"Jade," Justin's voice called through the trees.

Rayne stood up from her perch abruptly. Holden was at Jade's side with his right hand intertwined in her and his left hand around her hips; it had been only a day since the encounter with the wolves in the woods.

"What are you doing here...dog?" Holden hissed.

"Relax, bloodsucker," Justin barked back at Holden. "I have some news for you."

As Justin walked toward Jade, he caught sight of Rayne and she of him. Rayne stood hypnotized by the sight of Justin walking toward the beach where she stood. The sun catching his green eyes, his messy dark hair blowing in the breeze, watching him move in slow motion, Rayne had been paralyzed.

"I'm sorry, but I don't remember being introduced." Justin smiled looking at Rayne.

"Rayne," she answered, trying to break the eye contact that she seemed to be locked in.

"News," Jade interrupted, "what kind of news?"

"Well, after our little *encounter*," he laughed, "I talked to my dad about you and your family." He tried very hard not to look at

Rayne while he spoke, but his thoughts gave him away, and Jade chuckled at what she could hear.

"You spoke with your father?" Rayne interjected with intrigue, pretending as if she did not just hear what was going on in his head.

"Yah, I told him about your family." Still looking at Jade. "He would really like to meet with you; he has never known a vampire that didn't want to drink from humans."

"Justin, I would love to meet your dad and have a little chat, but we have some things we need to deal with right now. Our mother has been taken by supposed Guardians, and we need to get her back before they kill her." The words flew from Jade's mouth as if someone else was speaking. How could she be so strong at a time like this she was the youngest of her family; they should be the stronger ones. Yet here she was taking charge yet again.

"Jade, my dad may be able to help you with that too," he said with a smile. "Please just give him a chance to talk to you."

"Rayne," Jade turned in her sister's direction "please stay here with Holden and Adrian for a few hours."

"Um, yah sure...stay here," she mumbled, staring at Justin in a daze.

Holden tightened his grip on Jade. *I do not think this is a good idea; you going alone . . .* his thoughts echoed through Jade's head. She turned to him and kissed his lips then unlocked herself from his grip.

"It will be okay," she said to him. "Stay here with Rayne. I will be back in a few hours."

He gave her another kiss, and he let go unwillingly as she pulled herself back.

"Okay, two hours," Holden said, glaring at Justin. "Then I am coming looking for you."

Justin and Jade took off into the trees leaving Rayne, Holden and Adrian waiting on the beach, Justin moved very quickly through the trees even in his human form, but it was not hard for her to keep up with him as she had speed on her side. They ran for about five minutes; then Justin stopped suddenly.

"Okay, my house is just over that hill," he said nervously. "Please don't be frighten of my dad; he is very old."

"Old, what do you mean old?" Jade laughed. "I mean come on, it's not like I haven't seen my share of birthdays."

They topped the hill, and Jade saw a small wooden house with a man sitting in a chair on the porch facing east. As he turned his tired body, that looked leathered by the sun, Jade could see pain written all over his face.

Justin took her hand and walked toward his father.

"Dad, this is Jade."

"Nice to meet you, child," the man said softly.

"Nice to meet you as well, sir." Jade nodded.

"Well, Miss Jade, do you have a last name?" he asked.

"Yes, I am Jade Sullivan," she answered politely, "and you, sir, what is your name?"

"Logan Greene," he said.

"Well, Mr. Greene, Justin said you wanted to talk to me about our family?"

"My dear, sit with me, Justin tells me you thought you were the only ones of your kind; well, I can assure you, child, you're not."

Justin and Jade sat on the porch with his father as he told them about the Real World Order; this was an organization where vampires, witches, and shifters lived and interacted with the human world without most of the humans knowing that the creatures were in fact, not human. The Real World Order had been created thousands of years ago by the vampires who ruled the earth to instill balance between the species. Their mission was to keep order for the shadow creatures and allow the humans to live in peace, somewhat. The vampires now control most of the major companies that keep the world's industry running smoothly. There is a group of Guardians that oversee everything, kind of like royals in the Real World Order.

Jade sat and listened for almost an hour as Logan spoke; he told her things like the Real World Order created all the different religions to keep humankind "spiritually ignorant," so they would be able to keep the Real World Order secretive. They formed groups like the Illuminati, Freemasons, and other powerful and secretive organizations.

"How could I not have found this before?" Jade asked Logan. "We've searched for so long and found nothing."

"Because, child," he answered with a smile, "I don't think you were believed to be real vampires." He paused and took a breath. "Young vampires are very mischievous creatures; they trick the humans and hypnotize them, so they can feed. Most of them do not actually kill the humans, they just disorient them, and the most important fact is that they cannot come out in the sunlight. It *will* kill them." The lines on Logan's face softened. "So naturally, my dear, someone that can endure the sun, they would assume to be a *wanna-be vampire* there are so many out there now, pretending."

"So you're telling me that because we come out in the daytime and don't bite people, they all thought we were fake vampires...that live forever?" Jade laughed sarcastically. "Why could I not see any of this in my visions?"

"I would have to guess you couldn't see them in your visions because maybe your visions can only go as far as your knowledge for the world and the people around you," Logan guessed. "You, child, are what we call a watcher. Someone that can see the future can watch for danger and see the outcome of events for example, war. That is very useful to them, so it is very possible that this vampire that has your mother has tried to keep you from this world in order to keep the Guardians from finding out what you can do."

"I don't understand why Cavan would not want us to help them if they are so intertwined in the human world. Can we not do some good with all of this?" she questioned, already beginning to see visions of the past vampires they had actually met.

"I'm afraid, my dear; I cannot answer that, only this Cavan can." Logan took a deep breath, "Now that you know what you are looking for in your visions, maybe it will help you save your mother."

This was a lot to take in, everything Jade thought she knew for the past century and a half. *"How could I be so stupid, I should have seen this?"* Justin could see the hurt and confusion on Jade's face; he rubbed her hand and gave her a soft smile. "It's getting late, come on, Jade, let's get you back before soldier boy storms the forest looking for you." He laughed, trying to make her feel better no doubt.

"I don't know if there is much else I can tell you here, you have a lot ahead of you now."

"But what do I do now?" Jade asked, confused.

"My little Jade," Logan said softly as a smile crossed his tired face, "you don't seem to understand, you have now been *introduced* to the Real World Order...watch for the symbol, I have faith that you will see."

The possibilities ran through Jade's head, the visions began to flow clearly.

CHAPTER 14

Jade returned to the cottage with Justin, Holden was waiting very anxiously by the water with Rayne. He came running over as soon as he seen Jade through the clearing, taking hold and hugging her tightly. He glared at Justin with hatred in his eyes; Jade could not help but giggle. He was jealous.

She kissed Holden and whispered, "*You have nothing to worry about babe!*"

His grip on her loosened a bit, but only enough that they could walk down to the beach. Justin following with a smirk across his face, of course he could tell that Holden was jealous, but Justin was not interested in Jade in that way but that did not stop him from tormenting Holden.

"Justin," Jade said, turning to face him, "Rayne is down at the beach. I think you might want to go get to know her before . . . " She paused. "Um, never mind just go on down there and talk to her."

Holden and Jade went into the cottage and sat in one of the small rooms. He felt a bit more at ease once he figured out why she sent Justin down to see Rayne. They were connected enough that he understood Jade had had visions of Rayne and Justin *getting along*.

The two of them sat there quietly for a bit; Holden knew that when Jade was trying to induce her visions and see clearly the best thing for him to do was just sit back. Therefore, he did just that; he sat with his back propped up against the head of the bed, his legs stretched out in front of him, leaning back with his arms crossed behind his head. He looked so content sitting there staring at Jade silently, waiting for her to snap out of her thinking trance.

"Ah, I can't think straight," Jade growled after about an hour. "There is too much new information, I can't think . . . "

Holden sat watching Jade argue with herself for a few more minutes then with a seamless movement, he picked her up off the edge of the bed and laid her down. He was leaning over Jade now looking down with a seductive smile.

"What are you doing?" She hissed. "I have to figure out how we are going to do this."

"I know," Holden's voice was low and smooth, "but you didn't look to be getting too far with your little argument, so I thought I would help clear your head a bit." His eyes ran up and down her body slowly then met her eyes. His smile softened as he leaned down to kiss her.

"Holden," Jade breathed his name, almost inaudible.

"I know, babe." He sighed. "Just tell me when to stop; we both know I am strong enough now." Jade felt her body relax as they kissed; she held him closer to her than she ever had. There was so much going through her head, everyone's emotions and seeing other vampires in her visions, she felt different. Jade did not think this time would be a matter of Holden being strong enough to stop; this time, she was not sure she wanted him to. As they kissed, Jade could faintly hear the music playing in the background of the room, her thoughts now totally consumed by Holden's thoughts.

Jade pulled herself back; she could feel the frustration in Holden, but he understood why. He truly was a gentleman even if being a vampire did give him the instincts of a killer.

"I'm sorry, Holden."

"Don't be sorry. I know this is not the time or place," he said with disappointment.

"Holden," Jade called as he got up and walked toward the door, "please don't be mad."

"I'm not mad…just a little frustrated that's all," he said as he left the room.

Jade could read the thoughts in Holden's head, and she knew why he was frustrated, but it truly was not the time or place, and deep down, he knew that. She gave him this new life and everything that came with it including new emotions, urges and physical demands. Jade felt horrible; she knew she loved him, and she knew he loved her. Jade was plenty old enough now a hundred and fifty years of abstinences was pretty damn good. However, her values were still the same as when she was a child. Jade wanted to wait until she was married before she had sex, so why should that change now just because she was an immortal.

Jade sat there for a few hours alone in the room thinking about everything, Holden, her mom, Adrian, Justin, and Ezrabeth. The room got dark and quiet; the vision came so clear like she was right there. A castle overlooking the water, the room her mother was in, no windows only a small opening overlooking a dining area, the large wooden door that locked her in. Cavan telling her they were all dead. She looked so different now; her hair black as the midnight sky, hung lifeless down her back, her eyes empty and dark. Her mother's face broke; all of her energy washed away. She truly looked like death now.

"Okay, Jade, think . . . how can I stop it? I cannot let her think we are dead; I cannot let her feel that. Look harder where is she; there has to be a clue somewhere."

Jade watched her mother walking through a castle with Cavan, showing her around and laying out her boundaries; she watched the images of her mother trying to think of ways to end her immortal life and getting more upset every time she could not do it.

"No, I have to find her, look harder. I know there is a clue some-where; I just have to look harder."

"That's it! There it is! Mom, you are a genius, of course, you keep a journal. Keep writing, I can see it."

Journal entry,

In the dead of the night, I hear the wolf howl. In the light of the day, this world is empty. It is now the only time I can truly feel free for he cannot follow me around this prison when the sun is afire. Yesterday, I walked the grounds observing the view from the cliffs, thinking of a way to end my eternal hurt that now fills my existence. My family and my beloved Adrian are dead. I am now dead. This place surrounded by water, it seems to be a small island. The wolves that guard beyond the walls will not give me the chance to run; they just bring me back when I try. The view from the castle tower is all I can see. Nothing but trees and water, as far out into the water as I can see is empty, no other land, no life, just empty black water. There has to be something out there, something that can save me . . . or kill me, the only beauty I see are the black orchids in the gardens below.

Darkness is almost upon the sky again, and soon, he will rise; yet another night, I must endure.

Jorja Sullivan

"Thank you, Mom, I knew you'd send me a sign!"

Jade ran out of the room and down to the beach where everyone was sitting, "Justin!" she yelled as she ran. They all turned, Holden's eyes glared, but Jade ignored him this time, "Justin . . . wolf guards," she felt both excited and anxious while she said it. "Black Orchid's an island . . . "

"Whoa," Justin said almost catching Jade as she ran into the group of them. His face hardened as soon as she said *guards*. "Slow down, sweetheart, you don't want to go there . . . I like you." He paused.

"What's that supposed to mean, dog?" Holden hissed as he came closer to Jade and reached for her arm pulling her over to him.

"Easy, both of you," Rayne said as she watched her sister's face. She knew what Jade had seen, and she tried to read the journal entry in her sister's mind, but there were too many thoughts going through at once she could not make sense of it.

"Everybody shut up for a minute." Jade gasped. "Okay, Justin," she said, looking at him. "Where is there werewolf guards?"

"Not around here." He laughed. "My dad put a stop to that many, many years ago."

"Then I need to talk to your dad again . . . NOW!"

Holden was not happy, and Adrian was more confused than ever. However, Rayne seen the thoughts more clearly now; she knew Jade needed to talk to Logan to find out who still had wolf guards and where.

"If you want, but it's not really a subject he talks about nicely," Justin said sarcastically and shrugged his shoulders.

"Hold up just a minute," Holden said, pulling Jade to face him, "you have to tell me what's going on here; I don't like this."

"Holden, babe, relax. I think I know where my mom is, but I need some help from Justin's dad," Jade said, hoping Rayne would help explain things to him when Jade went to talk to Logan.

"I am coming with you." Holden hissed harshly.

"No, I'm sorry, please stay here with Rayne and Adrian. I know you are worried, but you don't have to be. I will be back soon."

Jade kissed him then took off in the trees with Justin again.

"Logan, I have some more questions if you don't mind?" Jade asked softly.

"Of course, little Jade, anything you like." Logan smiled.

"What can you tell me about wolf guards?"

"Guards . . . " he growled. "Why the hell are you asking about them? I thought you were different than the other vamps."

"I'm not trying to upset you, Logan, it's just that in my vision, I was reading a journal entry that my mother wrote and wherever she is, wolves are guarding outside the grounds walls." Jade stopped and looked at Logan and Justin, both of them were very upset with the topic, but Justin knew she was sincere.

"Dad," Justin said, "I know you don't like talking about him, but do you think that Uncle William might know something about this?"

"That idiot would not know his own paw if he punched himself with it," Logan barked. "If you think he knows where her mother is, then go ask him yourself."

Logan did not seem like he had much strength to do anything, but that did not stop him from almost lunging at Justin with the very thought of this uncle.

"Come on, Jade, let's go," Justin said harshly. "Let this old dog calm down; I have to talk to the rest of my pack."

"You want me to go see your pack?" she hesitated, from the last encounter they had, Jade knew they did not like her much; well, they did not like vampires very much.

"No, I want you to go back to the cabin and write out that journal entry, so I can read it and see if anyone in my pack can see any clues as to where Cavan's castle is." He started to walk away; then he stopped and turned to Jade. "You better get that boy of yours under control; we will meet you at the cabin tonight around midnight." Then he was gone through the trees.

"I don't trust him." Holden hissed. "I don't see how you can, I mean look at him, he is a damn dog for crying out loud."

"Holden, please," Jade begged. "You don't understand; he might be able to help us find my mother."

"I thought you could see the future; can't you just see where she is and how to get there?" He was being so sarcastic now it was beginning to just piss her off.

"I can't control my visions. I can only see the castle she is in not where it is." Jade hissed back. "*I can't believe we are even having this fight. Why can't he just understand, what does he have against wolves anyway?*"

Holden and Jade stood there staring intensely at each other in silence for a few minutes; then his face softened.

"I'm sorry, baby. I guess I still have a lot to understand and get used to," he said, putting his head down onto hers. "I didn't mean to upset you. I honestly don't know what I am supposed to do here. I don't know anything about being a vampire or wolf or anything like that. I'm a soldier that's all I know how to be." He sighed, bringing his eyes up to meet Jade's. "I guess I'm just scared; I don't want anything to happen to you . . . I don't want to lose you like I've lost everyone else." He kissed her forehead. "You are my life, Jade Sullivan . . . now and forever."

"Holden, I love you." Jade held him tighter. "Nothing and no one will ever change that." She kissed him back softly, but this time, she actually felt him, pulsing through her, she could feel his thoughts not just see them.

It scared her!

"Holden." Jade gasped as she tried to pull herself away just a bit, so she could think straight, but he did not let go. His grip on her got stronger, and her body tensed; as Jade pulled her head back, she could see his eyes glowing bright fire orange.

"Oh . . . you haven't fed today...This is so not good right now! Justin is coming tonight, and you are thirsty!"

The thoughts rang through Jade's head like a wrecking ball. Holden was letting his instincts start to get the best of him; she needed to get him out to feed . . . NOW!

"Holden, we need to hunt."

"Jade, what's wrong with me? I feel really strange . . . and thirsty." As soon as the words came from his mouth, he knew what was going on. They had not hunted yet today because she had been so preoccupied. Rayne and Adrian had gone out to hunt, but Jade and Holden had not.

"I'm so sorry, babe, we will go right now," Jade said.

"But what about Justin?" he asked, almost concerned. "Isn't he coming at midnight?"

"Yah, we still have a few hours. I am sure we can find something before then, come on."

Jade yelled out to Rayne and Adrian to let them know that they were heading out to hunt; but they were too involved in a conversation in the living room and just gave a wave on the way out the door.

It was about 11:30 p.m. when Holden and Jade got back from hunting; they both felt much better. They had come across a large bear, after all the purpose of coming here was to get Holden and Adrian stronger.

"You might want to get changed." Rayne laughed as they walked back in the door. "Justin will be here soon, and you look like crap." She looked at Holden. He was getting better at being more graceful with smaller animals, but the bigger ones still made quite a mess.

Jade was trying to give Rayne her space; she seemed to be bonding with Adrian, so she tried to stay out of the way. After all, when they find their mom, he was kind of going to be their stepfather.

Holden went to clean up, and Jade started to write out the journal entry from her vision while he got changed; it didn't take very long. Once Holden was all cleaned up, he and Jade sat on the bed propped up on the headboard.

"Jade, I am really sorry about earlier," he said sincerely.

"It's okay, it was my own fault. I should have taken you hunting sooner and not let you wait so long," Jade added.

"You have so much to worry about already. You don't need to be worried about me too, I shouldn't have snapped at you." He leaned the side of his head to hers.

"I know you did not mean it, but for future reference," Jade said, tapping her hand against his chest with a chuckle. "If you don't let me know when you need to feed, I'm gonna punch you in the teeth." She laughed. "I don't need you in a bad mood just because you are hungry."

"I know." He chuckled. "I guess it's a guy thing; well, that combined with a vampire's thing. I guess it doesn't make a good combination, does it?"

"So we have a deal, you will let me know when you are hungry, and I won't punch you in the teeth for being a jerk," Jade said plainly with a giggle.

"You've got yourself a deal, babe." He turned and kissed the side of Jade's head. "How did I ever get so lucky to find an angel like you?"

"Angel?" She raised her eyebrows and tilted her head. "Angels have wings, babe...not fangs." Jade flashed him her *killer* smile, and he laughed then shook his head at her and gave the same smile back; he looked so beautiful as he parted his red lips to reveal his perfect teeth. She did this; Jade made him into a monster just like her.

That thought made her a little sad, *I actually turned a human into a killer . . .*

"What are you thinking about right now?" he asked.

"You don't want to know," Jade said a bit ashamed.

"I wouldn't have asked if I did not want to know," Holden declared so tranquil.

Jade sighed. "I was just thinking that I am surprised with myself, that's all."

"Surprised at what? Everything you are doing to get your mom back?" he asked.

"No, not that, well, I guess I'm surprised at you actually." She looked up at him. "I turned you . . . I turned you into a top of the food chain killer." Jade let out a sigh, but before she could say anything else, he turned to face her and put her chin in his hand.

"Don't you even go there, Jade," Holden almost sounded angry. "I would not be alive today if you hadn't changed me. I would be a pile of mush on the rocks at the bottom of that bridge . . . You saved me."

"But you're not *alive*, you're a vampire. Your heart doesn't beat; your lungs don't need air to breathe."

"Stop right there." He put his finger up to her lips. "I know you have a lot on your mind right now with your mom, so I will let you away with this, just once. Chalk it up to some stress breakdown or something." Holden paused and stared in Jade's eyes. "You gave me the choice, and I took it; just because I don't have a pulse doesn't mean I'm not alive. I *AM* alive because I am here . . . with you!" He gave Jade a quick kiss. "Never forget that."

Rayne knocked on the door and waited for a response.

"Come on in, Rayne, it's okay," Jade answered.

"Justin and a few other people are here; I think you should come out." She looked a little uneasy. Justin had talked to her a bit before about being a shifter, but seeing more of them knowing what they were even in their human form did not really sit right with her.

"Okay, tell him we will be right there," Jade said; then Rayne closed the door. "As for you." Jade grinned, giving Holden a tap on the chest again. "Please behave; this might be the only chance we have to find my mom."

Holden took a deep breath and sighed. "You're lucky I love you; when I was a human, I did not back down from anyone. I guess that's why I liked the military so much." He laughed.

"So you will be nice?" Jade asked in a softer, more innocent voice then kissed his cheek.

"Yes, I promise I will be a good boy." He rolled his eyes sarcastically. "But only until one of them get out of line, then it's game on." He laughed getting up off the bed and taking Jade's hand to help her up.

"Justin," Jade called, walking out into the main room of the cabin. He was standing with Rayne, Adrian, and the others from his pack. They did not look happy to be there.

"Jade, this is Marc," Justin said, tapping one of the males on the shoulder. "He has a few answers for you."

"Hi, Marc," she said softly.

"Okay, first thing, I don't like vampires . . . " Marc said harshly. "I just want to make that very clear, but Justin said you're different, and I have to give you the benefit of the doubt."

Jade could feel Holden getting tenser; he did not like Marc anymore than he liked Justin but for way different reasons. Marc was an ass.

"Justin came and told me about your vision, and we went to my dad, Justin's uncle William to see if we could get some answers for you." He gritted his teeth looking at Justin. "Do you have the journal entry Justin told me about today?"

Jade handed Marc the piece of paper then took Holden's hand and sat on the couch beside Rayne with him. Marc read the entry aloud.

"Okay, this here." Marc pointed to the paper. "The only beauties I see are the black orchids in the gardens below." He paused looking at Justin who gave him a nod to tell him it was okay to continue. "Black orchids are the symbol of the Real World Order. There is only one place they grow that wolves have ever guarded, that is Castle Lear. It is on an island about halfway out in the North Atlantic between Nova Scotia and Ireland."

This was good, now at least Jade had an area to focus her visions. "Sign, Logan told me to look for a sign; this must be what he was talking about."

"Yah, maybe," Marc said, grinding his teeth.

"Marc, if the wolves don't want to be guards, and it is such a bad subject, why do they do it?" Jade asked confused.

"You think we have a choice," Marc barked back at her. "You think if it wasn't for wolves like Justin's dad and mine, we wouldn't be still under the control of bloodsuckers."

Justin cut in, "Easy, Marc, I told you these ones are different." He winked at Rayne. "They are not like the other ones." He walked over to Rayne and took her hand.

"Do you know who is guarding the Lear Castle now?" Rayne asked Justin.

"Marc," Justin said, turning his head with a smile, "I believe you can answer that one."

Everyone in the room turned to look at Marc as he grumbled under his voice.

"What?"

"My mother," he growled louder. "She is the pack leader guarding the Lear Castle now, and she has been there for the last nineteen years; she was ordered there after I was born along with a few others from around here and some they got from down in the U.S."

Marc's face was as hard as stone now; it hurt him a lot to think about the woman that left him as a child. That seeded his anger toward the vampires, and then as he got older and met more of them, it just got worse.

"Marc, do you think she would help us?" Jade asked, very unsure how he would react.

"How the hell do I know?" he barked. "I don't even know the woman. I haven't seen her in nineteen years."

Justin barked back at Marc, "Chill, man, she is just trying to figure things out. You don't need to be such an ass." He was still standing beside Rayne holding her hand in his. The wolves started arguing among themselves.

Adrian stepped in, after listening to everything that had been going on over the last few days, he had enough. "ENOUGH!" he yelled. "All of you, listen to yourselves. There is a good woman out there being held against her will, what difference does it make if she is a vampire, a human or a wolf?" Adrian looked around the room and had everyone's attention "We ARE going to find Jorja; you can either help us or not, but either way, you are going to stop this crap right now."

Jade smiled as she felt his emotion hit everybody in the room.

"We can either work together or not, that's your choice, but Marc, I'm sure you want to see your mother again, and I am sure she is not happy there either."

When Adrian stopped to take a breath, Holden cut in, "He's right, you know. Up until a few months ago, I didn't believe vampires existed never mind werewolves, but I have never met any humans more compassionate, more loving and more full of hope than I have in this family right here. They don't care that you're wolves, they don't treat you any different. How can you even put them in the same boat as the rest that you've met? They thought they were the only ones."

Jade's heart almost broke. *"My Holden, what an angel; he knows that it's not what we, or they are, if we were going to work together."* Jade squeezed his hand and smiled.

"Well, what do you guys say?" Justin asked, turning to his pack. "Are we going to help them or not?"

The group looked around at each other for a few minutes talking back and forth with their eyes. Finally, Justin turned to us. "Okay, we'll do it, you have our help, but on one condition," he said, looking at Marc. "We need Marc's mom out safe too."

"You bet, if you guys are willing to help us, then how can we say no to that?" Rayne added.

Everyone sat around the fire burning on the beach; Jade listened to the stories the wolves told about their past with the vampires and the Real World Order. The wolves explained how vampires had ordered them to guard many things over the years to keep the humans from finding out the truth. All the secret organizations and groups had wolves on the front lines to keep the humans at bay, maybe it was because the wolves were big and strong, or maybe it was because the humans subconsciously told them something was different and to stay away. Either way, it had been working for thousands of years.

Rayne and Justin were getting closer by the second; Holden felt more at ease with Justin as well he even struck up conversations with him about hunting. Holden was curious about how the wolves fed and the differences between their habits. Jade thought it was nice to see them getting along for once since they are both going to be around for a while. Adrian and the other wolves got in on the conversations too; everyone was actually having a good time.

As Jade was listening to everyone, her mind was reeling with visions again of all the vampires she had really encountered and how many of they had the black orchid symbol somewhere on them, either a ring or a necklace, even a tattoo. It made sense that they did not believe her family; they do not have the symbol, and then there was the coming out in the day thing too. With all the folklore and myths that they encountered over the years, it was no wonder the other vampires would not open up if they thought they could hurt them or worse. The other vampires really did need to sleep somewhere dark to keep from burning up and to reenergize. It was so fascinating, Jade thought, that they are the same creature but so different. Her family didn't sleep and got all their energy from the blood they drink; she wondered why other vampires didn't. Jade wondered if all the other myths were true, if garlic and crosses really bothered them; she felt like a child again reading her first fiction book. She remembered back to when she was a child and would ask her mother if vampires could be real and if they had enough garlic in the house to keep safe from an attack; Jorja would always laugh and tell Jade her imagination was working overtime.

The group watched the sun come up over the water's edge, what a work of beauty. Justin asked Rayne if she would mind him hunting with her and Adrian today; she wasn't really sure if it was a good idea since she had never hunted with someone other than her family before, and he did not hunt the same way she did. Justin was a wolf, and he does not drink the blood from the animals; he eats the meat. Justin thought they would be a perfect team; they both could hunt together. Rayne could drink the blood, and he could eat the meat.

No waste!

Rayne thought about it for a little bit, and after talking it over with Adrian to see how he felt, they decided to try it. After all, it could not be that bad if they were using the entire animal for feeding more than one of them, kind of like conserving food sources.

They left about midafternoon. Justin assured Rayne it would be safe; his pack had decided it was still too weird to eat with vampires, so they took off east to do their hunting while Justin, Rayne and Adrian headed west.

CHAPTER 15

Jade was having a major dilemma, sitting alone in the cabin with Holden, whom she felt she had been so unfair to over the last few days. Keeping him in the dark, running all over the place with Justin, not giving him the attention he so very much needed and deserved.

They sat, not saying a word to each other not because there was tension, but he just did not know what to say; he was confused about what he was supposed to do and how he was to act or react with everything that was going on. On top of that, he still had normal male urges to deal with that were magnified immensely now because he was a vampire. Jade listened to his thoughts for a bit; he did not make any effort to hide what he was thinking from her or try to think of other things just so she would not know how he was feeling. Jade thought he probably liked that she could read his mind; that way, he did not really have to say it aloud.

He was frustrated with himself for having sexual thoughts about HER; it was not really his fault, all men got thoughts like that about woman they were attracted to. Jade heard it in the minds of just about every human she had ever met. However, Holden was really bothered by his cravings and how they were getting stronger every time he touched her.

Then without having time to even hear or see it coming, Holden jumped up and took Jade's hand.

"Jade, I love you." He paused, clearing his thoughts that had now become a jumbled mess.

"I love you too, Holden," Jade said, a little shocked by his movement.

"Jade," he took a deep breath, "when this is all over and we have your mom home . . . " He paused again and stared at Jade almost waiting for her to finish his sentence.

"What is it Holden?" Jade really wished he would clear his thoughts he was beginning to scare her.

Holden growled for a second trying to think of a way to say it then he just blurted out. "Jade, when we have your mother home safe and everything is back to . . . well, normal . . . I guess." He paused again taking in a deep breath, not that he needs to breathe then said softly, "What I am trying to say, Jade, is . . . " He pulled a tiny box out of his pocket. "Will you...marry...me?" He did not move while Jade looked at the ring in front of her; she was speechless.

Two very long minutes passed as Jade sat there in shock. Was this really happening? Did Holden really just propose to her? Thoughts echoed throughout her head.

"Jade," Holden spoke nervously.

"Yes," she smiled.

"Will you?" he hesitated.

"Can I ask you something first?"

"Anything." He smiled.

"Just tell me you're not doing this because I changed you." Jade looked down into her lap afraid of his answer.

"Jade, you gave me a choice between living and permanent death. You didn't even know me, you didn't know who I was, or what kind of person I was; you just knew that I was there." He sighed. "I know that it's only been a few months, but I've never felt this way . . . Ever. So, if I live to be thirty or three hundred, my life will be pointless if I cannot spend it with you. I love you, Jade. I don't know how else to show you that."

This is the part where if Jade could cry, she would have. She reached out to him, wrapped her arms around his neck, and whispered, "Yes." He kissed her without thinking twice; she did not want to let go. They broke apart for only a moment while he put the ring on her finger, then he kissed her again.

"It's so beautiful, but where did it come from?" Jade asked, since they were in the middle of nowhere, it was not as if he had been away from her long enough to go shopping at all.

"I know this is going to sound a little morbid, Jade, but it was my wife's," he said, a bit ashamed. "I had it in my pocket the day we met on the bridge, and I have just kept it with me ever since." Holden sat staring at the ring for a moment. "I will buy you a new one, whenever we make it back to civilization." He tried to smile, but Jade could see the embarrassment on his face.

"I love it." Jade took Holden's hand. "And I love you."

Jade was so excited, but of course, they could not get married anytime soon; however, Holden was okay with that. Just knowing that she said yes, for now was enough for him even if it meant they wait a couple years for the actual wedding.

When Rayne got back from hunting, Jade could not wait to show her sister the ring. Justin took off to find his pack. Holden and Adrian went down to the beach to talk while Rayne and Jade stayed in the cabin for a little *girl talk*.

"Who would have guessed that my baby sister would be married before me?" Rayne laughed. "I'm so happy for you, and Mom is going to be ecstatic you know."

"Let's not get ahead of our self." Jade chuckled. "We are not doing it just yet."

Jade could see her sister's thoughts going back to Charles and the hurt that she felt after she lost him, the night they lost their father as well, but Rayne was happy for her sister just the same.

The vision came on so suddenly; it ripped through Jade's mind like glass cutting everything in its path. She gasped. "We have to leave first thing tomorrow." Then her face froze. "Cavan... Adrian is going to kill him." Jade's body started to shake. "Adrian is going to kill his father and the Guardians are there...and..."

Rayne tried to snap her sister out of it, but Jade's body was almost convulsing. Jade could no longer hear Rayne; all she could see was the vision of what looked like an army descending on Adrian as he stood over Cavan's ashes. Jorja was offering herself, her DNA, and her own destruction. For the Guardians to do with as they pleased until they duplicate the endurance gene for the sun. In exchange for letting Adrian go, so he could return to his daughter. This was not just a vision; it was so clear Jade felt as if she was standing right there beside her mother watching it all but could not stop it. *Mom, please! NO!* Jade could feel the tears pouring down her cheeks. *"But how? It is not possible I have not been able to cry since the day I died,"* the confused thought bellowed through her mind, only it was not water dripping from her face...it was blood.

A scream rang through Jade's ears bringing her back to reality, only to realize it was her own voice. Jade opened her eyes and looked around the room. Rayne, Holden and Adrian were all staring at her; their mouths open in awe.

"Jade . . . what . . . did . . . . you do?" Rayne whispered, terrified. "What is on your face?"

Holden stood back; his eyes fixed on hers. He was holding Rayne's arm in shock. Adrian was the only one to come to her; he wiped Jade's eyes with his shirt. "It's okay, Jade; you don't need to cry. There is no way I will let that happen."

Jade looked at Adrian puzzled then saw his shirt...there was blood all over it.

"Let what happen, and what is on your shirt?" She whispered in shock, did that blood come from her vision?

"I cry, the same way." Adrian comforted her. "I realized it years ago, it takes a lot of effort for it to happen and after seeing the vision you just had; you've been so brave for everyone it was bound to happen sooner or later." Adrian put his arm around Jade and gave her a kiss on the forehead like her father use to do, then lifted her chin up, so he could look her in the eyes.

"Do you honestly think I would let your mother take my place?" he raised his eyebrow.

"But . . . " Jade was so confused. "How did you . . . and the blood . . . what's happening to me? I didn't know you could see my thoughts. Why did you not say anything?"

Adrian chuckled and wiped Jade's face again. "You never asked," he explained plainly. "I could see you from the beach and came running, poor Holden is terrified." He chuckled looking over at Holden and Rayne who were still standing ten feet away.

"In over a hundred and fifty years, I have never leaked blood from my eyes, why now?"

"I am always the one that knows what's going on; I don't like not knowing." Jade could not hide her inner voice any longer from her sister; Rayne ran to Jade and hugged her.

"That is how vampires cry, but it takes a lot to get there, some never do. You saw it in your vision, and I guess that unlocked the flood gates, so to speak," Adrian explained. "But you're right, we have to leave first thing tomorrow if we are going to find her. Don't worry, honey, your vision is not written in stone; things can always change."

"How do you know all vampires cry if you have never met any others?" Jade whispered, feeling more emotionally drained than she had ever been.

"I am not sure, Jade, it just came to me when I wiped your tears," Adrian answered as he tried to recall how he knew.

Justin and his pack returned later that night; the group went over how they were going to get to the Lear Castle and how they were going to approach Marc's mother. Adrian called Ezrabeth to let her know he was safe and to make sure she was doing all right. However, like always, she was acting like the adult, she was fine; she had talked to the school and told them that Adrian was sick and would need some more time off. Ezrabeth was such a smart kid; well, she is not a kid anymore. Sixteen is an *independent* age, not quite a kid anymore, not yet an adult. She had it covered though; Ezrabeth had learnt over the last sixteen years how to cover up for things that were out of the ordinary with her father. He briefly explained to her that what was going on without giving her too much detail to worry about, but he assured her that he would explain everything when he came home. She was not very happy about it, but she knew she did not have much choice.

At first light, the four vampires got into Jade's SUV, while Justin and his pack followed in Justin's truck. The drive took almost seventeen hours to get from Algonquin to Halifax where they would get on a boat to go the rest of the way to the island. Jade stopped in Quebec, so they could fuel the SUV and quickly feed again. There is no way she was going to let any of them be weak; even Justin's pack hunted with them this time. They all had the same idea; if they had to fight, they had to be strong.

It was almost dawn when they finally reached Halifax; Rayne thought it best to rent a cabin, so the wolves could get a good sleep, and they all could feed again before crossing the ocean to the island that the Lear Castle was on. Since there were eight of them, she figured two family-size cottages should keep up the appearance. Justin and his pack took one and the vampires took the other.

"I guess you guys should get some sleep," Rayne said to Justin and the other wolves. "We don't hunt in the daytime; there is too much risk of getting caught."

"Yah, I guess you're right; we're so close we don't want to cause any unwanted issues," Marc answered sarcastically. Then he and two other wolves took off into their cabin. Justin and Rayne went into one of the rooms in the other cabin and left Holden, Adrian and Jade in the main room.

"Jade," Holden said as battle plans ran through his head, "how are we going to do this?"

"I don't know, babe, I really don't know," she answered quietly dismissing the actual plans.

"Um, Jade, you know how you can see visions, right?" Adrian asked.

"Yah."

"Well, do you ever see what's already happened?" he continued.

"I don't think so, not unless you count reading thoughts."

"No, this is different. It's like I get past visions of things that I couldn't possibly know."

"Maybe that's your gift, we all seem to have something a little different." Jade laughed.

"Maybe, but it did not start happening until you fully turned me, and it only seems to work if I touch something," Adrian added.

"What do you mean?" Holden asked curiously and a bit jealously.

Adrian looked at Jade. "Give me your hand, you're a hybrid vampire. You, your sister and your mother have lived many lifetimes. The Guardians of the Real World Order need the three of you, so they can fulfill the prophecy and finally come out into the world and live freely among the humans just as they did in the beginning, but the last time they tried, you all died. For some reason, I can't see how though. Your endurance gene can only be duplicated with the blood of the three of you combined together with your venom all in one; it is some kind of weird trinity. From the moment your mother gave birth to you in the very first life, Cavan has been trying to prevent this from happening. He does not want *all* the vampires to *"come out of the dark."* They went into hiding when the humans first began to turn on them. So in turn, the vampires set out messengers all over the world with new religions and began the new world to direct the humans' attention away from the supernatural. The humans took to these religions graciously as the great alternative to being ruled by vampires and treated as food. The new world grew over many thousands of years, and slowly, the vampires went from being the gods on earth to a myth in nightmares."

Adrian stopped for a moment and closed his eyes; his vision was a group of people sitting around a fire they were dressed in robes and reading from a book bound in what looked like skin. They read the prophecy aloud:

Three women to walk in the light will give the power to rise from the night! Within these three from their life combined will bring the light to all dark kind!

Adrian opened his eyes again. *"I guess* Cavan believes that with just Jorja alone, he can create what he hopes will be the *"day walker gene,"* if he can get this before the Guardians get the three of you together and fulfill the prophecy then he will have the power over the vampires, and in turn, he will have the power over the humans."

"How the hell can you know all that just by touching her hand?" Holden asked in shock. "You're making it up, you have to be, how can you know when you have never even met another vampire?"

Holden was getting madder by the second all this talk about hybrid vampires and special powers, reading minds and having visions, and now seeing the past. Holden was still without any thing he considered a *"special power."*

"I don't understand why I didn't see any of that in my visions." Jade crinkled her face trying to recall her visions and memories.

"It's like Logan told you, you only see what you already know and the possible outcome of that," Adrian answered back.

Holden stormed off into the other bedroom and slammed the door; he was so agitated that everyone around him had all these "powers," and he had nothing. He was a soldier; he knew how to fight, but in his mind even that did him no real good at that moment. Adrian and Jade sat out in the main room for a bit talking some more about visions and what he had just told them about the prophecy. After about an hour, Adrian said he would go in and talk to Holden, guy to guy. Jade decided to go outside and sit on the porch to try to clear her head.

"You know a lady shouldn't sit alone out here when *filthy dogs* can sneak up and attack," a voice said, laughing from the side of the building.

Jade turned around to see Marc leaning against the wall. "What are you doing out here? Shouldn't you be sleeping?"

"I don't sleep much during the day. I like the sun too much." He smiled. "Look, I wanted to apologize for acting like such an ass earlier."

"Don't worry about it! We all have our issues. I'd be pissed off at vampires too if I had grown up without my mother because of them."

"Can I be honest with you?" he said, sitting down beside her.

"Nope, I'd rather be lied to." Jade laughed sarcastically.

Marc's lips curled almost into a smile. "That's not the only reason I don't like vampires."

"Then what is?" Jade was curious about why, but she was more curious why he was sharing it with her...a vampire.

"I had this girlfriend a few years ago; turns out she was a vampire. After dating for almost a year, I thought she was the one for me, and I finally got up the nerve to ask her to move in with me." He chuckled. "I did not know she was a vampire; she was a waitress at the bar in town. Worked the night shift so naturally slept all day. I really should have put two and two together, but they do say love is blind." He took a deep breath. "Anyway, I figured, if we were going to have any kind of future together, I should tell her what I really am; but I guess the surprise was on me. She told me that her family would never let her be with a *dog;* they believed that the only thing we were good for was guards."

"Marc, I'm so sorry." Jade's face softened.

"Don't be, turned out for the best anyway. When I told my dad what she was, he lost it on me and told me what really happened to my mother, up until then, I thought she just took off on us." Marc leaned his back against the rail behind him, his eyes staring off as if he was remembering something, but Jade didn't bother reading his thoughts; she figured it was best not to invade any privacy. After all, he was actually opening up to her without being rude.

"But what happened to your mother was not that girl's fault," Jade told Marc. "It's not fair to blame her."

"No, you're right, but it did not make it any easier to get over her; I really did love her I thought." Marc shook his head. "Anyway, I just wanted to say I was sorry; you definitely don't seem like the other vamps I have met."

"Well, thanks . . . I think." Jade chuckled. "Maybe now you will be a little nicer to us."

"Well, let's not get ahead of our self here." He laughed. "But I guess this is a start."

Justin came out of the door behind Marc, with Rayne, both looking very surprised to see Marc and Jade sitting together.

"Does Holden know you're out here?" Rayne's eyes giving her sister that *what-the-hell-are-you-doing-out-here-with-him* look.

"I don't know, him and Adrian are talking in the other room, so I came out here to clear my head," Jade answered, sliding her body a little further away from Marc.

"Looks like someone else is trying to clear his too." Justin laughed, kicking Marc's foot as he walked down the step past him.

"Rayne and I are going for a walk; want to come?" Justin asked, looking at Marc.

"Na, I'm good right here," Marc answered with a smirk.

"Me too, I should go check on Holden soon, see if he is feeling any better."

"I'm feeling much better," Holden's voice came from behind her. "Adrian and I had a nice little chat," he said with a smile.

"Good, I'm glad," Jade said as she wrapped her arm around his leg.

"Before you guys take off Rayne, there is something I want to talk to you all about," Adrian said, following behind Holden. "Can you come inside for a minute? I don't really want to talk about this out here." The group of them came into the cabin and sat down, including Marc.

"Okay, where do I start?" Adrian said to Holden.

"How about the beginning, tell them what you told me. Start with the real Guardians in Ireland," Holden answered as he sat in the armchair and pulled Jade onto his lap.

"Alright, well, as Jade already knows, just like she gets visions of the future, I seem to get them from the past when I touch something relevant. It must have been Jade's blood, still on my hand because while I was talking to Holden, a vision came to me about the Real World Order and why the three of you were turned in the first place. The Guardians had known since the second birth of your mother's soul that she would be the one to have you girls and fulfill the prophecy. The three of you have been reincarnated many times over the past few thousand years, and until this last life, the Guardians were never able to turn you in time. The seers had foreseen Jorja's birth and come forth to the Guardians, and this time, they sent Cavan to search for her. It took him a little over a decade to find her, but when he did, he saw that you girls had been born already, and that the prophecy would be able to come true. Therefore, he turned your mother and then returned for the two of you. What he did not count on was falling instantly in love with her and want to take her for his own once the transformation was complete, so he told the Guardians that none of you survived the change. His internal battle for longing to control the humans and his love for Jorja kept him torn for nearly fifty years until he met my mother; unfortunately, he never got over his love for Jorja or his need for control, so once he found her again, he decided to have both. Hence he told her we are dead, if she thinks we are all dead, then she has no reason to try to escape she will be his forever."

"We have to get her out of there," Rayne growled. "Fast."

"We will, Rayne, you can bet my life on it." Jade hissed, agreeing with her sister. "I am not going to let this happen, if the vampires are meant to live out in the open and we can make that happen, then you bet your ass we are going to get our mother out of there and find the real Guardians."

"Okay, tonight, we will hunt and feed once more then at first light, we hit the water." Rayne hissed, and she stormed out the door Justin taking off after her.

"I'm going to try to get some sleep before tonight. Wake me up when you're all ready to hunt," Marc said as he headed back to is cabin.

"My head hurts now." Adrian laughed, trying to keep light on the situation. "I'm going to go lie down for a bit, give you two some time alone." He winked at Holden then went into one of the bedrooms and shut the door.

Holden and Jade were still sitting on the armchair in an empty room now; he just sat there holding her, not saying a word, leaving his mind open and thinking about the future, all the possibilities that could happen with everyone.

As the sun went down, Adrian came out of the bedroom and into the living room where Holden and Jade were still cuddled in the seat together. "If I did not know any better, I would think you two were sleeping." He laughed.

"I wish I was," Jade told him. "Maybe that way, I could stop all these visions and voices for just a few hours."

"Not me, I spent too many night sleeping lonely. I am quite content being awake holding my lady," Holden added with a smile.

"Are you feeling any better?" Jade asked Adrian. "Your head still hurting?"

"I think I'll survive; there are so many new things in the last few weeks. It's just a lot to take in all at once," he replied.

"I know what you mean," she added, rolling her eyes.

Rayne and Justin came in a few minutes later followed by Marc and the two wolves, Chris and Sage. Sage was the girl that Holden had attacked in the woods by the cabin in Algonquin the first day they met the pack. She did not hold it against him now, knowing that they don't feed on humans; she figured that it was the lesser of two evils for them to feed on animals even if they did feed on wolves in the past. The group sat in the main cabin going over the possibilities of what was going to happen once they got to the island and how they were going to deal with it, including the possibilities with Marc's mother.

They waited until a little after midnight before heading out to hunt; Marc and the other wolves went off on their own. Rayne and Adrian caught the scent of some deer heading west, and Justin followed them, while Holden and Jade took a path heading east stopping just short of a small clearing where the scent of moose wafted through the air. Being the gentleman that Holden was, he insisted that Jade take the first one.

Jade crouched down like a lioness watching the moose closely, her muscles clinching; the scent of blood wafting through the air. She kept her stance as still as stone until he was close enough for her to strike. Leaping out of the darkness into the air and catching the moose by the antlers twisting its head, clinging her strong body around the animal like a snake wrapping around him, overpowering him quickly. Jade sank her sharp fangs deep into the tissue of his throat. To Jade's surprise, the beast let out a large bucking movement; and before she knew it, he had hurled himself and her over the edge of the cliff that hadn't been seen through the thin tree line.

"JADE!" Holden yelled, closed his eyes and threw his hands up in the air as if to catch her.

Jade stopped in midair.

Holden stood there frozen for a moment then motioned with his hands as if he were pulling her back to him on the ledge of the cliff. Once Jade was standing back on the ground, in total shock, Holden came running and wrapped his arms around her so tight she thought he was going to crush her unyielding body.

"What just happened?" Jade was still shaking, but was it fear or excitement?

"I thought I lost you," his voice shaking.

"But how? I mean, you lifted me in the air and pulled me back." She tried to recall every second of what had just happened, to explain to herself, but all she could see now was Holden's jumbled mind.

"It felt like I was really holding you and pulling you back," he answered. "I just closed my eyes and pictured my arms stretching out to catch you."

"Holden, babe, if I needed air to live, you would be killing me right now." Jade tried to laugh.

"I don't understand, Jade, you're the one that knows what's going on all the time. How did I do that?"

"Well, babe, I think we might have found your specialty." She smiled.

After they had both calmed down a bit, they decided to head west to do the rest of their hunting . . . away from any heights, coming across some deer hiding among the trees. Feeling almost overflowing now, Jade and Holden walked back toward the cabin then stopped for a minute while Jade thought about how it was possible that Holden was able to move her . . .

"Can you try it again?" she requested.

"I don't know. I don't really know how I did it the first time," Holden replied.

"Well, you said you were picturing catching me, right? Well, how about you picture picking up that rock over there and bring it to us."

Holden stood still for a minute and closed his eyes and lifted his arms as if he was picking up the rock and pulled it toward himself and Jade; he opened his eyes when he heard the thud of the rock hitting the ground as he pictured dropping it at her feet. Jade was standing there with an immeasurable smile on her face, but Holden was in shock. He did it; he really moved the rock using just his thoughts. "This is too cool; I mean come on how handy would this have been in the military." The rest of the walk back to the cabin was entertaining as Holden was picking up rocks, leaves and just about anything else they came across that was not rooted into the ground. He was having a blast it took no time at all for him to grasp how to do it and keep his eyes open.

Holden and Jade were the first to arrive back at the cabin, so they sat on the porch and watched out over the moonlit water, watching boats sail in the darkness. Not long after Rayne, Justin and Adrian arrived back and joined them.

"Guess what," Jade blurted out as soon as Rayne sat down.

"Don't tell them . . . I want to show them." Holden interjected with a huge smile.

"Show us what?" asked Rayne curiously.

"Watch," Jade replied.

Holden stood up, lifted his arms and laughed. Rayne's jaw almost hit the ground as she sat there staring at Justin in the air, kicking and swearing at Holden. Adrian laughed as Holden put Justin back on the ground.

"How the hell did you do that?" Justin barked.

"This is too cool," Holden said, gleaming with a smile from ear to ear.

"Okay, so let me get this straight," Justin said, shaking his head. "Jade, you can read minds and see visions of the future; Rayne, you can read minds too; Adrian, you know, well, everything . . . and now, Holden can pick me up with his head."

Adrian laughed. "Well, first, I don't know *everything*, but Holden does seem to be telekinetic, and believe me, that will come in very handy in a fight."

"Well, just don't start playing games with me or any of my pack 'cause I'm telling you, you'll have to let your guard down at some point," Justin growled.

"Relax, dog, I'll behave," Holden said, still smiling.

CHAPTER 16

The sun came up across the harbor. The group packed up what little belongings they had brought with them, and Jade headed down to purchase a boat that would be large enough to fit all of them but small enough not to cause attention. She was speaking to a man at the end of Pier 4 who had the perfect boat for her. Jade had offered him a very large amount of money, a great deal more than it was worth. As he was graciously accepting her offer, a woman stepped up behind her and tapped Jade on the shoulder.

"I'm sorry, madam, but this man cannot accept your offer; and you must come with me at once," she spoke very softly as not to attract a lot of attention.

"I'm sorry, but who are you?" Jade replied, a bit more than shocked that this very human-smelling woman had been so brazen.

"Miss Jade, I must ask that you come with me please; it is very important," again speaking very softly. "Prince Edmond has requested your presence on his ship; we must not keep him waiting."

"Who is Prince Edmond?" Jade asked confused. "And who are you?"

"My name is Lylah; I am Prince Edmond's personal assistant. Now please we must not keep him waiting," the woman replied, putting her arm on Jade's hand.

Reluctant but very curious, Jade followed the tall woman to a large ship at the end of Pier 7; it was the only one there. Jade sent out a message in her mind to Rayne hoping that she would hear her and keep everyone inside the cabins until she could figure this out.

The woman, Lylah, led Jade onto the ship's deck then to an elevator and took them down three floors where the large metal door opened up to a grand hallway. Walking down the hallway, Jade realized that she could not hear this woman's thoughts.

"Right through this door, Miss Jade." She smiled and punched in the pass code for the grand door to open.

Jade stepped through, and her mouth hit the floor.

"Please don't be alarmed, Jade, I will explain everything." The man behind the desk stood up.

"How . . . is . . . this . . . possible?" Jade's eyes locked on a face she had known from many years ago, a face she believed had been dead for over one hundred and fifty years.

"Jade, don't be frightened," he said, walking around the large oak desk toward her.

"Charles," Jade whispered and immediately put up her mental walls to block out Rayne.

"This can't be, it's just not possible. I saw you dead," Jade tried to catch herself. "How?"

"I had to pretend to be someone I was not for many years. I never wanted to hurt any of you," he whispered.

"But I watched you grow up from the time I was a toddler, you grew up . . . I watched you get older every year until, until you were shot and killed." Jade gasped.

"Jade, please understand! I was not born into this world a human. I am a born full-blood vampire; I was not changed. With that, I am able to control my age both forward and back at my will. Please let me explain." Charles took Jade's hand and led her to a leather couch; he sat her down, still not letting go of her hand, he sat beside her and continued. "My father and I are the only ones in the entire vampires species that can endure the sun with no explanation as to why. None other, either born or bitten has ever been able to do that until you three. And no one has been able to since." He rubbed Jade's hand. "I had no choice but to make you all think I was dead. How would it look if I had got shot several times and just got up and walked away?" He closed his eyes pushing back a memory of that night. "We do have rules to follow when it comes to how humans see us, and if we die in front of them, we must act the part."

"But I don't understand, you were bleeding, the bullets penetrated you," still trying to comprehend what she was seeing.

"Yes." Charles laughed. "One of the downfalls of being born a vampire, all the human vitals are there, beating heart, blood pumping through my body, and well, as you saw, able to be shot." He blinked and shook his head repressing the memory. "But on the plus side, I can't die from it. I heal very quickly, and it doesn't really hurt . . . that much." He chuckled again. Jade supposed he was trying to prevent her from freaking out.

"Okay, so again, I don't understand why you are here now? Why not come to us sooner? We have been looking for others for so long and why did that lady call you Mr. Edmond?" Confusion was starting to get the better of her.

"Well, that's an easy one to answer." Charles stood up and bowed in front of Jade. "Let me introduce myself. I am Prince Edmond Charles II." He stood back up straight. "My father, King Edmond Charles I, was the ruler of all lands many thousands of years ago. I do believe you know the story about your mother; Lylah overheard the gentleman telling you the story regarding your mother's many reincarnations. When we finally found her, in this life, she was already married to your father, had given birth to Rayne and about to give birth to you. That is when I was *adopted*, so to speak, to the family in Halifax. They had no idea." His eyes fell to the floor. "I wanted to tell Rayne everything, and I knew I would be able to after our wedding."

Charles stopped and stared off as if he was reliving the moment. "Who would have thought it would all end the same night?"

"But what about Cavan? He turned us. He must have known who you were?" Jade asked sympathetically.

"He did know; that's probably why the bastard shot me!" Charles growled. "I thought you were all dead."

Jade could tell this was very painful for Charles, but where did that leave them? "Charles, or I'm sorry, Prince Edmond," Jade exhaled,

"It's okay." He chuckled. "Call me Charles."

"I still don't really understand. I mean there is my mom and getting her back . . . and what about Rayne?"

"I will speak with Rayne myself. I hope she will understand. My father and the rest of the Guardians have been trying to figure out a way to penetrate the Lear Castle for many millenniums. He has protection spells on it so that it can only be entered during the day as well he has guards, shape-shifting dogs that he has managed to keep all this time even after we had come to peace agreements and freed all the shifters that we had control over."

"Well then, there is no issue with that because we can go there in the daylight, and we know about the guards, and I think we have that covered," Jade said smugly.

"How could you possibly have that covered?" Charles laughed.

"We have Marc!"

"Okay, you lost me, who's Marc?" His eyes squinting together trying to figure it out.

Jade smiled. "Marc is the son of the pack leader guarding the Lear Castle!"

"The son."

"Yup, Marc's mother was forced there when he was young and has been there the last like nineteen years or so."

"I would like to meet this Marc, if that would be alright," Charles added.

"Hmm, I don't know; he's kind of has an issue with vampires, something to do with them taking his mom away," Jade said with her eyebrows raised.

"Yah, I guess that would piss him off a bit, but nevertheless, we will have to speak with him. I have to speak with my father; now that I know you're not dead, we just might be able to fulfill the prophecy," Charles said with hope in his voice. "Cavan did a very good job of convincing us all that you were dead."

"Um . . . there's more," Jade whispered.

"More?"

"Yah, well, it's kind of a long story, and I am not going to get into it all with you now. I am sure there is time for that later, but the basics are, there is more than just us that can handle the sun."

"What do you mean more than the three of you, Jade?"

"Well, let's see where in this jumble of crazy mess should I start. The gentleman your lady friend overheard, his name is Adrian, he is engaged to my mom. He is also the half-breed son of Cavan. I turned him full myself. There is also Holden. I found him from a vision I had and saved him from killing himself over the death of his family. Both of them seem to be like us; they have no issues with the sun. Then there are the four wolves that are with us as well."

"Hmm, I don't really know what to do about that right now, Jade. There are laws in regard to changing humans to vampires." Charles took a deep breath and let it out slowly thinking to himself. "Okay, I will speak with my father, and then we will need to meet these other ones, the wolves included."

There was nothing Jade could do; she knew that if they had any chance of getting her mother back, she was going to have to go along with this and let Charles meet the others, but that also meant seeing Rayne again.

"Charles," Jade said quietly in the elevator heading to the upper deck of the large ship, "what are you going to say to Rayne?"

"I am going to tell her the truth, I owe her that much, don't I?" That was more of a statement than a question.

They reached the top deck; Charles kissed Jade's hand then pulled her into his chest, squeezing her tight. "You have no idea how happy I am to have found you again, Jade, no idea at all." He took a deep breath. "Please do not tell your sister about me. She deserves the truth, but I need to be the one to tell it to her." Jade agreed reluctantly not to tell Rayne, but only because he was right; he needed to be the one to confess.

Jade walked slowly down the harbor and up to where everyone was waiting by the trucks. She could tell Rayne was trying to read into her thoughts, but Jade was not about to let her just yet. Holden reached for her, and she almost fell into his arms. Jade's mental walls were high, heavily guarded, with a mental barbwire, no one was getting in.

"I don't recognize his face, Jade," Adrian put his hand on Jade's shoulder. "Who is he?"

"Who's face?" Rayne was shocked how he could see past Jade's block, but she couldn't.

"Adrian, how can you see that?" Jade said quietly, her face still buried in Holden's sweater.

"Call it father's intuition." He smiled. "Ezrabeth hated it too, it seems a lot more vivid now."

"Great, just great, well so much for easing into this. Okay, well, I was hoping to do this a little different, but here we go." Jade slowly turned out of Holden's sweater and faced everyone who, by the way, looked very, very confused. "We can't leave yet."

"What do you mean, yet?" Rayne yelled. "We are going to get our mother back, and we are going to do it now."

Justin put his large arms around her shoulders from behind and cradled her.

"Easy, baby, let her finish. There has to be an explanation . . . right?" Justin said, turning his head to face Jade.

Jade explained about Prince Edmond and everything that he said, just leaving out a few *tiny* details that she thought would be better to tell Rayne in private.

"So this guy was born a vampire, and he and his father are okay in the sun too?" Justin clarified.

"Yes, but he explained that they were the only two of the entire line even his mother can't," Jade said.

"But why now? Why all of this, all now?" Rayne asked as she slumped back into Justin's arms for comfort. "We looked for so long for others."

"Rayne, we did not exist to them; we did not have the mark and only the Guardians knew about the prophecy." Jade tried to explain again. "To everyone else, we were humans; vampires can't come out in the daytime, and Cavan had them convinced that we died that night."

Adrian walked in between Rayne and Jade and put his hand on both their shoulders. "What is the next step, Jade?"

"We have to wait." She sighed. "Prince Edmond has to speak with his father because, well, I kind of did something I guess I wasn't supposed to." Jade's eyes hit the ground in front of her, ashamed.

"What weren't you supposed to do, Jade?" Rayne asked softly and concerned.

Jade turned and kissed Holden softly and whispered, "I made you," and let her eyes drop again.

"So you made a vampire that is immune to the sun; is that not what they are supposed to want?" Rayne asked defensively.

"There are laws . . . apparently," she added quietly.

"Big deal, if they wanted us to follow their laws, then they should have talked to us sooner," Rayne said harshly. "It's their own fault, not much they can do about it now."

"Yes, there is," Jade whispered.

"Not without going through me first," Adrian stated. He knew exactly what they could do; they could kill Holden, and they could kill Jade for making him, although Jade was pretty sure they would not kill her due to the prophecy.

"That won't be necessary!" The voice came from behind them.

A man that stood tall and sleek in black pants with a black shirt and no tie. Jade did not know the man's face but knew exactly who he was. His eyes gave him away.

"My dear Jade, I have not seen you since you were a baby. You have grown up to be a beautiful woman just like your mother," he said as he took a step closer. Holden and Adrian instinctively stepped in front of her and forced her back a few steps.

"There is no need for that, gentlemen, I mean you no harm, any of you," he said, looking at the entire group.

Jade stepped out from behind them and extended her hand to this man who took it gently and bowed.

"How do you do, sir?" she asked softly.

The rest of the group was getting very anxious and wanting answers! Jade gently looked up at the man in front of her and gestured with her eyes for him to introduce himself. Jade could feel the stinging of Rayne trying to poke through her mental barriers to figure out who he was and what was going on.

"Let me introduce myself," he said, looking around the group then stopping at Rayne. "My name is King Edmond Charles I, but please call me Edmond." He extended his hand to her. "As you may already know, I am head of the Guardians. I would like to invite you *all* onto my ship where I would be happy to explain further."

"Rayne," Jade whispered, looking scared for her, but Edmond interjected and told Jade not to worry, it would be all right. Then she got a mental message that felt like it was sent only to her, telling Jade he respects the privacy with Charles and Rayne, and that Charles will keep his distance for this conversation. That made her a little more at ease . . . but not much.

Jade looked at Justin a little worried. "Um, are you guys—"

He cut her off bluntly, "You're damn right, we are!" He looked back at the rest of his pack. "All of us," he said firmly then put his arm around Rayne protectively as they all followed Edmond down the harbor to his ship.

CHAPTER 17

The room was large with wooden panel walls, large landscape paintings hung from the walls and an oversized rectangle redwood table in the center between two large windows overlooking the water.

"Please have a seat," Edmond requested once everyone was in the room. "First off, I just want to let you all know that neither myself, nor any of the other true Guardians mean any of you harm." Edmond smiled softly then continued, "I have waited many thousands of years for this prophecy to come true, and now that we are so close, I am not going to waste time on minor details about permissions to turn. We are very lucky to have all of you."

Edmond walked around the room; of course, the wolves were very uneasy with it all, but they would get over it. Justin stood behind Rayne who sat at the table. He refused to let his guard down and for good reason. Holden and Jade sat side by side; Adrian sat across from them beside Rayne, while the wolves stood with their backs to the wall.

"I think that we have been kept in the dark long enough," Rayne said with a sigh. "Can you just be straight with us? I think after everything, we at least deserve to get some real answers." She looked over at her sister still trying to read her thoughts, but Jade couldn't let her in, not yet. Jade could see that Rayne was getting upset even if she did not show it on the outside, she could feel it on the inside.

Edmond sat at the head of the table and began to speak; he told them the details of the prophecy, the history of the vampires expanding on what Adrian had told them. Adrian was very pleased with himself and his gift to have known all this.

"If it is okay with all of you, I would like you to meet the rest of the Guardians," Edmond asked.

Jade's heart felt like it was going to jump out of her chest as she began to think about how Rayne would react if Charles were to walk into the room right now.

The room went silent as darkness rolled down covering the exposed windows and inner lighting came on; then twenty-five men and women entered the room all ranging in looks of age from about seventeen to eighty years old. Rayne and Jade were shocked; they had met everyone of them at some point in the last hundred and fifty years. The sisters looked at each other as the faces from their past walked through the door. *"How could this be possible? How could we have met these people throughout our life and not known what they were or better yet how did they not know who we were?"* Rayne's inner voice rang loud in Jade's mind, all the questions, all the years, Rayne and Jade looked at each other as the Guardians sat around the table with them and began to introduce themselves by name. Once they were all sitting, Edmond began to speak.

"You wanted answers and you wanted the truth, this is all the truth we have." He paused and pulled a tattered scroll from the sideboard drawer and placed it on the table. It was the prophecy. Edmond read it aloud

> *Three women to walk in the light,*
> *Will give the power to rise from the night!*
> *Within these three from their life combined,*
> *Will bring the light to all dark kind!*

Attached to the bottom of the scroll was the formula to combine the blood and venom along with some herbs to create an elixir so powerful that only a drop was needed to allow any vampires, born or bitten, to be able to walk in the daylight for the rest of their existence . . . or so the scroll claimed.

"I understand that your venom is very strong?" Edmond questioned. "So strong that with only a single bite, your prey will die within seconds." He looked at Rayne and Jade, waiting for an answer.

"Yes, although we've kept away from biting humans for many years. That's how it seemed to work in the beginning anyway, that's why we chose to feed on animals or blood bank bags," Rayne answered with shame.

"Don't be ashamed, my dear," one of the female Guardians said softly. "You took control over your need for the blood and chose not to kill the humans for it, not many of our kind can say the same."

Edmond clarified that the rest of the vampires do have venom; however, it is not near as toxic, and when they bite into a human, the venom causes the bite area to go numb and relaxes the humans like a drug. Most of them end up passing out, and when they wake, they have a mild headache and little to no memory of the encounter. Therefore making it easy to feed regularly and not be found out. Some humans, however, are stronger than others are, making it a little harder to cover their tracks. Edmond explained that once they were finished feeding on a human, they would simply lick the wound, and their venom would heal it closed and erase all traces of the bite.

"Okay, let me get this straight," Rayne said, shaking her head, "you don't kill them when you bite?" Jade knew her sister was angrier with herself now more than ever for the trauma they caused in the early years.

"Oh, but, my dear," one of the elderly ladies chimed in, "we can kill them if we take too much blood; we have to control ourselves when it comes to feeding on the humans, and that can be very difficult at times." She paused. "As you well know from your younger years when the thirst burns you drink until it stops, sometimes, depending on how long we wait between feedings, it can be very hard to stop before killing the humans."

Jade sat back in her chair looking at the twenty-five men and women trying to read them, trying to figure out if they were sincere or if this was just some trap like her mother was in. However, she could not read any of them, not even one. She locked eyes with Rayne for a moment and asked her if she was having the same issue... she was.

"Okay, what's the next step?" Rayne did not know if she should be mad or scared, but either way, she knew they had to save her mom.

Edmond let out a sigh. "I was hoping you had a plan."

"Well, going in during the day sounds like the best option since Cavan will be asleep," Jade started. "And it might give us a better chance to talk to the guards."

They sat there for a few hours mapping out the route there and the best plan for them to enter since the rest of the Guardians could not help in the daylight; it would be only the wolves and the vampires and...Charles!

The name screamed through Jade's mind without warning, his face was so clear, she threw up her mental walls again but not fast enough. Rayne's eyes locked with her sister's faster than Jade could react.

"Jade!" she yelled. "What the hell!"

Immediately, Jade's hands covered her mouth, everyone in the room was staring at them, Holden and Justin included. Trying to figure out what was going on.

"I'm sorry, I don't know what happened," Jade cried.

Edmond looked at them both with a soft smile. "Would you two ladies please join me in the next room?"

Without a second thought, Holden and Justin both stood up in defense mode. The sisters just stared at each other while Jade mentally apologized repeatedly.

"I'm sorry, gentlemen, but you will have to stay here; this is for them to work out on their own," Edmond said sternly.

Adrian stood up and looked at both of them; he could see what Jade was hiding, no matter how hard she tried to hide it. He put his hand on both boys' shoulders. "Guys, its okay, they will only be in the next room, and trust me, these walls are not that thick if you need to interrupt."

"What the hell is going on?" Justin demanded.

Holden held Jade's arm. "Jade, what's going on? I'm not letting you out of my sight."

She couldn't answer him; she really wanted to, but when Jade opened her mouth, nothing came out. Rayne and Jade just stared at each other. Finally, Edmond cut in between them, "Ladies, please." As he held out his hand toward the door, Jade turned to Holden and whispered, "I'm sorry," and slipped out into the hall; Rayne followed. Before the sisters entered the adjoining room, Jade grabbed Rayne's arm, "Rayne, I'm sorry, but I did not know until just a few hours ago." Jade could tell by the energy flowing out of her sister . . . she had a pretty good idea what was about to happen, and she was pissed!

The room was empty, only a few pieces of art on the wall. The sisters both turned to Edmond blankly and said at the same time, "Get it over with."

Jade mentally spoke to her sister, *I'm sorry, Rayne, I truly did not know until a few hours ago, and he made me promise not to tell you. He wanted to tell you himself.*

"Jade, I don't know how to feel right now, just let me process it all."

When Charles walked into the room, he was silent, just looked at them both. Rayne's thoughts flowed into Jade with no barriers; she did not even try to block it.

"Rayne," Charles whispered, "I'm so sorry; I truly thought you were dead."

Rayne did not say anything; she just stood there for a few more minutes . . . staring. Charles started to speak again, but before he could get the first word out, Rayne hauled off with a killer right hook and connected with his jaw; it made the loudest crack Jade had ever heard. Jade was sure they heard it in the next room. He stumbled back a few steps, but before he could open his mouth, Rayne was already heading for the door.

"Rayne, STOP!" Charles demanded.

Rayne slowly turned to him with dripping blood-red eyes and said dryly, "I mourned you for over a hundred and fifty years." And that was it, she walked into the hall.

"Charles, please understand how hurt she has been," Jade said softly. "Just give her some time to process this."

"Jade, I know she is hurting, but so am I. I thought you were all dead too," Charles pleaded, trying not to sound defeated.

"Let me talk to her, but for now, I think we just need to focus on getting my mom back." Jade leaned in and gave him a hug and whispered, "If she didn't still care for you, she wouldn't have hit you . . . give her some time to take it all in; that's all."

Jade walked out into the hall where Rayne was standing; she could tell her sister was hurting so much. She stepped closer and put her arms around Rayne; Jade took a deep breath, and they slid down the wall and sat together on the floor.

"Rayne, I wanted to tell you."

"I wouldn't have believed you even if you did, Jade," she groaned. "I'm sorry for getting pissed at you in there; it's not your fault he lied about dying."

"Sweetie, in his defense, he thought we were dead too," Jade reminded her. "So what do we do now?"

"We save our mom . . . he stays the hell out of my way, and when we are all home safe, maybe just maybe, I'll give him the chance to explain!"

Rayne was a very strong woman she had worked very hard over the last century and a half to put her human emotions behind her, and in one swift punch, there they were again; Charles would be a huge help to getting her mom back, and Rayne knew that. Jade just hoped everyone else saw it that way.

"Well, sis, you know we need his help; you don't have to like it or even talk to him, but you can't deny that the more we have on our side, the better off we're gonna be." Jade squeezed her sister tighter; Rayne could feel Jade's energy wrapping around her like a blanket.

"I hate when you're right . . . How do we tell the guys?" She laughed.

They decided that it would be better for Jade to have a quick chat with Charles before bringing him in to meet the others. She asked him just for the time being if he could leave the past behind them. He knew it was going to take a lot for Rayne to forgive him, but he also knew that saving her mom was a damn good start for him to get back in the good books.

Rayne's eyes followed Charles and Jade, as they entered the room, with daggers. Adrian and Holden stood back waiting for the bomb to drop. Just because Holden could not read minds did not mean he couldn't clearly see the tension as they walked in.

"Hello, a pleasure to finally meet you all," Charles said.

Rayne sat glaring at him, so many thoughts ringing through her head. Adrian stood beside her with his hand on her shoulder like any protective father would, seeing the hurt in her, wanting to do something but having no clue what to do.

Edmond stood up at the head of the table. "Thank you for joining us, my son." Charles nodded and then sat beside him.

The obvious tension aside, they needed a plan. Rayne and Charles did not say much; he just stared at her from across the table while the rest of them worked out the best way to get on the island without detection.

"Okay, I'll be the one to point out the obvious here," said Marc. "They are going to see us coming miles away, a big ship like this it's not like we will be able to sneak up on them."

"He has a point." Jade looked over to Edmond. "We need to be a little more discreet than just pulling up on a huge ship."

Charles broke his eye contact with Rayne for a moment. "We need to send the wolves in first." He was so calm. "You are the ones that are going to be able to reason with the guards that are protecting Cavan."

"Of course, it made so much sense why did I not think of it," Jade's mental voice annoyed Rayne, but she had to admit, it did make sense. Justin and Marc could go in first, find Marc's mother and try to talk some sense into her. The rest of them would hold back and wait for the wolves to clear the way. They decided to take two smaller separate boats; the first boat would have the wolves and the second the vampires.

"I'm going in with Justin," Rayne demanded, "on the first boat."

"Rayne, what if the guards attack you?" Charles interrupted. "I won't let you do it."

"If I recall correctly, you don't get to tell me what to do anymore." She hissed. "You gave up that right over a hundred and fifty years ago."

Up to this point, no one dared to ask what happened earlier when she and Jade left the room, but Justin seeing how hurt she was, jumped in, "Care to explain?"

"NO!" Rayne spit out. "I'm going on the first boat," she glared back at Charles. "End of discussion!" And she stormed out of the room.

Jade got up to follow her sister, but Edmond stood just as fast. "Allow me; the rest of you please let Lylah show you to your rooms. You should get some rest."

Holden and Jade finally alone sat in a quiet room. She knew what he was thinking, so before he even asked, Jade told him the truth, she told him who Charles was, and that he and Rayne had been engaged but only for a few short hours before he was shot and thought to be dead alongside their father.

"How could he do that to her?" Holden asked. "Rules or not, there is no way in hell I would ever leave you like that."

"It's not totally his fault, babe; he thought we were dead too."

The door opened just a crack. "Jade, are you in here?"

"Yah, come on in, Adrian, we're just talking."

"Have you heard from Rayne since she walked out?" Adrian asked. "I can't find her anywhere."

"Come to think of it, no." Jade had not heard from her sister, nothing through her thoughts at all. Jade called out to Rayne in her mind, but got nothing back. "I don't like this. I'm going to look for her." She got up off the couch. "Stay here please," Jade asked them both. "She is upset; she's not going to want everyone in her face."

Adrian only agreed because he could pick up Jade's thoughts, and she promised them both that if she was in trouble, she would call for them. Jade started walking around the ship calling out for Rayne in her head with no response. She hit every level she could get to without an access code until running into Charles on the upper deck leaning on the rails looking out into the water.

"Stupid question, but have you seen my sister?"

"Yup."

"And where is she?"

"Right now, she and that *dog* are out taking a walk."

"What did you expect, Charles, you were just going to walk in, and she was going to be all over you again?" Jade took a deep unneeded breath. "She never stopped loving you, not for one day, not for one hour, not for one minute."

"Then why is she with him?" he growled.

"You were dead for over one hundred and fifty years, Charles... you were dead."

"But I'm not dead, Jade, I'm standing right here."

"Charles, she is hurting right now and confused. You have to give her some time."

"I never stopped thinking about her, you know."

"I know, just give her some time." Jade gave him a hug and headed for the ramp off the ship.

CHAPTER 18

"There you are." Jade walked up to Rayne and Justin sitting on the end of one of the docks. "Got a minute?"

Justin looked a little concerned Jade read his thoughts for a moment and seen that he had been trying to talk Rayne out of going with him and Marc on the first boat; he was scared that the guards would see her as a threat and attack her, the same concern the rest of them had.

"Jade, if you're here to give me a hard time too, I'm not interested in hearing it."

"Actually the opposite . . . I have a plan."

Rayne and Justin looked both intrigued and nervous at the same time.

"Well, I do think it's a bad idea that you take the first boat with the wolves alone; they are right, it will be seen as a threat."

"I told you, Jade, I don't want to hear it," Rayne began.

"Let me finish . . . jeez." Jade laughed. "I'm going with you, just the four of us on the first boat the rest can follow for backup."

"Four of us, as in?" Rayne asked.

"As in you, me, Justin and Marc."

Justin chimed in, "And you think that's a better idea?"

"Yes, I do; once we are on the island, we will be close enough that Rayne and I can call out to our mother through our bond while you and Marc confront the guards."

"I knew it was only a matter of time before you ladies tried to get us alone," Marc crept up behind them laughing. "Told ya, dude, she wants me."

Marc and Justin laughed while Rayne and Jade stared at each other trying to figure out if he was serious. "I hate to burst your bubble, sweetheart, but I don't think that's what she had in mind." Rayne laughed. "But I guess it's always good to have a dream."

"So how are we going to make this breakaway happen without all the others putting the kibosh on our little getaway plan?" Marc asked sarcastically.

"Well, we are all here . . . " Jade raised one eyebrow. "Once we are in the water, I'll call out to Adrian and let him know what we're doing."

"You're not leaving without me." Charles walked up behind her on the dock.

"You just keep popping up today, don't you?" Rayne snarled.

"I'm not letting you go without me. I lost you once Rayne, I'm not losing you again."

"What the hell are you talking about?" Justin looked back and forth between Rayne and Charles.

"I take it you did not tell him about us?" Charles replied staring at Rayne.

"*Us*, what us, there has been no us to tell about in over a hundred and fifty years; remember you would rather pretend to be dead!" She hissed.

"Okay, clearly I missed a huge piece of this puzzle." Justin took a step back. "Rayne, what's going on here?"

"I don't have the time or the patience for this right now." She turned to walk away; Charles grabbed her arm. As fast as that, Justin was on him, and they were in a full-blown scrap on the dock. Rayne and Jade stood there in shock for a second until Marc tried to jump in.

"STOP!" the sisters growled at the same time. "Both of you, enough!" Charles and Justin stood up both breathing heavy and still eye to eye. "You don't get it, do you? Either of you."

Jade took Rayne's arm; they looked at each other and in their mind shared the same thought. With a sharp glance at the guys standing on the dock, they smiled and dove in.

Since they do not need air to breathe, the two girls could swim underwater as long as they needed to; to be out of sight, they resurfaced a few miles out to sea.

"Rayne, I am truly sorry."

"I know, it's not your fault."

"Do you have any idea how far out we are?" Jade asked, looking around and seeing no land anywhere.

"Nope, but when has not knowing ever stopped us from doing anything before." They both laughed. "I can't believe we just left them there on the dock; they are probably freaking out right now."

"Well, we are already this far out; we might as well keep going. There is no way Cavan's guards will see us coming if there's no boat, right?" Rayne added.

They went under again and swam as fast as they could; if they could just make it close enough for their mother to hear their thoughts, she would know her daughters were not dead.

Rayne and Jade swam for miles still no island. They resurfaced again to try to figure out where they were and where the island was; it has to be close they had been swimming for hours. Just as the sisters hit the surface of the water, a speedboat came out of nowhere; two arms snagged the girls out of the water and into the boat. Before they had a chance to see what happened, they were heading back the way they just came.

"What the hell!" Rayne hissed as she looked up to see Justin and Marc standing over her.

"Are you both insane?" Marc growled. "We've been circling around out here for hours looking for you."

"You should have just let us go." Rayne hissed back.

"Not a chance." Justin leaned in to put a blanket around her.

"I don't need that." She spat back pushing the blanket away.

"What's your problem, Rayne?" Justin barked. "I thought we were cool, or is it because I punched your boyfriend?"

"Pardon . . . " Jade knew this tone in her sister's voice all too well.

"You heard me." Justin didn't back down.

Rayne stood up faster than either of them could move and backflipped back into the water.

"Wrong move, I appreciate what you're trying to do, guys, but way wrong move." Jade followed Rayne back into the water and under she went.

She knew they wouldn't follow her in, but that did not mean they wouldn't follow them to the island. In their own testoster-one-filled way, they thought the two wolves thought they were help-ing. The sisters swam down until they hit solid ground. They opened their minds so that they could talk without taking in the water.

"What now?"

"I don't know."

"They don't seem to be going anywhere, and I'm sure Charles told the others what went down."

"I don't even know what direction is the right way anymore."

"You know if we go back to the surface, they are going to pick us back up."

"Ya, maybe that's not such a bad idea."

"I just can't deal with them fighting, and Charles, well, I can't deal with that at all."

"I know, Rayne, but let's be real here; we can't stay down here for-ever. Let's go find the boat get dry and figure out a real plan."

No sooner did the girls hit the surface, Justin and Marc were there again. "You ready to get back in the boat?" Justin asked softer now.

They helped them in and headed back to shore.

Holden and Adrian were waiting on the dock; Charles was behind them. "I told you we would find them," Marc snarled.

"Dog's got a good nose even in the water." Charles hissed.

"Don't start." Jade hissed back at him as she and Rayne got out of the boat, walked passed everyone and headed for Jade's SUV.

"Where are you going?" Justin hollered behind them.

"To get dry clothes, if that's alright with you, guys," Rayne mumbled back.

Jade sent a mental message to Adrian as she passed them asking him and Holden to meet her back at the cabin. She didn't really know what they were going to do next, but she knew the four of them needed to figure something out, without the tension of Charles and Justin.

The second they hit the cabin, Holden grabbed Jade and squeezed so tight she thought he was going to break her in half. "Why?" Holden growled. "Why on your own?"

Rayne jumped in right away in her sister's defense. "It wasn't her fault. They were pissing me off."

Adrian stepped in the middle. "Rayne, you are going to have to figure out a way to deal with your feelings . . . for both of them. Like it or not, the more help we have, the better our chances of getting Jorja home." He was right, but Rayne wasn't going to admit that right now. The girls got changed, and Jade grabbed her cell phone out of the SUV and headed back to Edmond's ship. It dawned on her that her mother had her cell phone when she left; maybe just maybe she still had it.

Mom, are you there?

Jade waited a few minutes, no luck. It was a long shot, but she had to try. Jade stuck her phone in her back pocket and walked up the ramp onto the ship.

Edmond was waiting on the deck for them. "Ladies, so nice to see you return safely." Jade could see he was genuinely concerned for their safety. The wolves including Justin and Marc were sitting on a bench talking until they saw the girls getting back on the ship.

Justin slowly walked over to Rayne. "I'm sorry." He took her hand. "I was out of line. I have no right to freak out on you."

"You're right, you don't, neither of you do." She pulled her arm away and headed to the elevator but not before snagging Jade's arm on the way by. Adrian stayed on the deck with the rest of the guys. He knew when to give a woman her space. Holden, on the other hand, was still learning; as he attempted to follow them, Adrian quickly put his hand out.

"Um, trust me, man, stay up here." Adrian laughed. "If I've learnt anything in my life, it's when a woman used that tone . . . keep a little distance for a bit."

"But Jade's not the one upset, Rayne is," Holden responded confused.

"Doesn't matter, women run in tighter packs than we do." Justin laughed.

Rayne and Jade got off the elevator, walked down the long hallway to the board room where they first came in and met everyone. Rayne dropped down into one of the large chairs and let out a growl.

"I don't get it."

"What?"

"Why we did not make it to the island or at least see it; we swam for hours before those guys picked us up. How far out could it really be?"

"I wish I knew, honey, I wish I knew." Jade put her head down on the table.

The sisters sat in the dark room for a few hours; Jade guessed everyone figured giving them some time to themselves might prevent another mutiny. Rayne and her sister did not talk much; Jade was trying to induce her visions with little success. Not entirely sure how much time had passed as the room's windows were still covered, so Jade had no idea if it was day or night, when the phone in her pocket buzzed.

I'm sorry, she's dead!

Rayne and Jade looked at each other, red tears filled Jade's eyes. Rayne reached for the phone and typed back.

Cavan, for your sake, I hope you're lying to us, or you're gonna want to start praying to whatever gods you think will protect you. We are coming for her!

She put the phone down, wrapped her arms around her sister and focused all her energy into Jade like a blanket protecting her. Before either of them knew what was happening, a vision came crashing through both their heads.

(Jorja knocked on a cabin door; the woman that answered looked puzzled when she opened the door but invited Jorja in anyway. "So, Jorja, what brings you by this evening?" The woman laughed.

"Koko, I can't stand it anymore, I need to get out of here. I can't survive this way anymore." Jorja sighed.

"Jorja, really . . . What do you think I can do about this situation you are in?" The woman that Jorja called Koko said softly,

"I mean really, I can't get you off the island. The only boats in or out of here are heavily guarded and overseen by Cavan." She took a deep breath. "Believe me, if there was a way to get out of here, I would have taken it a very long time ago."

"Why haven't you at least tried? If there are boats, there has to be a way to get away from him."

Koko paused for a minute staring out the window. "I did try . . . about a year after I got here."

"What happened?" Jorja asked softly.

"He caught me and had me beaten and left me for dead!"

"But I don't understand, are you not the head of his so-called security?"

"Yes, now I am. After they left me for dead, I crawled into a cave on the south side of the island." She sighed. "It doesn't take long for my kind to heal when given time to rest. So I hid there, ate the few rats and birds that I could find; and when I was strong enough, I came back and told Cavan I would do whatever it took to let me back in."

"But why would you want to if you were already in hiding?" Jorja asked confused.

"Because even though I was not under Cavan's slavery at that point, I still couldn't get off the island, I can't swim that far, and there is no way to get on the boats." She answered, "Even the years when Cavan was gone, he still had his so-called helpers that would deliver the food to us, and they would not help out of fear that he would kill them too," Koko continued to tell Jorja about how she was forced to leave her husband and son when he was very young; the two most important people in her life ripped away from her. Jorja's icy heart felt for her, knowing that her family is alive out there and not being able to go to them or to see her little boy grow up. She actually felt Koko's pain thinking that her family is dead her children and her beloved Adrian, knowing that even if she manages to escape off this island, she will still be alone. But for Koko, they are still out there waiting for her to come home someday.

Jorja stood up to leave as the sun began to light up the sky, turning to Koko, she said, "You know Koko if there was a way to get you back to your family." She paused and took a deep breath. "I would help you get away from here."

"Jorja, you know as well as I do that he would have me killed if I tried to leave again."

"I will fight for you, your family needs you, Koko." Jorja gave her a big hug. "You are the only friend I have here even if you are supposed to keep me from escaping again." She laughed.

"Jorja, you know it's kind of funny, but you are the closest thing I've had to a friend in almost twenty years, but I am still not going to let you escape." She sighed. "He will kill us both."

"Not if we killed him first . . . " Jorja smiled and turned out the door. "See ya later, Koko, I need to see what I can find to eat out here. There has to be some kind of animal on this rock even if it's a bird."

"Jorja," Koko reach for her arm before she was all the way out the door, "be careful."

"Don't worry, darling." She smiled and took off into the trees.

She's alive!

Rayne and Jade sat there still holding onto each other with smiles ear to ear.

"Cavan is not going to win this," Rayne whispered in her sister's ear. "Our mother is way too strong willed; we should have never doubted that."

Adrian was standing in the doorway when the girls looked up; Jade knew that he had seen the vision too. He just smiled in amazement. "If I hadn't seen it myself, I might not have believed it." He turned back out of the doorway and headed to the elevator. A few minutes later, he returned with Holden, Justin, and Marc. Edmond and Charles followed behind them. Once everyone was sitting at the large table, Adrian asked the girls to repeat what they had seen in the vision. Marc's face was as hard as stone as he listened to what they said. He knew exactly who Koko was; Jade could feel the rage pulsing out of him with every word she spoke. This was the woman he thought abandoned him. Hearing that she had been beaten and left for dead because she tried to get home to him just made his blood boil. Jade locked eyes with him from across the table; his thoughts were a jumbled mess of anger, hatred and revenge. She had to admit his thoughts were not too far from her own.

Adrian looked at both of them. "We need to be smart about this; I know what you both are thinking, but we need to be smart if we are going to save everyone."

Out of nowhere, Charles cleared his throat, took a quick glance at his father and stood up. "I have an idea." He looked at Rayne and Jade with a half smile. "We need to give Cavan what he's been after all this time." Not breaking eye contact with Jade, he lowered his mental walls for her and Rayne to see his plan. "We give him the magic, we give him them." He nodded still not breaking eye contact.

"Are you freaking crazy?" Justin growled.

"Not a chance in hell," Holden added.

However, Jade could see, she could see exactly what Charles had in mind; up until now, she had not been able to see into Charles's mind. Charles had no intention of actually handing the sisters over to Cavan, but he did have the intention of awakening the magic in them. One of the advantages of being as old as he was she guessed, he showed her the power that she and Rayne could access when they put their energy together. Something the sisters had only scratched the surface of when they connected for the vision.

"Is that real, Charles?" Jade asked.

"More real than you could ever imagine." He smiled.

Everyone in the room, still very confused, was now watching them.

"Charles, what are you doing? You know it's not safe to tell them," Edmond bellowed. "Do you remember what happened last time?"

"Yes, Father, but this time is different. I can feel it . . . they can feel it. They are so much stronger this time. How else did you plan on breaking the barrier surrounding the castle without their power?"

Images Jade did not recognize entered her head, images of them, Rayne, Jorja and Jade in a former life.

"Charles, I don't understand. I don't recognize any of that," Jade said, but Rayne just kept silent.

Everyone in the room started to buzz, wanting to know what was going on. Charles kept his walls down while he continued to show images of a life with Jorja, Rayne and Jade. However, this was a life they did not remember.

"Stop it, Charles, right now!" Edmond growled, and just like that, the room was silent again. Jade turned to Rayne, and Rayne looked at Charles, through venomous teeth, she growled, "Someone better start telling us the truth, and they better start doing it NOW!"

Edmond stood up and asked everyone to leave the room, so he could speak with Rayne and Jade in private with Charles.

"NO!" Jade slammed her hand down on the table.

"Jade, what are you doing?" Charles pleaded.

"I'm tired of this, tired of the games, tired of the secrets, and for damn sure, tired of the lies," she demanded. "They stay, or we all go!"

Edmond was furious; no one talks to him like that, period. However, Jade did . . . she was not about to back down. If even a fraction of what Charles had just shown her was true, then she had no reason to be afraid anymore, and he knew it.

"Ladies, please, I know you're upset. I know all of you are," Edmond said, looking around the room defeated. "And, Charles, we are not just going to hand them over to Cavan, but I think you may be on to something if everyone will just calm down for a moment. I promise, ladies, I will tell you everything, no more secrets."

Adrian sat back down beside Jade while Justin and Holden stood behind them. Marc and Charles sat on the other side of the table. None of them were going anywhere until they got some answers.

The prophecy was just a small piece of the puzzle. A very long time ago, a powerful witch wondered the earth she went by the name

Lilith. Edmond began with Lilith, as she was the very first vampire. There are thousands of stories about how she actually became a vampire. It's said, however, that Lilith finally became lonely and tired of being the only of her kind and chose to mate. Since she had immense power, she thought that all her offspring would be born with the same power, but that was not the case.

The first of her born was a baby girl, born of little strength and power. However, as the child grew, so did her power. Lilith had also given birth to five other children; none of them had any of the power that the first was developing. They did, however, all have the vampire's curse. This made her children the first-born vampires in history. By the time the first child reached her teens, Lilith had grown so afraid that the child's power would overpower her own that she ordered the girl to be killed. Not having the courage to kill the child herself, she sought out a witch to do it for her; this witch had many abilities one of them was seeing a life path of one's soul. She could see that this girl's soul was destined to conceive two children, both female; she could also see that somewhere in the future of this young woman's soul, she would change the world forever. The witch knew she had to save this child's soul somehow, but she also knew that if she did not kill her, Lilith would hunt down the witch. So instead, the witch put a spell on the child's soul to be reborn as a woman over and over again until the time would come that she could finally bring light to the darkness Lilith was creating. The witch etched the scroll and had it passed through generations until Edmond came across it some three thousand years ago and began to look for Jorja. He knew that by finding her and her daughters, he would ensure the scroll's writings would come true. Charles agreed as it meant the prophecy in the scroll could be fulfilled, and the night-bound vampires could be free. Only it backfired. The first time Edmond found Jorja and her daughters, he told them about the prophecy, and that they had the power to change the life of all vampires. What he did not count on was that they already knew about their magic and had become drunk on the power they had, they became out of control. The more the three of them used their powers, the more out of control they became until the fatal night it blew up on them, the night they were to be turned into vampires. Edmond did not understand how it happened; he only knew that the three of them had generated so much power, and for whatever reason that was, the earth opened up fire bellowed from the hole and consumed the three of them; and just like that, another life was over.

"I don't understand," Rayne confessed, confused.

"Edmond, how can you expect us to believe any of this?" Jade added. "I mean really, if it went that bad before, why risk telling us this time?"

"You're different this time. Both of you are, I can feel it in you," Charles said as he stood up. "I know this is a lot to process, but please believe me if you can tap into that power again without killing yourselves, you just might be able to save your mother, and we will finally be able to fulfill the prophecy." He took a deep breath, looked at the sisters then walked out of the room. Edmond followed not far behind him. They were smart men; they knew that by giving them another option to save their mother, the girls would probably take it. Rayne and Jade closed their eyes and spoke only in their minds to each other while the men stood blankly not knowing what to do next.

"Rayne, I don't know what to do."

"It's okay, Jade, as long as we stick together; there has to be some truth to what Edmond said, or we wouldn't have been able to see it in Charles's mind, right?"

"But how, Rayne, how is it possible that we could even have a fraction of the power he was talking about and not even know it?"

"Well . . . I don't know, but I do know that you changed Holden, and he is like us, maybe can't hear our thought, but he has the mind power stuff, and both him and Adrian have no sun issues."

"I guess."

"And don't forget the vision you had we did that together."

Rayne and Jade started to giggle louder and louder as they thought about all the possibilities that ran through their heads, magic, power, and so on. The guys looked at them like they were crazy but did not dare speak a word.

CHAPTER 19

Jade wondered the ship on her own looking for Charles. Rayne and Justin went and found a quiet place to talk; she figured she should probably fill him in on why she is so hostile with Charles. It did not take Jade long to find Charles; he was in the large office that Lylah had brought her to the first time she was on the ship, sitting at the oversized solid oak desk.

"Why is everything on this ship so exaggerated and over the top?" Jade said as she leaned against the doorframe.

"Jade, I was hoping to see you." Charles stood up and walked over to the door to welcome her in. "Please come in, sit." He pulled a chair out for her and sat down in the one beside it. "Jade, I can't begin to imagine what you're feeling right now, but please believe me when I say that I never intended for anything to ever happen to either of you."

"Charles, please, can we just cut right to it? I know the speech. I just want to get my mom back and go home." Jade knew she was being harsh with him, but enough is enough.

"Look, Jade, believe me. I want to get your mom back just as much as you do, but we can't just sail up to the island and storm the shore. He has spells protecting it, so even if we tried, we couldn't get on to the banks; we have to break whatever protection spell he has on it first, so we can at least have a fighting chance." Charles was being genuine.

"And how do we do that?" Jade turned to Charles.

"*We,* don't . . . "

"What do you mean we don't, what do we do then? There has to be a way." Jade could feel herself being worked up again, so she took a deep breath, closed her eyes and slouched back in her chair. "Charles, I can't take any more cryptic games, just please be straight with me . . . please."

"I showed you the vision of the power you had before; I opened the door for you. You have that power in you. You know you do because you can feel it; it's how you were able to see the vision of your mom and how you know, in your heart, right now, if you and Rayne were to hurl enough power at that island, you would break the protection spell, and we would be able to get on to the island."

"But how? I don't know how to use it, and for damn sure don't know how to control it. I don't want to end up being sucked into the earth like I saw in your memory." Jade scoffed.

"Jade, you're different this time; you have lived a very long time. You do not live that long and not get some wisdom out of it. I have faith in you, in both of you."

"But that still doesn't tell me how to do it." She sighed.

"I have some books, they are very, very old they may help. You are more than welcome to stay here and read through them if you like." He opened a locked cabinet behind his desk then left the room giving Jade some privacy, shutting the door behind him.

Jade skimmed through the books for hours; she was so focused on the one she was reading; she did not hear the door open.

"Jade."

Jade nearly jumped ten feet in the air.

"Holy crap!" Rayne said, laughing. "I'm so sorry I thought you heard me come in." Rayne nearly fell over she was laughing so hard.

"Not funny, Rayne." Jade hissed.

"Whatcha reading?" Rayne tried to regain her composure as she walked around behind Jade and leaned over her shoulder; clearly she was in a much better mood then before.

Jade showed Rayne some of the books that Charles let her read; there was a ton of information in them on original witchcraft dating back thousands of years. After a few hours and many books, they finally came across what they were looking for.

The book was not very big by comparison to the others, but the information it held was far greater than a thousand books in this library. In the front of the book, it stated that this book was rewritten from ancient scrolls. The sisters read through what appeared to be a journal, the names were not familiar, but the events were almost word for word as Edmond had described them. The daughter of Lilith, from birth to death, a day-by-day log of her progression. The powers that grew inside her were being fueled by her hatred for her mother's need to dominate the human race. On the day Lilith ordered the child to be killed, she called upon a witch named Aura. The journal was very detailed about the spell that had been casted on the child and her descendants. The more Jade read, the clearer it became.

Rayne and Jade put the book down, looked at each other; they shared the same thought, pointed their hands at the door and willed their combined energy through it . . . Nothing happened, the sisters tried again this time, they stood up side by side, joined one hand and pointed the other hand at the door, and with every bit of emotion they could muster, they pitched a ball of energy at the door and blew it open.

Charles stood on the other side of the now empty doorway with a smile ear to ear. "I told you, you had it in you!" He winked, then walked in the room and sat on the leather couch that was against the wall. "Now all we need to do is figure out how to amplify it, so you can break the protection spell."

"Why didn't you tell us before that there was a spell covering the island?" Jade asked. "Don't you think that would have been important info to share?"

Charles laughed. "I guess timing is everything, so can we figure out how to break the spell?"

"This book tells us how to break protection spells," Rayne snapped. "Where did you get this from?"

"Some secrets are not mine to tell, Rayne," he answered softly. "Now how do we break this particular protection spell?"

Jade showed Charles the pages where it described how to break the spell; it seemed like a very simple process, the question was, could they drum up enough power between the two of them? There was only one minor setback; they needed a black orchid to channel the spell through, and the last Jade remembered, they only grew on Lear Island.

Charles leaned back on the leather couch and sighed; he closed his eyes for a moment scanning through his own memories to see if there were any other possible places that they could find this flower. Quickly running out of ideas, he growled and opened his eyes again. Unfortunately, centuries ago, they were all ordered to be destroyed, as they held too much power for any race, human or otherwise to control.

Charles stood up, more frustrated with himself than anything, spun around and put his fist through the wall, letting out an animalistic growl and stormed out of the room. Jade watched Rayne, watching Charles leave. Jade did not have to read her sister's thoughts to see that it excited her to see Charles a little out of control; Jade had to admit it excited her too. Rayne and Jade stood in the room a little while longer, clearly, Charles was not coming back any time soon, so they took the book and went to find Adrian and Holden.

The sisters reached the main deck of the ship and found everyone there except the Guardians and Charles, even Edmond was there talking to them. Rayne and Jade had to show them what they had found; with any luck, someone would know where they could find even one single black orchid.

"Where did you find this book?" Edmond asked strangely.

"I've not seen it in a few thousand years?"

"Charles let me go through a bunch of old books he had in his study," Jade answered slowly meeting his eyes, hoping to get a glimpse of what he was thinking. "When I asked him where it came from, he told me it was not his secret to tell."

"This is impossible," Edmond said, shaking his head. "This book was consumed by the earth the same day you three were. Your mother was clutching it in her hands when the fire reached up for you." He stared closely at the worn book again trying to remember any possible way that it could have survived, but he could see nothing.

"Jade, can I see it for a moment?" Adrian asked as he stepped forward. As he touched the book, his finger grassed Jade's and a face rang through her mind as clear as day. Ezrabeth!

Jade jumped, startled at what just happened, Adrian looked at her just as confused. "I don't understand," he said, staring at her; then all the sudden, the visions came in as clear as could be.

The black orchid in this spell was not a flower per se but something that loomed inside of Ezrabeth. When she was very little, her mother used to feed her herbal teas at night before bed to help her sleep. These teas were infused with many different flowers one of which was the black orchid. Her mother would get the teas from a local Pagan woman back in Madoc whom she had met almost by accident one evening while she had been taking Ezrabeth for an evening walk trying to get her to fall asleep. They had become close friends, and the woman offered the tea to help, seeing clearly that the child was not completely human.

"That woman, do you know her?" Jade asked Adrian.

"Yes, I remember her; she was friends with my wife not too long after Ezrabeth was born." He strained trying to picture the woman and trying to remember anything else he could about her.

After reading Jade's thoughts, Rayne quickly grabbed a blank piece of paper from the back of the book and began to draw the face; she could see in Adrian's mind, in hopes that maybe one of the Guardians may be able to identify her. No sooner did she lift her pen from the page, her eyes widened, and the sisters looked at each other. That woman, the one Rayne had just drawn, "Grandmother!" Rayne and Jade said at the same time. "But that's impossible," Rayne said, staring back up at her sister.

Charles walked up behind them. "Nothing is impossible," he said, clearing his throat. "Clearly neither of you have been paying attention these past few days."

"Excuse me." Rayne hissed.

"Well." Charles laughed. "Clearly, you haven't because if you had been paying attention, you would not be so surprised with reincarnation."

"Reincarnation," Jade repeated, remembering the words she had read about her mother's soul being reborn time after time of course it made sense, "*but why our grandmother, and why feed the orchids to Ezzy?*" Jade's inner voice pondered.

Adrian, still unsure why Ezrabeth, shook his head. "The only reason I can possibly come up with is that this woman knew that there would be some importance to this, and she found a way to hide the flower's power where no one, human or otherwise, would think to look."

Out of nowhere, Justin reached for Rayne's hand. "Obviously," he said matter-of-factly, "the three of you are destined for something big. We have beliefs in my tribe; when you are put on a path for whatever reason that is, certain people are set along the path to help you. In your case, it just happens to span over many lifetimes."

Why did it have to sound so simple when Justin said it?

"Adrian, I will call in and order Ezzy's plane ticket if you will let her fly alone? If you're not comfortable with that, then I will go back for her, but either way, we need her here," Jade told him.

"I don't like the idea of her flying alone, and I'm not entirely sure how she would even get to the airport," he answered.

"Hmm, I guess I really did not think that part out. Okay, well then, I will fly back." Jade felt foolish for a moment, of course, she knew that.

"That won't be necessary," Edmond said. "I will send my helicopter for her. There is only enough room for one of you to go."

The obvious person to go was Adrian being that he was her father. Edmond called in his pilot, and the helicopter arrived within the hour. Adrian called Ezrabeth and explained a little bit to her about what was going on and told her to be ready when he got there. Jade gave Adrian a small list of things to grab while he was back in Madoc to help with the spell before he left. Since Adrian would not be back until the next day, Rayne and Jade decided to take some time and do a little hunting; Holden, Justin, and Marc came with them. Edmond advised them they did not need to hunt; his ship was well stocked with more than enough blood to satisfy their thirst. Rayne politely thanked him but declined for the time being. The hunt was what they needed.

"Rayne, I'm so happy to see you," Ezrabeth cried as she got out of the helicopter practically leaping into Rayne's arms. "I've missed you so much."

"I've missed you too, Ezzy, I'm so sorry we had to leave the way we did." Rayne apologized, hugging her back.

"It's okay, I was just so worried about all of you," Ezzy added. Ezrabeth turned and looked at Jade with a smile. "I told you, you were different."

Jade smiled and gave her a hug and then turned to Adrian who handed her a small bag then gave a quick wink. The ship set out into the ocean; once they were far enough out that they could no longer see land, the ship stopped moving. Rayne and Jade had taken Ezrabeth into one of the rooms to explain to her what they needed to do and how. Ezzy surprised the sisters when Jade told her what the ritual would require of her; she thought for sure Ezzy would back out once they told her that in order to channel the orchid's power, Rayne and Jade would need to drink her blood. Knowing that their venom was fatal to humans but not to Adrian when he was a half-breed, Jade did not know if it would kill Ezrabeth or not. Jade really expected her to back out.

"Does my dad know this part?" Ezrabeth asked.

"No, we wanted to give you the choice before telling him and having him choose for you," Rayne answered softly. "We wanted it to be your choice..."

"What will happen if I don't have the same tolerance as he did?"

"Then you will die," Rayne whispered.

Ezrabeth sat there for a few moments in silence; Rayne could read what Jade was thinking, and her eyes lit up.

"Is that a possibility?" she asked, looking at her sister, hopeful.

"I'm not sure, the process would require one of us to complete it once her life force was almost gone; and if we are focusing on breaking the spell, I just don't know if I will be able to save her in time," Jade said, looking up at Ezrabeth.

"Wait, are you saying that even if I am not immune to your venom, there is still a possibility I could survive?" Ezrabeth smiled ear to ear.

"Well, that would depend on your definition on surviving," Charles interrupted as he entered the room. "Your venom may kill her, but if she so chooses, I could turn her while you two are completing the ritual."

"Why do you even care?" Rayne snapped.

"Rayne, please," Ezrabeth whispered and stood up. "Who are you?" she asked Charles.

"My name is Charles, I am an old friend that just wants to help make things right," he replied.

"Charles!" She turned to Rayne. "As in *the* Charles?" Rayne rolled her eyes.

"Yes, I suppose I am *the* Charles if you mean Rayne's Charles." He laughed.

"Rayne, I thought you said he was dead?" looking at Rayne, she asked.

"He is dead . . . apparently, he just doesn't like to stay that way," Rayne sarcastically snapped.

"Okay, do we really need to do this right now?" Jade hissed. "Ezrabeth, the choice has to be yours. We never had that choice, and I swore that I would never take that choice away from anyone."

"Jade, I appreciate your concern, but really, everyone I care about is a vampire." She sighed. "I'm not scared, and I'm not backing out. I will do whatever it takes, and if I have to become like you in the process, then so be it."

"Ezzy, are you sure?" Rayne asked, squeezing Ezzy's hand.

"One hundred and fifty percent," Ezrabeth replied with a smile. "Now if you all will excuse me, I should really go talk to my dad and tell him what's going on. Oh, and by the way, it's a pleasure to meet you, Charles . . . I've heard a lot about you." Ezzy smiled at him and left the room to find Adrian.

Before Charles had a chance to make another smart-ass comment, Rayne spun around and followed Ezrabeth out of the room. Charles raised his eyebrows. "She hates me," he added as he sat down beside Jade.

"She doesn't hate you." Jade laughed. "She loves you, and that hurts her more than hating you right now."

"Jade, I don't know how to make things right with her, has it been too long? I mean she seems to really like that dog she is with." He sighed.

"Charles, please be fair; it's been over a hundred and fifty years, and she finally met someone that she can be honest with about what we are, and then all the sudden, here you are. She's just confused. I'm sure you've loved and lost many times in your life as well, so please try to understand," Jade replied with a half smile trying to comfort him.

"You're right; I have loved and lost. If I am to be totally honest with you, over the thousands of years I have been alive, you and your family have been reincarnated many times, and I have loved you all at one point or another, so forgive me if I am trying to hang on to her now that I know she is still alive." He slumped into the chair. "For each lifetime that we have met, none of you remember the past, and I am forced to pretend I am someone new again and again; this time I don't. She may hate me for being gone the last century and a half, but at least this time, I am still remembered." He leaned in and kissed Jade's cheek then got up off the couch to leave the room. As Charles reached the door, he turned and smiled at her dropping the guards of his mind just enough for her to see a brief life that she had shared with him before another untimely death. Then the walls were back up again, and he headed for the hall.

"Charles, wait! Your father, does he know?" Jade asked as she followed him into the hall, confused since Edmond's story did not seem to include any of their other lives.

"No, not all of them, he doesn't," he answered, turning back to face her. "Some secrets are not meant to be told." His eyes met Jade's, and for a brief moment, she was lost; and within seconds, she blinked, and he was gone leaving her with images in her mind of so many deaths and so many lifetimes of hurt. Too many times, he had let himself love one of them just to be left alone and empty again. Jade leaned against the wall and slowly slid down until she was sitting on the floor crossed-legged with her back to the wall trying to process the images that Charles left her with; she closed her eyes and just sat there.

"I thought you said we don't sleep . . . "

Jade's eyes opened to see Holden sitting across from her; she must have been lost in thoughts because she had not heard him sit down.

"We don't, I'm sorry, babe, I am just trying to get my head straight," she said, reaching across for his hands. "Come on, let's find somewhere else to be. I'd like to get some fresh air."

"Jade," he said, wrapping his arms around her once they stood up, "I love you."

"I love you too, Holden." Jade must have had a look on her face because Holden dropped his head to hers and kissed her and then whispered, "I thought you needed to hear it. There is a lot of crazy crap going on here, so I just thought you needed to hear it." Holden squeezed Jade tighter and kissed her forehead. Since the ritual could not be performed until the next full moon, they had almost four weeks to prepare. It was the longest four weeks of her life.

CHAPTER 20

After what felt like an eternity of silence, Jorja began to hear voices around her, but she could not open her eyes; everything was black. *"What's happening? Where am I?"* Her own voice rang loud in her head. Jorja could feel sharp pains, like needles puncturing her skin, followed by a warm sensation flowing into her arm; it felt much the same as when Adrian injected her with his venom. Still not able to open her eyes, Jorja could feel her body tensing as the warm liquid made its way through every inch of her stone body. The voices became clearer.

"This is amazing . . . ," a woman cried.

"Yes, after all these years . . . " a man's voice said.

Jorja did not recognize either voice. *"Where is Cavan? Why did he let this happen to me?"* Jorja tried to move her arms, but they felt heavy, almost like she was nailed down to whatever she was laying on. Her body now feeling like it was on fire, she remembered the night Cavan created her this was much the same feeling. Jorja fought to open her eyes. She could feel them flutter just a bit.

"Her eyes, look at her eyes!" the woman's voice squealed.

"Inject her again," a harsh male voice hissed. *"We are so close we can't have her wake yet."*

"STOP IT! You're killing her," another man growled; Jorja knew this voice, it was Cavan. *"This has gone on long enough; this entire thing will be pointless if you kill her!"*

In the darkness, Jorja heard the commotion, breaking glass, shouting, loud growls and hissing. Her body, being pulled in all directions like a rag doll, all of a sudden, she felt her body tensed, her spine felt as if it had been snapped in half, then a strong cold wind on her face. She was falling . . . Everything stopped and went dead quiet, still pitch-black and stayed that way for what seemed like ages, and then finally, Jorja heard a faint voice.

"Jorja, my love, please wake up, you're safe now. I am so sorry, my love, please, you must wake up . . . I won't let you die!"

Jorja's body slowly began to regained awareness, but she felt very weak. She tried to open her eyes; they flickered just a bit, and she could hear a faint voice telling her to wake up, but it seemed so far away.

"Jorja, my love, please wake up, you're safe now," Jorja heard the voice again this time a little closer. She tried to speak, but her throat burned she could hardly make a sound.

"Don't try to talk, my love, you need to regain your strength." This time, the voice was much clearer, and now she knew it was Cavan.

Jorja tried to open her eyes again, but they seemed to be glued shut, and again, she felt them flicker just a bit. She would have to try much harder. With every ounce of energy in her, Jorja finally forced them open. The room was dark only distant flickers from what looked like a fireplace burning. She tried to sit up but felt a warm hand grab her arm.

"Hold on, my love, you must be careful."

"Cav—" She tried to speak.

"Jorja, don't speak, you're too dry," he said. "Please, my love, you need to drink before you try to do anything," he continued as he helped her sit up. Jorja leaned back against a very large wooded headboard, and Cavan handed her a goblet full of blood. Her throat burned hotter than anything she had ever felt; she took the goblet eagerly and drank it all. No sooner did she finish it, he handed her another. Slowly, the burn started to subside.

"Cavan," Jorja said, still trying to focus on the room around her, "what happened?"

"Shhh, my love, we can talk when you are stronger," he said in a concerned voice.

Jorja looked around the room. She did not recognize anything. The room was very large with extremely high ceilings; it looked very old with stone walls and an oversized fireplace on the wall at the foot of the large four poster bed that was curtained with transparent purple and red sheers. She did not see any windows, only candles hanging in indents in the stone walls.

"Where am I?" Jorja's voice was very dry and cracked.

"That's not important, love, drink some more," Cavan replied, filling up her goblet from a copper urn on the table beside the bed. "I will explain everything, Jorja, I promise; please just drink up now you need it."

Jorja drank the entire urn of blood; when she finished it, she set the goblet on the bedside table. Cavan took the urn out of the room, once the door shut behind him, she tried to stand. After a few minutes of struggling, Jorja was finally able to put her feet on the floor. She held onto one of the bulky pillars of the bed to help herself up. Legs trembled beneath her, Jorja stood for a moment to catch her balance and scan the room again; there was a lot of old Victorian-looking furniture. The room looked like something out of a gothic fairy tale. Slowly, she made her way from the foot of the bed to a small window like opening in the wall that overlooked what seemed to be a grand dining area. Below, she saw an old woman lighting oil lanterns that hung from the stones; she turned and looked and immediately call for Cavan. Before Jorja could turn her still very weak body around, Cavan was behind her. "Jorja, please, what are you doing out of bed?" he asked as he took her arm and helped her to a scarlet-colored velvet chair.

"Cavan, I need some answers," Jorja pleaded dryly. "What happened? Where am I?"

"Ireland, love, we are in Ireland," he replied and turned his head to stare into the fire.

"Ireland?" she asked confused. "What am I doing here?"

Still very reluctant to give any answers, Cavan replied, "I *will* explain everything, love; we have plenty of time for that . . . later; but for now, you need to rest and get your strength back."

"I don't want to rest, Cavan, I want answers. What happened, where is my family?" Jorja demanded in what tried to be a harsh tone but hardly came out as a whisper. "Where is Adrian?"

"I TOLD YOU TO REST!" Cavan growled then stormed out of the room, locking the door behind him. "*Am I now a prisoner to this room?*" The longer Jorja sat there, the more she began to remember. She remembered leaving her home to come with Cavan to Ireland to see the Guardians, but she didn't remember actually seeing them; come to think of it, she didn't remember even getting on the plane. Every thought in her head was so hazy; every sound she tried to remember was muffled. "*What did he do to make me feel so foggy?*"

After a few hours, the old woman Jorja had seen earlier in the dining area came to her door; she unlocked it with a rusty antique-looking key then quickly closed the door behind her, locking it from the inside this time.

"Here you go, my dear," she said, handing Jorja a tray with another urn and goblet.

"Who are you?" she asked quietly, hoping the woman would stay and speak with her.

"Hush," the old woman replied, placing her wrinkled finger over her mouth, "he will hear you."

"Cavan?" Jorja whispered.

"Yes," the woman replied quietly. "My name is Aura," the old woman continued as she set the tray down on the bedside table. "But please try not to let him catch you speaking to me, it will upset Lord Cavan."

Lord Cavan, Jorja laughed to herself. "*I want answers. Where is my family? Where is Adrian? What the hell am I doing here? I have to find a way out.*" Aura left the room just as quickly and quietly as she arrived, locking the grand wooded door behind her. Jorja drank the blood in the urn a little slower this time as she walked around the room looking for any other way out. No windows to the outside, one locked door and one very small opening into the grand dining area. She staggered slowly back to the velvet chair and finished her drink.

It had been sometime since Cavan had stormed out of Jorja's *prison cell*. Aura came in regularly to bring more blood. Jorja could feel herself getting stronger, after being completely alone in this large room with only a few very brief visits from Aura, Jorja was beginning to think she was going to go mad.

Expecting Aura, it was like clockwork when she would arrive with a single goblet, the door to Jorja's room opened, turning to greet Aura, Jorja caught sight of Cavan's crimson eyes.

"How do you feel, my love?" his voice was low and somewhat pained.

"I feel just fine," trying to keep her hatred from showing. Not sure what to say or do next, Jorja simply walked over to her chair, sat down and stared at him.

"I know you are angry with me, my love," he began, "but it was the only way to keep you safe."

"Safe from what?" she replied in a monotone voice.

"This is very hard for me to say...Jorja..." He paused, walking over and taking her hand. "They are gone."

"Who is gone?" she asked, knowing that she really did not want the answer to this; Jorja knew very well who he was talking about.

"Rayne...Jade...all of them," he said, still holding her hand very firm, as if trying to make sure she couldn't run away.

"What do you mean they are gone?" Trying to keep composure as rage hit Jorja's voice.

"The Guardians...I'm sorry they, they tried to find you, but the Guardians got to them first." He stared into her eyes. "They tried to fight . . . But the Guardians were too strong for them, I am sorry, my love, but they are *ALL* dead." That very moment, Jorja felt every inch of faith, hope, honor, trust, and love drain from her body.

"We must stay here Jorja; the Guardians have agreed to allow your existence to continue if we send them regular samples of your blood."

"Regular samples of my blood," she spoke through her teeth, "why do they need that? What did they do to me to make me so weak?"

"Jorja, my love, they were doing a tremendous amount of testing on your blood and venom to try to find out why you could endure the sun." Cavan replied, "But they still could not find the answers. I convinced them if they did not let us go, that you would surely die, and they would never have their answers." He stood up and took Jorja's hand lifting her off the velvet chair that she had been perched on. "Come, my love, I will show you around *our* home."

Jorja could not believe this was really happening, truly, her life was over. "*Cavan should have just let them drain me dry rather than make me continue without my family! My girls were my soul, and Adrian was my heart. With every beat of his half-breed heart and every breath in is half-breed lungs, I felt more alive than I had in over a century and a half.*"

Jorja followed Cavan through the antique castle halfheartedly as he advised her to stay within the castle gates. As they walked around the desolate castle, Cavan rambled on about its history, how it had been in his family for many, many years. When the last living heir passed away, he came back to claim what was rightfully his for eternity. It was a very beautiful building, Jorja had to admit that, but she could not enjoy the beauty as her heart had turned to stone once again. The castle looked over the blackest water Jorja had ever seen, and she wondered to herself, "*Is it possible for a vampire to drown?*" As Cavan walked her around, Jorja went over the voices in her mind, the last words she spoke to Rayne, Jade and Adrian. "*Could this really be possible? I had finally found a love, and now it was gone forever. Now I truly am...dead!*" Jorja's inner voice echoed through her mind.

* * *

"My love, when will you open up to me?" Cavan asked as he moved a strand of hair away from Jorja's face.

"Stop calling me that, why do you keep asking me? You know how I feel." Jorja hissed turning her head away from his direction and walked over to the window facing the ocean. The view across the water was beautiful from Cavan's room, with the moon sitting on the horizon.

"Jorja," Cavan said harshly, "it's time to get over it and move on; they are gone, and nothing will bring them back. Are you going to keep yourself locked up forever?"

"I don't keep me locked up, Cavan, you do," she snapped and walked out of the room toward the east side of the castle to watch the sun come up; one of the few delights he could not take away from her.

Without her daughters, Jorja was nothing; it was because of their strength that she made it through the last century and a half. She was so isolated on this island, nowhere to go, and nothing to hunt. All meals brought to her by Aura, the servant woman, but even she had blocked Jorja out at Cavan's orders. Jorja felt she was going insane; there was only one other creature on this entire island that Jorja had spoken to and even she was harsh most of the time. This creature went by the name Koko; she told Jorja her name means "the night." She was a very beautiful creature, one like Jorja had never seen before. When she was not patrolling the castle, she takes on the form of a woman. Her skin was a golden tan with black hair that reached down almost to her hips. However, during her patrol, she takes on the form of a large and very dominating wolf. Never had Jorja seen a creature that was able to shift from human to animal; she was very intriguing.

Koko caught Jorja the first time she tried to escape, only a day after Cavan had shown her around the castle; she made it as far as the cliff on the north side. Jorja had planned to jump and hoped to swim or die whatever happened first; however, Koko was very fast, caught Jorja in midair. Jorja thought Koko was going to chew her leg off, but she just called to the others, and they brought her back to Cavan. She had shifted into her human form to speak with Cavan and let him know where Jorja had been found, but before she turned to leave, she whispered softly to Jorja, "I'm sorry," then shifted back to her wolf form and took off into the trees. Since then, Cavan allowed Jorja to take walks around the island during the day, but only if she were accompanied by Koko, as he felt Koko would keep Jorja "in line" and make sure she didn't do anything brazen like try to jump off a three-thousand-foot cliff again.

The days ran into the nights then into the days again. Jorja had no idea how long she had been a prisoner anymore, nor did she even care. Her family was gone; Cavan assured her that the Guardians would not try to hurt her again so long as she keeps giving them regular samples of blood and venom. Who knew there was such a thing on this earth that could penetrate her skin, but Cavan had a needle; it looked like a fang, and it seemed to have no problem poking her at least twice a day. Sometimes, she felt he was taking more blood out than he was giving her to drink, trying to keep her weak, so she could not get away. He told Jorja it was for her own safety that she must stay at the castle, but some days, she just wished he would have handed her over to the Guardians and let them kill her.

Jorja sat in the dining hall in a large red velvet high-back chair staring into the fire that Aura had lit only moments earlier. It must have been close to dusk. Every day, Aura did the same routine; about half an hour before dusk, she would go room to room lighting the lamps and starting the fireplaces, it was how Jorja could tell night from day when Cavan had secluded her to her chamber. Not long after Aura had left to finish lighting the rest of the castle, the large door to the east wing opened.

"Good evening, *my love*," Cavan whispered as he crossed the hardwood floor. Jorja was sure he only called her that now because he knew how much she disliked it. "How was your day?"

"It was fine," she answered dryly.

"Just fine, what did you do today?" Cavan tried to engage conversation, but Jorja was too depressed to humor him.

"Yes. Just fine, I did the same thing I do every day here," she said a bit harsher. "I walked around the island while being followed by dogs, then came back in and sat here by myself."

"Jorja," he said, putting his hand on her shoulder, "it is safer here, I know you are lonely, but if you would just open up to me and let me into your heart, you would see it's not really that bad being here." The lies flowed all too easy from Cavan's mouth.

"Let you into my heart...now that is a joke," a sarcastic tone escaped Jorja's mouth. "I have no heart!"

"Don't say that, you do have a heart," Cavan said, moving his hand to her leg as he knelt down in front of her. "I know you do because I can see how broken it is."

"Is there something I can do for you tonight, Cavan?" Jorja hissed.

"Well, since you ask," he smirked, "why don't you take a walk with me?"

"I am getting really tired of walking NOWHERE," she snapped. "I want to hunt, I NEED to hunt."

"Jorja, I already told you, you can't hunt anymore, and that is final," Cavan growled.

"You can't keep me here forever, Cavan. I will find a way off this island, and I don't care if the Guardians find me. I will let them kill me...gladly." Jorja hissed back and turned to walk out of the room.

Cavan grabbed Jorja's arm spinning her completely around and stared her square in the eyes. His eyes were a deep blood red, and his grip tightened on her arm. If she were human, her arm would have broken for sure. They stood face to face, eyes locked, rage elevating. Then with one blurred movement, he wrapped his arms around her body and kissed her, hard. So many thoughts reeled through Jorja's head, the first being how easy it would be to rip his arms off and beat him with them, but as she was considering all the painful things she could do to Cavan for what he was doing to her, Jorja realized that as he kissed her, she was not pulling away. For reasons she could not begin to understand, the anger, rage, hurt and just about every other emotion contributing to this kiss . . . she did not let go!

After a few moments into a very passionate kiss, Jorja pulled her head back just a bit and looked at Cavan; he opened his mouth to speak, but she put her finger on his lips.

"Don't . . . say . . . a word." Trying very hard not to look him in the eye, Jorja unwound herself from his arms and left him standing in front of the huge fireplace and walked out into the west hall. Once she was out of his sight, Jorja leaned against the cold stone wall, put her hands over her eyes and took a deep breath. *I need to get out of here, there is no way I will let myself enjoy anything that involves Cavan. I don't care how lonely I get and that's final!* Jorja stood there only a few moments longer then went to look for Koko.

CHAPTER 21

Jorja knocked on Koko's cabin door; Cavan would not allow the "dogs" to sleep in the castle. She looked a little puzzled when she opened the door but invited Jorja in anyway. Koko knew there was no point turning Jorja away because she would only be sent to find her later, at least if she was there, Koko could keep an eye on her and not have to worry about Cavan freaking out.

"So, Jorja, what brings you by this evening?" She laughed.

"Koko, I can't stand it anymore. I need to get out of here. I can't survive this way anymore." Jorja sighed.

"Jorja, really...what do you think I can do about this?" she said softly. "I mean really, I can't get you off the island. The only boats in or out of here are heavily guarded and overseen by Cavan." She took a deep breath. "Believe me if there was a way to get out of here, I would have taken it a very long time ago."

"Why haven't you at least tried? If there are boats, there has to be a way to get away from him," Jorja questioned, as she took a seat at Koko's kitchen table.

Koko paused for a minute staring out the window. "I did try, about a year after I got here."

"What happened?" Jorja asked softly, fidgeting with a napkin.

"He caught me and had me beaten and left me for dead!" Koko's eyes looked through Jorja as if she was reliving the memory.

"But I don't understand, are you not the head of his so-called security?"

"Yes, now I am. After they left me for dead, I crawled into a cave on the south side of the island." She sighed. "It doesn't take long for my kind to heal when given time to rest. So I hid there, I ate the few rats and birds that I could find, and when I was strong enough, I came back and told Cavan I would do whatever it took to let me back in."

"But why would you want to, if you were already in hiding?" Trying to understand why she would come back.

"Because even though I was not under Cavan's slavery at that point, I still couldn't get off the island. I can't swim that far, and there is no way to get on the boats," Koko answered. "Even the years when Cavan was gone, he still had his minions that would deliver the food to us, and they would not help out of fear that he would kill them too."

Jorja understood Koko's situation; it is better to be the right hand of evil, keep your friends close but your enemies closer, right?

The more Koko and Jorja sat and talked, the more Jorja understood her. Koko was no different from her in some ways, a prisoner. She told Jorja she had been forced to leave her husband and son when the child was very young; the two most important people in her life ripped away from her. Jorja's icy heart ached for her, knowing that her family is alive out there and not being able to go to them or to see her little boy grow up. She could feel her pain knowing that her own family was dead, her children and her beloved Adrian, knowing that even if she did manage to escape off this island, she would still be alone. However, for Koko, they were still out there waiting for her to come home someday.

Jorja stood up to leave as the sun began to light up the sky, turning to Koko, she said, "You know, if there was a way to get you back to your family," Jorja paused and took a deep breath, "I would help you get away from here."

"Jorja, you know as well as I do that he will have me killed if I try to leave again."

"I would fight for you, your family needs you, Koko." Jorja gave Koko a hug. "You are the only friend I have here even if you are supposed to keep me from escaping again." She laughed.

"Jorja, you are the closest thing I have had to a friend in almost twenty years. But I am not going to let you escape." She sighed. "He will kill us both."

"Not if I killed him first..." Jorja smiled and turned out the door. "See ya later, Koko, I need to see what I can find to eat here; there has to be some kind of animal on this rock even if it's a bird."

"Jorja," Koko reach for Jorja's arm before she was all the way out the door, "be careful."

"Don't worry, darling." Jorja smiled and took off into the trees.

* * *

Jorja could hear the rustling about fifty feet to her left, all this time trapped in this prison, and as weak as she was, her senses were still as sharp as ever. The only thought in Jorja's head was, "I don't care what it is I'm going to eat it . . . " Jorja waited, crouched down ready to attack.

Jorja tried not to feel bad about finishing off the entire litter of rabbits; she could not help but wonder as she lay in the clearing letting the sun beat down on her, why she felt so different. The blood that Cavan gave her did not taste even close to the same as this, she had almost forgotten what animal blood tasted like but from what she could remember, the human blood had a different taste as well. Jorja started to wonder what blood Cavan had been feeding her since she woke up on this island.

It was relaxing laying there in the sun; Jorja had almost forgotten how angry she was at Cavan for kissing her the night before, almost. She closed her eyes envisioning her family, her beautiful girls and her

Adrian. Jorja could almost see Jade and Rayne bickering about some movie they just seen and how the visual effects were subpar or how they would sit for hours like old ladies and talk about how much times have changed. They look so young, but to live as long as they had, it takes a toll on the mind, making you look at the world in a different way. Then there was Adrian, Jorja missed him so much. She missed how careful she had to be with him all the time and how mad he would pretend to get with her for not letting go of her control. If he only knew how close she was all the time.

The longer Jorja lay there, the more she thought about them and the angrier she got with Cavan again for taking her away from them and not being able to protect them.

With the fresh blood running through her, Jorja could feel the difference in her body, her strength, and her heart, it felt strange almost alive again. Now all she had to do was keep her little feeding fest to herself and try to find more, even if it is one rabbit at a time; Jorja needed this blood if she was going to be able to have the strength to get Koko and herself off the island.

The sun began to set as she laid on the grassy clearing looking up at the sky, not too long after, Koko came looking for her. "There you are, Jorja, I was beginning to think you left without me." She laughed.

"Not gonna happen, darling, if I get off this rock, you're coming with me." Jorja smiled.

"You really should get back, Cavan is up, and he's looking for you," Koko said, rolling her eyes.

Koko walked Jorja back to the castle, talking and laughing as if they had known each other forever. Jorja did not get too far into the castle before Cavan flew over to them and ordered Koko to wait outside for him. Giving Jorja a strange look, Koko turned and went back outside.

"What the hell was that for?" Jorja hissed. "Am I getting too close to having a friend here?"

"Jorja, my love, we need to chat." Cavan took Jorja's hand, walked up the grand stairs and down the long stone hall toward her room. Jorja tried to ask him what was going on, but he would not give her any answers. He just kept saying, "We need to chat." When they got to the door of Jorja's room, she walked in ahead of him, but before she could turn to ask him again what was going on, Cavan shut the door and locked it behind her.

"What the hell, Cavan!" Jorja yelled through the door. "Don't play games with me." He did not answer. Jorja yelled louder, but it made no difference; she knew he was gone. With nothing else to do but sit and wait for him to come back and open the door again, Jorja decided to write some more in her journal.

Jorja did not know how much time had passed; it could have been days or even weeks, she had no idea. No blood was delivered, no light was given, just the occasional steps could be heard outside her door, how long could a vampire survive without blood? Jorja wondered as she laid on her bed drifting in and out of consciousness.

Jorja realized that she was surely going to die in this room; however, what comforted her most was the realization that she was okay with it. Knowing that maybe in death, she would see her family again brought Jorja peace; as she lay in the blackened room, Jorja started to think she could hear her girls again. Their voices rang through her thoughts; they were laughing and singing and carrying on as they did when they were children. Then the laughter changed, and the voices were clear, Jorja heard Jade calling . . . "Mom, where are you?" She thought surely she must be in heaven now. She smiled softly in the dark, lying still on the bed, Jorja closed her eyes one last time and whispered, *I'm right here, I'll always be right here. I love you, girls.*

CHAPTER 22

On the open deck of the ship under a glowing full moon, Adrian cast the circle the way his aunt taught him to during the many full moon ceremonies they would do when he was a child; he called the corners and asked the spirits to help then stepped aside. The circle was cast around the four of them, Jade put the herbs in bowls at each of the corners, Rayne held on to Ezrabeth's arm tightly and whispered one last time that she could back out, but she was not listening. Ezrabeth was solely focused on Charles's face as he stood in front of her, his hands firmly on her hips for support. Rayne and Jade began to recite the ancient text in a language long forgotten, and Adrian began to burn the herbs in each of the four corners from outside the circle. The sisters called upon their strength together as one in unison; as Ezrabeth stretched her arms out wide from left to right, Rayne took one arm, and Jade took the other, and in one sharp motion, they bit into her wrists together and drank. The feeling was so euphoric the sisters nearly lost sight of what they were trying to do. As they drank the blood, Ezrabeth's body went limp; Rayne and Jade let go, and Ezrabeth fell into Charles's arms. He could clearly see she was dying and did his part in her transformation, while he did, the sisters chanted again, this time their arms locked in with each other. The energy between them growing in to a large ball of fire, bigger and bigger, as the light filled the circle pushing at the thinning veil that contained it within. Then with no warning, the energy ripped itself from the sisters, up toward the full moon above. Fully exhausted,

Rayne and Jade both dropped to the ground, and Jade began to lose consciousness but not before seeing the island slowly forming only a few short miles away, the moon lit it beautifully; then before Jade knew it, her eyes closed, and no matter how hard she tried, they were not opening.

* * *

When Jade came to, the sun was high in the sky above her; she blinked in a panic as the sun began to burn her eyes. Jade could feel herself starting to freak out, groggy, unsure where she was; she reached for Rayne beside her, but there was nothing. She sat straight up and looked around; it seemed she was on a balcony, as Jade began to focus more, she realized that she was on a lounge chair on the lookout deck of her room on Edmond's ship.

Holden walked out on the deck beside her and reached for her hand. "How are you feeling, babe?" He asked softly. "You scared the hell out of me when you collapsed."

"What happened? Where is Rayne? . . . Oh my god, where is Ezrabeth?" Jade cried in panic. "Please tell me she is okay," she cried.

"Jade, baby, relax, it's alright; they are all fine." He straddled his legs over the long lounge chair and sat down facing her, one hand on hers and the other on her cheek. "Rayne is fine, the last time I saw her, she was with Justin heading to her room; Ezrabeth, well, all I can say is she is an amazingly brave little girl. She is with her father and Charles right now."

Jade let out a small sigh of relief. "Did it work?" she asked, looking down at Holden's hand intertwined in hers in her lap.

"Yah, babe, it worked." He smiled and brought Jade's hand up to his mouth and kissed it gently. "You were amazing, you all were."

"How long was I out for?" Jade was curious especially since she had not slept in over a hundred and fifty years.

Holden chuckled a little when he said, "Eighteen days."

LIES

"What? Eighteen days, are you kidding?" Jade's eyes opened wider than ever. "What a waste of time, we have to get moving."

"Relax, babe, we've been working on our plan of attack while you were out. I have to admit I'm a little jealous; you didn't tell me that you guys fought in a war." His eyes lit up a bit. "Your sister has some great strategies."

"That's because when the military doesn't know you exist, you have one hell of an upper hand." Jade laughed. "We should get a move on though seriously, I'd like to see Ezzy."

Holden and Jade walked on to the main deck. Rayne and Ezrabeth were talking, but as soon as Jade's foot hit the deck floor, Ezrabeth leapt from her seat and nearly knocked Jade over. "Jade, you're up!" she screamed. "I was so worried about you." Ezzy's arms wrapped around Jade like a snake squeezing tighter with every second.

"Ezzy, strength, remember," Rayne said, giggling.

"Oh, sorry." Ezrabeth let go quickly. "There is a lot to get used to."

"It's okay." Jade laughed. "I'm just glad you're alright."

Justin walked over as well and gave Jade a hug; he did not speak any words aloud, but in his mind told Jade he was glad she was okay. Jade smiled and kissed his cheek.

Rayne stepped forward. "Enjoyed your nap?" She smiled.

"Just tell me where we are at now, with all of this. I just want to get her back and go home; I've had enough of this crap to last me five lifetimes." Jade sighed.

They went down into the meeting room where the Guardians were to show Jade the plan they had laid out. A voice of apology hit Jade's mind and without even thinking, she looked up and met Charles's crystal blue eyes across the table. She did not think anyone else noticed, as they were going over plans and strategies. Charles told Jade he was sorry for the images he had left her with on the many times they had spoken over the four weeks leading up to the ritual.

Jade nodded with a small smile letting him know that everything was okay, but she could see the concern still on his face.

The safest time to hit the island would be at dawn, Charles and Holden prepared the smaller boats for the water. By the time they were done, it was late afternoon; Edmond offered the vampires a drink from his blood bank in the ship's hold. Of course, he was very refined about how he had it served to them, warmed and in a crystal glass. The wolves were catered to as well with a steak dinner prepared by a chef that Edmond employed. As they all sat around the large table in the dining area, small talk was being made but Jade did not say too much; she scanned every vision she could possibly see trying to see the outcome of tomorrow, but nothing she did could make her see it, total emptiness, darkness, nothing . . . The more Jade tried the more frustrated she got with it. Holden put his hand on Jade's lap and gently rubbed her leg, no doubt trying to make her feel better but even that did not help. Jade gave Holden a quick kiss when she finished her glass then excused herself from the room. Still long before midnight, the sun had barely set, after wondering the ship for a bit Jade found herself back on the main deck leaning over, watching the black water below splash against the ship. "*Eighteen days I've slept, eighteen days I've wasted,*" she let out a growl. "*If I were stronger, we could have saved her by now.*" Jade could see the faint outline of the island in the distance; they were just far enough away to stay undetected. "*Mom, I miss you so much.*" She let out an unneeded breath. "*I should have never stayed away so long; I should have seen this coming sooner. I should have been stronger for you.*" Jade's head hung down facing the water again, she began to cry, not just feel like crying, those blood tears that seemed to flow so easily now falling from her face into the black water below.

"You're wasting your dinner."

Jade did not bother to turn and face the voice that snuck up on her, there was no point; she knew it was too late to hide from him.

"What do you want, Charles?" Jade said softly still not turning around to face him. "Why do you keep popping up at all the wrong times?"

"Just lucky . . . I guess." He laughed. "Or maybe it's you that is following me, being that I was out here first and all."

"Then why did I not see you when I came out?" It came out a little harsher than she wanted. "I'm sorry," Jade said softer. "I did not mean it like that." She sighed still facing the water; she did not want to look at him.

"You don't need to be sorry, Jade; you did not see me because you were looking in the wrong direction." He smiled as he leaned in beside her, now facing out over the water, like she was. "I have this favorite spot on the ship. I like to come to when I need to clear my head sometimes." Then he pointed up. Jade's eyes followed Charles hand up to a very small wooden perch at the top of what looked like an antenna; he must have sensed her confusion since there was no stairs or climbing pegs going up the pole. Charles chuckled then with a little push off the floor, he jumped straight to the top and landed on his feet, square in the middle of the tiny perch, and with the same effortless motion landed back beside her. Not a sound made.

"Impressive," Jade whispered, still trying to keep her blood-streaked face in the opposite direction of his.

"You know," he said, clearing his throat then handing her a chunk of material. "If I remember your mom correctly, she'd be kicking your ass right about now if she heard you talking like you were."

Jade took the material and wiped her eyes clear with it before she turned to face him. She was about to give him hell for eavesdropping on her when she realized the chunk of material he gave her was his T-shirt.

"Why did you do that?" Jade questioned.

"Do what, eavesdrop on you or give you my shirt?" He chuckled.

"I don't know, either, both, I don't get anything you do." Jade let out a defeated sigh.

"Well, I gave you my shirt 'cause you needed something to wipe your tears, and I think it would have been a little weird for you if I was still wearing it while you did that." He chuckled again. "And the eavesdropping . . . well, that wasn't my fault, you came out here, where I already was, remember?"

Jade was getting even more frustrated than she was before, but was she frustrated because she still could not see the outcome of tomorrow or because as pissed off as it made her, she had to admit he was right. Jade handed Charles back his shirt then turned to walk away. She did not get more than three steps before she felt his hand on her shoulder, and Jade froze instantly.

"Relax, Jade," Charles said calmly. "I'm sorry, I know you're worried about tomorrow, but you don't need to be." He took his hand off Jade's shoulder and moved around in front of her. She was now face to face with Charles well face to naked perfectly sculpted chest. Jade took a step backward to put a little distance between them, the visions of the past lives he had shown her still very clear in her head, Jade really did not want to give Charles any wrong ideas.

"How can you be so sure of that?" She cleared her cracked voice. "I can't see any of it, not the dawn, not landing on the island or my mother . . . Any of it."

"I've known you a very long time Jade, many lifetimes, and if I know anything about you, it's that no matter what happens or how hard things get, you'll never give up." He took a step closer and pulled her chin up softly with one finger so that she had no choice but to look him in the eyes. "No matter what happens tomorrow, no matter how things play out one thing is for sure, and that's we will not be leaving that island without your mother, *period!*"

"I hope you're right," Jade said almost in a whisper as she closed her eyes. Jade felt Charles's arms wrap around her like a blanket, firm yet soft, confident. She started to melt into him; then all the sudden, she stopped and looked up at him. "Why are you doing this, Charles?" Jade's voice was almost inaudible.

"Doing what?" he whispered, keeping a steady rhythm to his breathing.

"This, here, holding me, it's wrong; and you know it, so why?" Jade stared at him trying to read his thoughts. His mind was more guarded now than ever. Charles let out a small moan mixed with a low growl and squeezed Jade tighter for a moment then let her go. He stood in front of her for only a moment staring into her eyes before turning and walking away. Jade looked down at her left hand, the hand that wore Holden's ring; she sighed not knowing what Charles motives were, why he was acting like that now after telling Jade how happy he was that Rayne still remembered him, and Jade could not even talk to her sister about it. She leaned back over the side of the ship focusing on the island in the distance, pulling every bit of energy she had and yelled out in her mind.

"Mom, where are you?"

And clear as a bell, Jade heard her mother's reply . . .

"I'm right here, I'll always be right here. I love you, girls."

WHAT? Jade had heard her mother. She yelled out again; this time she got nothing, but Jade didn't care, she got her once that was enough for her.

"She is ALIVE!" Jade screamed as she ran back to the room where everyone was still chatting trying to keep things light before the big day.

"Jade, what the hell?" Rayne said, turning around to see her sister. Jade grabbed on to Rayne's arms and cracked her mind just a bit so that Rayne could see that her mother had answered. Jade had a smile ear to ear; she was so excited she almost did not see Charles come in behind her.

"See, what did I tell you?" He smiled.

Holden gave Jade a quick worried look as his eyes went from her to Charles. Quickly, Jade reached for him and pulled him up beside her, putting her arm around his waist.

"Jade, what happened?" Adrian asked, coming closer.

"I was leaning over the deck watching the water, getting more and more pissed that I couldn't see anything about tomorrow. So I yelled out in my mind to my mother . . . and she answered." Then all of the sudden, Jade stopped and looked at Rayne; she knew exactly what her sister was thinking. Jade was so excited she actually got a response that she did not really listen to what her mother had said.

"She was saying good-bye," Jade's heart sank. "How could I be so stupid? She thinks she is dying, that's how she could hear my voice."

Holden tightened his grip on Jade's slowly slouching body; she brought her hands to her head and closed her eyes. Jade could feel Charles's mind from across the room trying to comfort her without getting physically close. Jade let out a growl, harsher than she had felt come from her before; she stared straight at Charles and hissed. "Get out of my head" then took off back to the room she had woken up in earlier. Jade could hear the voices start to argue behind her, but she didn't care; she needed to be alone.

A few minutes later, there was a knock on the door followed by an arm waving a white cloth. "I come in peace." Rayne chuckled as she slowly stepped in the room. "You left quite a commotion back there," she said, sitting down beside Jade on the bed. "Wanna talk about what's going on?"

"I'm just stressed with all this," Jade's voice was low and cracked, and her cheeks were streaked with red lines.

"I think it's more than that, sis." Rayne put her arm around Jade's shoulder. Jade could feel her sister's mental probes trying to get into her head and see what was really going on.

"I can feel that you know." Jade turned to look at Rayne. "You really don't wanna see it, trust me."

"If it's upsetting you, yes, I do want to see it. You're my little sister."

Jade looked at her sister again and took a deep breath. *What choice do I have? She's going to figure it out sooner or later why not get it over with while I'm already a mess.* Jade sighed. "You asked for it." Jade let down her walls and showed Rayne everything . . . Everything she had tried to keep from her sister about Charles, about her past lives, even the encounter on the deck . . . everything. If Jade had learnt anything over the past century and a half, it is they only have their family, so there was no point keeping secrets or lying; it only makes things worse. As the images passed from Jade's mind to Rayne's, the few past lives that Charles showed her as well as the most recent events of this evening, Jade could see the hurt building up in her sister.

"I'm sorry, Rayne, I never meant for any of this," Jade said with her eyes to the floor, too embarrassed to look at her sister.

"Jade, I love you, no matter what." Rayne smiled and put her arm around Jade's shoulder. "I'm not mad at you, honey. You did not do anything wrong, well, maybe you did do one thing wrong." Rayne squeezed her sister tighter. "How could you have ever doubted your-self? If mom was here, you'd never hear the end of it." She laughed.

"I know." Jade giggled a bit with her. "We've got a great team of strong people with us on this ship, all of whom are willing to risk it all to help us save her; unfortunately, Charles is one of them." Rayne moaned, "But we will deal with that later, right now, you need to go back to that room, wrap your arms around your fiancé and tell him you love him 'cause trust me, sweetie, that boy is a keeper." She smiled then stood up and pulled Jade up beside her. Rayne hugged Jade so tight if she were human, she would have snapped in half. "I love you, sis, no matter what."

Holden was pacing back and forth behind Adrian and Ezrabeth when Rayne and Jade got back; he looked up at her when she walked in but did not move a muscle; he froze midstep the moment Jade walked through the door. Rayne went over to Justin and whispered something in his ear; Jade did not even bother to try to listen, her focus was on Holden. Jade walked over to Holden and put her arms around him; he let out the breath he was holding in with a huge sigh and wrapped his arms around her. "I'm sorry," Jade whispered. "I love you."

Adrian piped up. "I don't know what's been going on here today, but since Charles bolted out of here almost as fast as you did, I can only guess." He stood up and reached for Jade's arm. "I hope that things are all good now; I don't really want to have to kick his ass for messing around with my daughters' feelings." Adrian smiled and kissed Jade's forehead.

"It's fine, Adrian," Jade said still locked into Holden's arms. "Nothing that will prevent us from hitting that island in a few hours." She smiled. "Now if you don't mind, I'd like to steal you for a little bit before dawn," Jade whispered to Holden. Rayne gave her an approving smile wink combination as Holden and Jade headed back to their room.

"I don't know what all that with Charles was about, and if you don't want to talk about it, you don't have to," Holden said as they reached the room. Jade wrapped her arms around his and took a deep breath.

"How did I get so lucky with you? Most guys would be freaking out right about now."

"I'm not most guys," he answered simply. "But I do have some excess energy I'd love to let out if you know, you need me to kick his ass or anything." They both laughed. Holden held Jade for a few moments longer then leaned down and kissed her. Before she knew it, he had lifted her up so her legs wrapped around his waist then he sat himself down on the edge of the bed and continued to kiss her. *"If he is trying to keep my mind off tomorrow, he's doing a damn good job."* Jade's mental voice faded as things heated up quickly. Jade's mind raced; did she really want this to happen here . . . now? However, before she had a chance to give it a second thought, Holden guided their actions to a slow halt; by this time, they were laying down.

"What's wrong?" Jade questioned, hoping she had not done something wrong.

"This is not at all how I want our first time together to be, Jade." He took a deep breath and propped his head up on a pillow; Jade sighed and moved her body so that she was lying on his chest. "Are you mad?" Holden whispered as he played with her hair.

"Not a chance." Jade smiled. "How can I be mad when I am the luckiest girl in the world?" She turned her face inward and kissed his chest. Holden and Jade stayed in that exact position holding each other until Rayne knocked on the door just before dawn. "We are getting ready to hit the water," she told them. "I just wanted to give you a heads up."

"We'll be right there, Rayne," Holden and Jade said at the same time.

"Holden, no matter what happens today, I need you to know that I love you . . . " Holden's finger gently fell on Jade's lips, and a smile crossed his face; without saying a single word, he stood up and lifted her to him, he kissed her so softly, so carefully, his feeling flowed through Jade's body like a waterfall of emotion, nothing else needed to be said.

CHAPTER 23

The small and somewhat overcrowded boats drifted to the bottom of a large cliff. They needed to climb up the side of the rock face since Cavan would no doubt have the guards on full alert now watching the main dock on the other side of the island. Climbing was not a difficult thing for the vampires to do. Charles went up ahead in a swift jump making sure the way was clear; Edmond followed him with the same effortless movement and then tossed down ropes to help the wolves climb. The vampires climbed up easily digging their fingers into the cliffside like hiking picks. When everyone reached the top, they split up in groups to cover more ground. Edmond had provided them with small two-way radios, so they had a way of communicating since not everyone could hear thoughts.

The wolves stuck together in one direction while the vampires went the other. Ezrabeth, on the other hand, was made to stay on Edmond's ship where she would be safe. Adrian was not going to allow her to be put in harm's way no matter what. She did not like the idea of being stuck on the ship, but deep down, she knew it would be safer.

Rayne and Jade reached out with their minds trying to find their mother, calling out to her as well as trying to feel her presence with no success. They walked further and further inward until finally, they came to the castle wall; Jade put her hand on it ready to climb and jumped back just as quickly.

"What happened, Jade?" Holden gasped as Rayne grabbed her sister's hand that was now smoking.

"I don't know, it...it burnt me," confused, Jade's eyes went back and forth from the wall to her hand.

"It's spelled," Charles growled. "We are going to need to find another way in."

The group followed the wall around until they came to the front gate. It seemed too creepy, no guards at all. They took a few steps in then in a blur of fur and growls, wolves leapt out faster than Jade would have ever imagined. In full form, they circled the vampires, the same way Justin and his pack had done. However, before Jade had a chance to say a word, the wolves were on them. The vampires fought back as much as they could; finally, Holden was able to make his way away from the crowd and focused all his energy on forcing the wolves to the ground. It worked briefly until another wolf leapt on him from behind and broke his concentration. The wolves were back up again. Jade radioed to Justin letting him know where they were, and within seconds, his pack was there. They sprang onto the guards that were attacking, leaping out of the trees, Justin and his pack shifted into wolves midair. Shocked at what was happening, the guards recoiled for only a moment, which was long enough for the sisters to take off into the castle leaving the rest of them to sort out the guards. This was not the original plan, but sometimes, you have to play it by ear in battle. The castle was deathly silent. Rayne called out in her mind again for their mother and still got nothing.

"You won't find her that way," a woman's voice came from a large hall to the left of them. Rayne was on her faster than Jade could blink. The woman's neck now clutched in Rayne's hand and her back to the wall, Rayne hissed. "Where is my mother?" The woman gasped trying to speak so Rayne let her grip go just a bit.

"I knew you would find her," the woman began, "you are stronger this time."

Rayne hissed again. "Where is my mother?"

"Rayne," Jade put her hand on her sisters' arm gently. "This is Aura," Jade read the old woman like an open book, and Aura made no efforts to shield her out.

"I don't care who she is, where is my mother?" Rayne hissed again.

"Rayne stop, she's not the bad guy here." Jade forced the images she pulled from the old woman's mind into Rayne's head, and her hand dropped immediately.

"You, you are the one who put the spell on her, the one we read about in the book Charles had." Rayne gasped taking a step back.

"Yes, my dear, I am, I've been doing everything I can here to help Miss Jorja until you could rescue her." The old woman straightened her dress. "But it has not been easy; Cavan keeps her locked up in a room feeding her only small amounts of watered-down animal blood laced with toxic herbs."

"Where is she now?" Jade whispered. "And where is Cavan?"

"Cavan sleeps in the lower level of the castle during the day now, and Miss Jorja was moved last night into his chamber."

"Well, where is it?" Rayne hissed.

"Follow me!"

Rayne and Jade followed Aura through long and dark halls then down many flights of stairs. This was not just a lower level; this was a dungeon! Jade reached out to Adrian and Holden in her mind hoping they would see where she was and be able to find them if things went bad. A moment later, Jade heard a voice calling for her, louder and louder in a panic, it was Charles. She looked at Rayne hoping that she heard it too, but she did not seem to or at least she did not make any effort to let Jade know she did. Jade called back to him, *"Where are you, Charles?"*

"I'm close, Jade, I feel your energy." As they turned down another corridor, they ran smack into Charles, followed by Adrian and Holden.

"Where are the wolves?" Rayne demanded.

"They are outside explaining everything to each other. I have the radio if we need them," Adrian answered. "Now I assume you know where Jorja is?" he said, looking at Aura. Jade could see the worry in her wrinkled face; she tried to read the woman's thoughts, but as Jade suspected, she had put her guard back up. Charles could see the expression on Jade's face and knew exactly what she was trying to do.

"Aura, please," he pleaded, "tell me what you're hiding." Charles looked deeply into Aura's eyes.

"He is not alone in there with her; he has followers that believe he is the one that will free the vampires from eternal darkness." Aura let out a shallow sigh. "Charles, I've helped you before, but this time, you know I'm bound."

"I know," his voice was low and guarded. "I know." Charles hugged the old woman closely in a protective grasp and kissed her forehead then whispered something to her in another language Jade did not understand. "Now go, be safe."

Without another word, Aura disappeared down the dark hall from where they had just come. Speaking only in his mind, Charles told Rayne and Jade that he would explain later, but they must let her go.

"What the hell was that? What did you say to her?" Adrian growled. "Where is Jorja?"

Charles ignored his first questions but pointed to a large door to answer the last. "Rayne, your distaste for me put aside at the moment. I need you to focus. Do you remember what you did to my door on the ship?"

"What kind of stupid question is that? Of course I remember." She hissed back at him.

"I need you to take all that emotion that is building up inside you right now, both of you, and throw it at the door just like you did back on the ship," Charles pleaded.

Holden stepped in between and grabbed Charles's arm pulling him back away from Rayne and Jade a few feet. "What are you not telling us? How do you know all this stuff?"

Charles looked at Jade with sorrow in his eyes. "Some secrets are not mine to tell," then just as fast, the emotion was gone from his face, and his features were like stone. "Now," his tone was just as determined and hard as his body "I don't know how many of them are on the other side of that door, but if I know Cavan, he will be hiding behind Jorja. He knows we won't hurt her."

"That doesn't really help now, does it?" Holden hissed.

"Actually, soldier boy, that's where you come in." Charles gave a twisted grin. "You will need to do your mind thing to pull him away from Jorja long enough for one of us to grab her and get her out of there."

"Then what?" Holden growled. "We just run out of here with her?"

"No, then the girls make sure Jorja is safely out of the way; then we eradicate Cavan and anyone else in there!" Charles answered; before anyone could say another word, he pushed Rayne and Jade closer to the door.

Jade grabbed onto Rayne's hand looking back at everyone watching them and then focused every bit of anger she had for Cavan, and within a few seconds, the thick wooden doors blew into tiny pieces. The men rushed in front of the sisters like a football defense line. Immediately, other vampires started coming at them, and the fighting began. At first, Jade couldn't see how many there were, but once she was completely inside the room, she was shocked

LIES

to see there were only twenty maybe thirty at most, and Charles had been right, in the far end of the room, their mother laid on a hospital-type bed unconscious with Cavan less than a foot behind her. Jade pushed her way through the fighting vampires, her eyes fixed on a single set of red eyes in the distance. She was so focused on those eyes; she did not see the quarterback-looking guy to her left about to connect his oversized fist into her ribs. She thought he must have been more surprised than she was when he connected his fist to her ribcage with a loud crack, and she did not even miss a step. Holden jumped on him within seconds, taking him to the ground, lecturing him on hitting a woman in the process. With the growls and hissing of the vampires fighting behind her, Jade finally reached her mother and Cavan. Rayne was only a few steps behind her.

"If you think you will make it out of this room alive, ladies, you are sadly mistaken." Cavan laughed.

Jade looked down at her mother's body, lying still on the bed in front of her. If it were not for the almost inaudible whispers, Jade could hear in her mother's mind, she would have thought her mother had died. Rayne reached out for her mother's hand, but Cavan jumped in between them pushing Jorja's body away from them. Behind the sisters, Charles yelled to Cavan breaking his focus on them long enough for him to realize that most of the twenty or so vampires that were on his side were now in a pile on the floor about to be set on fire. Holden used his mind to lift Cavan into the air pulling Cavan away from the sisters. Edmond grabbed on to Cavan's hands forcing them behind his back. Cavan fought and twisted, but he could not break free from Edmond's hold. Adrian, who was now helping Rayne and Jade, lift their mother's body, made sure they had her secure then, went straight for Cavan. Edmond warned Adrian only once that the Guardians will need to take care of the punishment, and that he could not interfere. Adrian not even pretending to listen to Edmond hauled off and connected his fist with Cavan's jaw breaking the bones on contact. Cavan let out a scream in agony, but within seconds, his jaw was back in place, and the bones healed.

Edmond laughed. "I told you, the Guardians will take care of his punishment; he heals very quickly, and after what he has done, I want him to suffer for a while before we give him the mercy of putting him to death."

Adrian punched Cavan one more time rebreaking his jaw before he nodded to Edmond then turned back to Rayne and Jade. The room was now full with the scent of burnt flesh and dark smoke. Adrian lifted Jorja out of the girls' arms and carried her out.

When they reached the castle entrance, a woman came running to them, tears streaming down her face. "Jorja, please be okay, I'm so sorry." Adrian froze and let out a hiss at the woman.

"Adrian, it's ok, it's Koko." Jade warned.

Everyone stood as still as statues, as Adrian laid Jorja's body on the soft grass, they all thought the same thing, but no one would dare to ask...*is she dead?*

EPILOGUE

Rayne and Jade sat by their mother's bed for over a week. The Guardians set her up with an intravenous made up of the same material that Cavan had used to drain her. Every day, she was fed three bags of the purest blood Edmond stocked on his ship, and each day, there was a little more improvement until finally on the ninth day in the early morning hours, a whisper came from Jorja's mouth. "Am I in heaven?" she asked dryly.

"Mom, you're awake." Rayne jumped up knocking the chessboard that she and Jade had been playing on over onto the floor. "No, you're not in heaven, you're alive."

"Alive?" she replied confused. "How?"

"Shhh, Mom, we will explain everything later." Jade wrapped her arms around her mother, and Rayne wrapped her around the both of them.

"Where are we?" Jorja asked, trying to focus her eyes. "I thought you were dead . . . all of you." A look of terror flowed across her face. "What about Adrian?"

"I'm fine, my love," Adrian answered from the doorway. "You have a bit of a welcoming party out here in the hallway." He laughed as he crossed the room and sat on the bed beside her. "How do you feel?"

"Confused," she answered groggy. "I don't understand; he said you were all dead."

"You taught us better than that, Mom." Rayne laughed. "It takes more than some jackass power-hungry vampires to kill us."

"You have yourself some very strong and determined young ladies there, Jorja," Edmond said as he walked into the room. "Even when Cavan told them you were dead, they still did not quit!" Jorja smiled softly.

"I suppose I should introduce myself." Edmond laughed.

"No need, I remember you," Jorja replied, "Twice a year, you would sail into Halifax. I believe you went by the name Quinn."

"Yes." He smiled. "Even then, I kept an eye on you."

"Three white candles and a bag of white sage leaves, every visit," Jorja whispered with a smile.

"You still remember."

"The same order twice a year for almost fifteen years tends to make an impression." Jorja turned to Rayne and Jade. "I suppose there is a lot we need to discuss, but if it's alright with all of you, I would like a few moments alone with Adrian."

Rayne and Jade kissed their mother one more time, and they each sent her their own mental messages of love before getting up and taking everyone out of the room with them. Ezrabeth waited until everyone had cleared out before she came in, she reached for Jorja's hand. Jorja was more than surprised to see Ezrabeth there transformed into a vampire but with a quick glance into her thoughts, Jorja knew instantly what she had sacrificed.

"I'm so sorry, baby," she said dryly. "I . . . "

Ezrabeth smiled and wrapped her arms around Jorja and squeezed her tight. "I missed you."

Jorja hugged her back taking a deep breath. "I missed you too, sweetheart."

Ezrabeth got back up, kissed her dad and followed Rayne and Jade into the hall. Edmond signaled the girls to join him for a moment in his office. They left Adrian and Jorja who were wrapped in each other's arms tighter than a boa constrictor. Rayne and Jade took a seat in the office across the desk from Edmond and Charles.

"This is about doing the ritual for the prophecy now, right?" Rayne sighed.

"Yes," Edmond answered, "but we will need to wait for a while to do it."

"Wait . . . why?" The sisters asked together both confused, "but we thought . . . "

Charles quickly cut them off. "Your mother needs to rest, to regain her strength. We have waited thousands of years to be able to do this. I am sure a few months more will not kill us. Besides, we will need some time to get everything ready and prepare the rest of the Guardians. This will be a big change for our kind."

"So what do we do in the meantime?" Rayne asked. "I mean, do we stay here? Do we go home? Do we go into hiding or something?"

Charles laughed. "*We* go home. I'm told there is a soon-to-be-empty house that needs my immediate attention." He winked at Ezrabeth. "And besides now that I found you three, I don't plan on letting any of you too far out of my sight."

Rayne and Jade looked at each other and just shook their heads.

"Don't worry." Charles laughed. "I promise I'll behave, maybe even try out school again. I'm sure it's changed a lot since the last time I was there."

"Charles," Jade started but was cut off quickly by Ezrabeth giving her a sharp poke under the table. Jade could not help but let out a giggle. "Just behave, please," she continued while Ezrabeth smiled, and Charles gave her a sideways smile.

"So I guess there is nothing left to do right now but head back home and hope that things go back to normal, well as normal as they can be. My mom has Adrian, I have Holden, and Rayne, well, Rayne has some choices to make, but I guess there is plenty of time for that while we prepare for the prophecy!"

ABOUT THE AUTHOR

April Rodgers has been writing short stories and poetry all her life. In 2009, while battling depression for many years, April decided to use writing as a creative outlet to channel her depression resulting in writing *The Black Orchid* novel *Lies*. She then filed it away, having done the job that she set out to do. After a few years and a lot of support from her family and friends, she decided to bring it to life and share it with the world. With the help of her two amazing daughters, she has gained the confidence to continue writing these characters in the hopes that you enjoy seeing them grow in the upcoming series.

CPSIA information can be obtained
at www.ICGtesting.com
Printed in the USA
BVHW081523171218
535790BV00007B/452/P